# The Ghosts of Level Nine

Brian Bennett

ISBN: 978-1-7395446-4-5

# SYNOPSIS

This is a book of death and retribution, fast pace with plenty of twists and turns and full of ghosts from the beginning all the way to the end, but ask yourself this, are they all good ghosts or very bad ones. Kevin West is superficially timid, an introvert. Not good looking. He is thin, slight bodied, almost bald, and wears goldfish bowl glasses.

His wife Madge is a complete contrast. She is six foot and grossly obese. She is so domineering that in the end Kevin believes he has no choice but to do away with her. Having made all of his arrangements beforehand, he steals a lot of cash and goes on the run. He takes refuge on the top floor of a derelict, soon to be demolished hospital. He had been warned about the supposed ghosts which he laughed off. That is, until he finally meets them face to face. The dead sisters are friendly.

They tell him their deathly secret. Together they track down and take drastic revenge on their murderer. Other dead victims come forward.  Kevin and his friends then become unexpected vigilantes and do a lot more tracking and taking revenge. After the demolition, life for Kevin and his deceased friends takes an unusual turn which pushes them in a direction that they could never have foreseen.

# CONTENTS


Chapter 1 – 6

Chapter 2 – 15

Chapter 3 – 19

Chapter 4 – 23

Chapter 5 – 25

Chapter 6 – 31

Chapter 7 – 33

Chapter 8 – 35

Chapter 9 – 37

Chapter 10 – 40

Chapter 11 – 42

Chapter 12 – 45

Chapter 13 – 52

Chapter 14 – 53

Chapter 15 – 57

Chapter 16 – 62

Chapter 17 – 66

Chapter 18 – 71

Chapter 19 – 75

Chapter 20 – 83

Chapter 21 – 95

Chapter 22 – 99

Chapter 23 – 105

Chapter 24 – 113

Chapter 25 – 115

Chapter 26 – 125

Chapter 27 – 129

Chapter 28 – 136

Chapter 29 – 139

Chapter 30 – 144

Chapter 31 – 151

Chapter 32 – 157

Chapter 33 – 162

Chapter 34 – 167

Chapter 35 – 172

Chapter 36 – 177

Chapter 37 – 187

Chapter 38 – 195

Chapter 39 – 200

Chapter 40 – 204

Chapter 41 – 213

Chapter 42 – 216

Chapter 43 – 222

Chapter 44 – 227

Chapter 45 – 235

Chapter 46 – 239

Chapter 47 – 244

Chapter 48 – 253

Chapter 49 – 258

CHAPTER 1

A tiny grey haired man of only 5 ft in height walked down West Street towards his home, a home that he loathed and hated, he carried a full Tesco shopping bag in each hand. He was heading for number 46 which you could not mistake as his because of the run down state of the house itself. The house needed double glazing throughout, painting and repairs to the broken guttering that was hanging off in places and his green and black rubbish bins stood proud from the wild vegetation that grew all around the front of his house.

Brambles and other sharp objects snatched at his trousers as he picked his way along the front path towards the red door of the house. He placed the key in the lock and then just stood there staring at the peeling red paint and he said a silent prayer. He prayed that 43 year old Madge, his wife would be laid on her bed as dead and as cold as she possibly could be, because he hated her, loathed her and wanted her dead.

 Kevin took a deep breath and opened the door, the first thing that hit him was the smell of her, he tried to hold his breath as he walked down the passage way towards the tiny kitchen, he placed the two bags on the work surface. "I'm home dear" he called out, "Where the bloody hell have you been, Im bloody starving here, cook my tea and hurry up about it" came the tart reply, "Yes dear, coming up dear". He walked back up the passage and hung his jacket up, he picked up the post from the floor, and dropped it on top of the mound of other post that he had not even bothered to open. This mountain of post covered the bottom three step of the stairs.

Kevin had not been up the stairs for a good two years simply because they lived down stairs, she had one room, he had the other room and the use of the kitchen and bathroom, what more did they need.

Kevin turned the old dangerous electric cooker on, but to get the cooker to stay on he had to place a can against the switch, tilted in a certain position, he placed the chip pan over the biggest hot ring and began peeling potatoes.

Twenty minutes later he carried the fully laden tray into the room where his huge wife sat up on her bed. "About bloody time" she snapped, he placed the fully laden meat serving dish in front of her, it contained two full pans of chips, eight sausages and six fried eggs, the whole lot was smothered in tomato sauce and vinegar, another plate that he placed by her side contained half a loaf of bread and butter. Madge ate like a pig at a trough and he loathed the fat bitch with a vengeance. He sat on a wooden chair eating a ham sandwich, watching his wife, she had egg yoke, tomato sauce and hot fat running down her treble chins, soaking into her already stained night dress. Half way through her meal she slowed down and began to nod off, a tiny cough from him to revived her, and she would be off again, shovelling food into her mouth like a pig.

When she had finally finished eating her main course, he removed the tray from her and asked if she would like desert. "What do you think?" He took the whole warm apple pie out of the oven, placed it on a dinner plate and poured a full tin of hot custard over the top, and carried it through to his obese wife.

Kevin did not stay and watch he demolish her pudding, instead he returned into the kitchen and turned the kettle on, he filled the bowl with soapy warm water, this was the part he hated the most, washing her smelly, sore covered bulk. You see it was like this, when he first met Madge, he fell instantly in love with her size, she stood an inch under six feet and weighed in at twenty-one stone and was as ugly as sin, his perfect woman. They were married within a few months and he began to feed her, the bigger she became the more he liked it, until she became very domineering, it got to the point where she had ordered many different uniforms and outfits from the internet, for him to wear. He was forced to strip naked then wear these clothes while tending her various needs, she had whips and straps and would punish him if he did the slightest thing wrong, taking great delight as she whipped his bare buttocks, or hit him with a strap across the bare legs, anything to belittle him, make him feel small.

The last time that Madge had been weighed she was thirty-four stone, that was about four years ago, now she must be close to fifty stone and she smelt worse than a dead dog and he really wanted to kill her. Kevin took the bowl of warm water into Madge's living room, his first task was to remove her stained night dress, he would have to stand on the bed and literally drag the garment from her stinking body.

Madge was too big now to stand on her own two feet, she could roll slightly, but that was about all the help that she could give him, all the time that he was washing her, she complained, threatened him, slapped him and belittled him.

He began to wash her fat face, she had red looking sores in the rolls of flesh round her neck that oozed pink pus, the smell of which made him feel sick, he had to use both hands to lift just one of her huge breasts from the bed, which would reveal even more puss covered sores, the flabby orbs were so big that each one lay on the bed, underneath her huge arms.

Next came the worst part, he had to change her soiled nappy pads, she would cackle like an old witch whilst he did this, because she knew just how much he hated doing it. He would have to hold her drooping stomach up with his shoulder just to wash her down there, and the smell, it was truly awful and made him gag. How he kept his sandwich down he had no idea, all the time he did his work, she would be complaining about him hurting her and being too rough, she would start punishing him with a strap or a whip, which she always kept within easy reach of her bed.

Getting a clean pad onto her was really difficult, because she had not got the strength to lift her bulk from the bed, so he had to sort of use a sawing action to get the pad into place, which brought even more punishment for the tiny man, but he would get his revenge, and very soon.

Her room was the brightest room in the rundown house, it was painted white, her huge double bed was in the centre off the room, a flat screen TV was positioned high on the wall opposite her and turned on 24 hours a day, she had placed around her bed, a fridge in which to keep her canned drinks cold, a table to hold her lap top computer and other bits, and a tall gun like cabinet, that was where she kept the items that she punished Kevin with.

A wardrobe stood against one wall, not for her clothes, because she no longer had anything that would fit her. No it was for all the outfits that she had bought for him to wear, each one of them purchased from the internet. The only problem was that Kevin hated her with a passion, and had a plan to rid himself of her, permanently!

Kevin West was 40 years old, whippet thin, tiny and not a good looking man in any way at all, he nervously worked at an old brown oak desk, a desk that had seen better days, this had been his same work station of the last twenty plus years, and was situated in the furthest corner of the cramped office, and as far away from the office managers inner sanctum as was possible.

This freshly decorated managers office held not only a new teak desk, but all the latest mod-cons, the surface of his designer desk was covered in different coloured files, most of them rested in the in-tray, and very few in the out tray as the young manager in his early thirties, sat in his swivel chair with his feet up on his desk, his eyes closed as he talked into his mobile phone.

The small man sweated profusely, and was doing his very best at trying to concentrate on the many columns of blurred numbers on the sheets that were lay in front of him, rows of numbers that all melted into one. Pages and pages of scrambled figures, pluses and minuses that lay in front of him by the hundreds, all waiting patiently for him to put them into some sort of order.

He worked for HWSO Accountants PLC in Northfield, Birmingham. The company had been formed by two brother's Edwin and Richard Southern, way back in 1907 and at the present time the company was very successful, turning over £2,000,000 plus annually, and had been doing the same for the last 4 consecutive years of the companies long life. 40 year old Kevin West had worked for the company for twenty one long loyal, laborious years, and had never stolen as much as a paper clip, but today his mind was in turmoil, as he contemplated stealing £400,000 and leaving his fat, hateful bitch of a wife behind him forever. Kevin who was almost bald, not handsome, a stick thin man, that weighed less than 7 stones, lifted his thick lensed glasses and rubbed his tired eyes yet again, on top on his bad looks he had a long pointed nose under which sat a thin grey moustache, his mouth was a thin pink unattractive slit.

When she was finally finished with him, Kevin would go to his bedroom and lie down on his bed in the dark, close his eyes and let his subconscious take him back to happier times in his childhood, a time when his parents loved each other. His father was a big, broad shouldered man, he was a few inches over six feet tall and it was the work at the coal face that gave him his huge muscular build. His mother on the other hand was a small good looking woman of five feet four inches in height, she was of slight build and worshipped the ground that her husband walked on.

The problems began when Kevin had his tenth birthday, his

father stood on the sideline at the school football match, that was the moment when the big man realised that Kevin was not a good looking lad and so spindly that he was virtually useless at anything physical, he soon began to accuse kEVINS mother of all sorts of unfaithfulness.The big angry man would go out drinking, as soon as he returned home, Kevin would hide under the bed covers as his drunken father began screaming at the top of his deep voice, asking her who the father was, saying things like, how could he possibly be the father? Just look at the size of him and then look at the size of Kevin and how was it possible for him to produce something so weedy, so utterly ugly and useless.

Kevin began to notice the odd bruise on his mother, she tried her best to hide the deep purple masses, but Kevin knew that his mother was being abused by his father. Things began to deteriorate further for Kevin who he was about eleven years old, his father would make a point of sitting next to him on the settee. As soon as his mother would stand up and leave the room, his father would turn to him and punch him hard on the arm, or dig him in the ribs if he could, anything to hurt him, saying things like "you ain't no son of mine, you weak ugly bastard". "You won't never amount to anything, I wish you had never been born" The beatings and verbal abuse for Kevin and his mother became a daily event until one day, his father just wasn't there any more, he had just upped and left them.

The big man walked out of the house one day, saying that he was going for a drink and that was the last that they had ever heard of him. Where he went and who with, was a complete mystery but good riddance. Kevin and his mother soon became very close and relieved that the bully had gone and the loving pair did everything together, and did it without looking over their shoulder's all the time. Life was now perfect for Kevin, and then he began to wear thick lensed glasses.

The school bully Jamie Holmes was two years older than Kevin, he was just under six feet tall but a big fat lump of lard. Jamie would use his sheer size to make other kids give him their lunch boxes and their dinner money, any objections were usually met with a belly flop. As soon as he saw Kevin wearing his new glasses, the abuse began "four eyes, four eyes" he would shout as he pushed the weaker boy around, "it looks like you are looking out of the bottom of a coke bottle" he would shout out at the top of his voice, and then his followers would all join in with the hurtful chant.

What could Kevin do?, Nothing but take what was being dished out. James had a sister who was a year older than her brother, but was easily as big as him, Diane Holmes was the back of a bus ugly. But Kevin found her fascinating, he wasn't really sure why, it got to the point where he would sit a draw sketches of her in class instead of doing his work, he would follow her around and watch her huge bulk as it rippled up her body every step that she took. Kevin was 15 and a half years old and was following Diane along the street at what he thought was a safe distance, when she stopped, turned around, looked him right in the eyes and offered."Hey Kev, do you want to meet me down by the bridge, if you bring a big bar of chocolate we can go for a walk down the fields". Kev blushed down to his shoes but nodded his head in agreement.

With the arrangements made Kevin rushed home, changed his underpants, took some money out of his money box, crept into his mothers bedroom and took one of the condoms that his father had left behind just in case, and headed for his rendezvous.

Diane had changed her dress to a bright yellow affair, that to be honest did not do her any favours, she stood and looked down at him and then at the bar or chocolate. Without saying a word she took his small free hand in her sweaty ham like fist and led him into the fields.

She lay down in the long grass, opened the buttons at the top of her dress, just far enough to show the side of her huge orbs, took the chocolate from him and left him to get on with it whilst she stuffed her face. From that day forward, it was the sight of all that flesh that would stay with him forever. That was the best summer holidays of his life, and he bought an awful lot of chocolate bars.

Kevin's memories would always be the same and he would always open his eyes with a broad smile on his face, but the reality of his present situation would suddenly hit him, as he thought about the fat evil lump next door.

Madge would order ever more depraved items of clothing for him to wear from the internet. This was OK at the beginning, but as she had become more dominant, she became more abusive to the point that she had bought herself a long thin painful leather studded whip, the instrument of his pain had 4 thin strands of leather at the tip. Madge would cackle out aloud as she whipped his bare buttocks, marking him, making him cower every time he walked passed the end of her bed.

Madge hardly ever moved from the king sized double bed these days, simply because she was to fat to do so, she would lay there in her stained night dress day after day, he would look at her with hate and distaste in his eyes, and she would smile back at him when she saw the loathing and disgust on his face, enjoying every second as she forced him to feed her and wash her loathsome, naked bulk.

Kevin would look at her unsightly fat breasts with disgust, the saggy orbs that he once loved were now spread out sideways from her huge body, so much so, that the flabby sacks would disappear underneath her huge arms and rest on the bed by her side. He knew just from the smell of her that if he lifted either of her huge flaccid breasts, he would see the green weeping sores that hid themselves, underneath the unfeeling mammary glands.

Madge's legs were so thick at the tops, that it was impossible for her to place her feet or her knees together, the sheer number of rolls of fat at the top of her thighs prevented this from ever happening again. She wore thick sanitary pant like pads, and would intentionally stay in the same one all day long, she would smile happily to herself, because she took even more sick pleasure as she watched him wash and dry her down there.

She would smirk her thanks every time he changed her, which he was forced to do on a daily basis, this task would be done on his return from work, thankfully Kevin's only saving grace was that he was not allowed a mobile phone of his own, but why would he need one, he had no friends, no family, no-one.

Kevin loathed his wife and tormenter with a passion, he detested the unwashed, sweaty stench of her hairy body, the red blotches that covered her huge torso, some of them had even begun to ooze pink putrid puss. He smiled to himself as he sat on his bed in the darkness of his tiny room, this was where he had planned the best way to get his final life ending revenge on his tormenter.

All that was left to do was put a few more strings into place at work, when this was done, that was when he would finally make his move, then the fat cow would know who was really in control. He closed his eyes, smiled to himself and pictured in his minds eye, her terrified eyes bulging with fear, when she finally realised that she was going to die.

# CHAPTER 2

Kevin had very carefully set up a fake bank account in an assumed name, he sat nervously looking around the bustling office as he was about to transfer the first part of £400,000 of company funds into the false account. Sweat appeared on his furrowed brow, because he was certain that every other persons eyes in the office suddenly fell upon him, but he had set up the hidden account in such a way that only small amounts of money from large company accounts would be transferred automatically, and at various times of the day.

Once the transfer had taken place then the total amount would be held in a holding account, there the money would stay until all the gathered cash would be automatically transferred into his secret account, hopefully within 7 days, and without anyone else in the office noticing.

Sweat begun to run down each side of his brow as he nervously sat looking at the computer screen, because he knew that once he pressed the send button to make the transfers, there would be no turning back, and he would have no choice but to follow through with his revengeful plan. He knew that when his wife's body was discovered, the police would be searching everywhere for him, he had watched enough police programs to have a modicum of knowledge that because he didn't drive, the bus and train stations would be under immediate surveillance.

He would have to hide somewhere fairly close by, and for long enough that he could remain hidden away until the police had stepped down their search for him, and he knew just the place.

On his daily walk to work and for the thousandth time, he passed the old grey, run down derelict hospital. A high green chain link wire fence had been placed there to protect both the public and the building itself, he ran his fingers along the wire that surrounded the concrete structure with its many broken windows and "danger no entry signs," as yet again he studied the highest floors of the old building. The weathered red danger signs were hanging every few yards, in a bid to keep uninvited visitors out.

Many times he had stood in the shadows, and watched the druggies as they disappeared into the lonely looking 9 story uninviting building, he imagined that they went in there to take their illegal drugs, and then sleep off the effects in the darkness of the cold, damp grey underbelly of the hospital. One day he plucked up the courage and followed one young lad through a hole in the fence. Once inside he found out that the druggies only used the bottom two floors, but when he asked why, the long haired spotty youth wouldn't tell him, he just gave him a warning about venturing too high, because of the ghosts.

Kevin shrugged of the warning and walked quietly but nervously up the stone stairways to the upper floors, as he climbed ever higher, he stopped on the 8th floor and with the wind blowing into his face, he looked out of a glassless window at the busy streets far below, he could easily make out his own home, a home that he couldn't wait to rid himself of, a home that he loathed with passion. Kevin would be able to watch from this vantage point as the police went about their forensic business, he could also observe the police cars coming and going as they searched high and low for him. He moved from that floor to the upper most floor, and then from room to room, some but not all, of the windows had been smashed and some rooms were missing their doors.

There was old dusty rubbish laid all over the grey concrete floor. Empty beer cans, wine bottles and fast food containers spread all over the dust covered floors, all left behind by past uncaring uninvited visitors, youths that had once painted the walls with lots of abstract graffiti, none of which made any sense to him at all. He stopped occasionally and admired various bits of the artwork, but as he walked towards the end of the grey dust covered top floor, the graffiti suddenly stopped in mid word, and the last drawing seemed to have been left half finished.

He looked closer and at the end of the final drawing were the hurriedly sprayed words *watch out for the ghosts* he immediately stopped, and nervously looked around the cold concrete corridors, and saw millions of minute dust particles floating in the rays of sunshine, shards of bright light shone through the broken windows, his eyes searched every shadow and doorway of the long eerie corridor, he literally flinched at every unknown sound. He reassured himself when he could see nothing to worry about, but still he smiled to himself, because deep down, he didn't believe in ghosts or any other such hokus-pokus.

Kevin searched the cold dust filled rooms one by one, and in the very end room he found a pile of old blue and white striped mattresses, one or two of them were still wrapped in thick plastic, and looked as if they were brand new. He wondered why the druggies hadn't taken the mattresses down to their own level and made use of them.

He turned around suddenly, the hairs standing up on the back of his neck, because he sensed that he was being watched, but having looked everywhere, he smiled to himself for being so stupid. He shrugged his narrow thin shoulders, and continued looking out of the window at the view below. A warm southerly wind blew through his thinning hair as he stood there with his chin resting on his forearms, as he contemplated his future on the run.

The strange looking little man was deep in thought, as he planned the murder of his fat stinking bitch of a wife. With this plan now set firmly in his mind, he felt suddenly relaxed as he stood there staring into space with the wind in his hair, carefree and happy in his own company. He felt his mouth turn into a snarl as he thought of the fat bitch that would be laying there on her bed, waiting for him to return home, just so she could torture, cause him pain and humiliate him even further.

# CHAPTER 3

Madge had him dressed in her favourite blue and white short nurses outfit, he had stripped her rolls of flab naked and was in the midst of giving her a much needed bed bath, which she just loved him to do, simply because she knew that he hated doing it, she just lay there cackling out loud as he busied himself around her, she held a short whip in her right hand, and took great pleasure in striking him just hard enough across the naked buttocks to make him wince, she did this every time he leaned forward and stretched over her huge bloated body.

Kevin loathed her more and more each day, he longed for the upcoming time, when he would take his deadly life changing revenge. He would stare into her pudgy eyes as the fear inside her mounted, especially when she realised that the worm had turned, knowing that he was about to kill her, finally taking her useless life and he would smile to himself, because every second that he held the pillow over her fat face, she would be struggling with her very being to take another breath. Every slow second that it took for the very life to drain out of her huge body, he would feel relief, elation, happiness and at last freedom.

He suddenly stopped what he was doing, and with glazed eyes stood looking down at the fat bitch, his tormentor that he loathed with every fibre of his body.

"Why have you stopped, slave?" she demanded nastily, he turned away from her foul smelling breath, smiled his best smile and answered meekly,

"I thought that we might try something a little different tonight, my love?" her fat face seemed to roll outwards as she smiled, and answered nastily,

"You may, but if I don't like it, you will suffer, you do know that you skinny little weasel, but carry on with what you want to do to me, and we will see if you can actually please me for a change" Kevin went into the linen cupboard and collected the strips of torn up sheets that he had prepared earlier, this was a game that they had played and enjoyed many times before, especially when they had first married and had loved each other with a passion.

Kevin walked back into the room and roughly grabbed her thick left ankle and loosely tied the strip of sheet around it, dragging the huge leg to one side, he then tied the loose end to the metal bed post, when he did the same to the other ankle, she smiled up at him and said,

"You are a naughty boy, Kevin. I had forgotten all about this game, it has been such a long time since we have played it, just the thought of it has made me go all tingly inside" He moved to the top end of the bed and as he did so where she held her fat arms out willingly, she smiled as he did this to allow him to secure them to the bed posts, when she was bound at each corner, he stood with his hands on his hips looking down at her squirming form, he was quite pleased at his handy work, he smiled broadly to himself, because this would be the main part of his end game, Madge smiled up at him and said,

"Don't forget to blind fold me as well, you naughty boy?" he wound a black silk scarf around her huge head and as he looked at her round swollen smiling face, he wanted to punch her as hard as he could, and then murder the fat cow here and now, but it wasn't the right time, he was yet to put the final part of his plan into action.

He did what he always did on such occasions, he walked over to the food cupboard and took out two hand full's of different chocolate bars, and a large box of chocolate cup cakes, he then went to the refrigerator and took out two extra large pots of cold lemon yoghurt. Back in the bedroom Madge squirmed as she waited for him to begin feeding her. She made loud guttural noises as she devoured everything that he held to her mouth, when she had had enough, she stopped him by simply holding her mouth closed.

Now he removed the top from the yoghurt pot and poured the cold creamy lemon yoghurt all over her fat stomach, and then used both hands, as he rubbed the thick creamy liquid all over her breasts and body. Madge squirmed and moaned out loud with pleasure as he continued his ministrations, the next part of his pleasuring her was the part that he had been dreading the most, Madge suddenly shouted,

"Now, do it now" he closed his eyes as he began licking the yoghurt from her writhing rippling body, at the same time he was forced to pleasure her. When she was finally satisfied he quickly left the bedroom, and then staggered into the bathroom and threw up, emptying his stomach's contents into the white toilet. He gagged as he slid to the floor and loathed himself for doing it, but he needed to do it as it was an essential part of his final plan to kill her. Having pleasured her this way today, she would willingly let him tie her up again, as long as he promised to do the same disgusting things to her, and then that was when she would be at her most vulnerable, and at that very moment, he would put his plan into action, she would then be a willing participant in her own death.

Kevin held his breath as he washed and cleaned her writhing body, he did this unpleasant task whilst she remained tied up, she fluttered her eye lashes at him, and asked him if he wanted to have sex with her, but he refused, saying that he was exhausted after such a hard day in the office. When he untied her, she grabbed him and held him hard against her flabby body, rubbing her soft podgy hands all over his thin cringing frame.

"Are you sure you don't want to do it to me, my darling?" she asked hopefully, but was even more disappointed this time, when he said sternly,

"Quite sure my dear, but thank you for the offer" with that she bodily pushed him away from her, so hard that he fell backwards onto the floor, she shouted out angrily,

"Then piss off you useless fucking wanker" he smiled up at her and answered,

"Yes, dear" Smiling to himself as he turned away from her, he left the room with the vision in his mind of her reaching down, and playing with herself just as soon as he was out of the sight. He climbed into his bed and dreamt of the day when he would finally be free of her all together, and when that day came, it would be the beginning a whole new life for him.

<h1 style="text-align:center">CHAPTER 4</h1>

Over the next few days Kevin bought more essential items, useful things that he would need for a prolonged stay at the abandoned hospital. He bought warm clothing, a small camping stove, canned food and plenty of bottled water, he even thought about buying himself a mobile phone but what was the point when he didn't have a single friend in the whole wide world. As an afterthought he decided to fill a back pack with as much of Madge's chocolate stocks as he could and take that with him, after all she won't need it, will she, especially after she was dead. The next day at lunch time he bought a disposable chemical toilet, and a digital radio. He then made his way back to and then entered the derelict hospital by climbing through the ready made hole in the wire fence. He was met just as he stepped inside the fence by an unkempt young white youth of maybe 19 years of age, he had a few pink sores around his mouth and long unwashed hair, he looked at Kevin and asked,

"Are you the dude that is moving in up-top?" Kevin said that he was, the young lad then smirked,

"Best of luck with that mate, I only went up there once and nearly shit myself when that crazy ghost started chasing me, I ain't the only one that has been chased by it, why do you think that none of the lads ain't living up there?" Kevin smiled,

"You don't really believe all that ghost stuff do you?" the lad shrugged his shoulders and turned away saying,

"Don't say that you weren't warned, mate!". Kevin carried his things up to the top floor and stowed them away in the only room that had all of its windows intact, he looked at his supply's and mentally checked that he had everything that he would need to fulfil his needs. Happy that he had everything in place, he was just about to turn away when the hairs suddenly stood up on the back of his neck, he could definitely feel that he was being watched, but where from and who by, he didn't know. He slowly turned a full circle and scanned every inch of his surroundings, seeing nothing to be afraid of, he convinced himself that the lad down stairs had planted a ghostly seed in his head, and at the slightest sound, he had reacted to it.

## CHAPTER 5

Kevin woke up in a cold sweat, because this was the day that the money was being transferred into his bogus account, he would then remove just enough cash to last him a fair while, and then he would finally put his murderous plan into play. He had barely arrived at work that morning when the old phone on his desk rang as he was summoned into the managers office, he was literally trembling and crapping his pants, as he walked towards the fragrantly smelling office, surely his plans hadn't fallen through at the first hurdle, he asked himself.

He sat down in the rickety wooden chair opposite his boss, he could feel beads of sweat forming on his brow. Tom Bent the office manager looked Kevin up and down before saying in a soft almost feminine voice,

"Now Kevin, it seem's that we have a problem, and that problem was that you haven't had a pay rise for 4 years and as from today you will be promoted to office supervisor, that will give you an extra 25% on top of your salary, and we would like to thank you for all your honesty, loyalty and hard work over these many long years" With that the he looked down and carried on with his work. Kevin looked at the top of the other mans head, taking that he had been dismissed, he almost bowed as he whispered his thanks, before he quietly left the office.

He sat at his desk and looked down at his shaking hands, he rung them together out of sight of the other office workers. He closed his eyes as a single droplet of sweat dripped from his right eye brow, and landed on the back of his now trembling hand.

Now he was in turmoil, he felt hot, sick and thought that he was about to faint, could he stop the transfer of money, could he put up with Madge and her tormenting ways for the rest of his life, did he really want to stop the money transfer? "'NO' he certainly didn't" Kevin smiled wickedly to himself as he decided to continue with his original plan, and murder the fat bitch, so smiling to himself, he pressed SEND on his computer, it was too late now.

Kevin walked away from the bank with £40,000 in cash, which felt as heavy as lead in the brand new blue holdall which he had bought especially for the job, he whistled nervously as he swung the bag, back and forth in his sweaty right hand, he studied each passing face to see if they were looking at him or about to arrest him. He smiled to himself as he rounded the corner and left the bank behind him, it was as though he had been holding his breath since he had left the old building.

 Kevin stopped walking, leant against a wall and took some deep breaths, he smiled to himself because the first part of his plan had been a complete success. He would love to tell someone, anyone, a friend that he had £360,000 in the bank and It was all his, to do with as he pleased. But he knew the he had to hang onto the money just in case of an emergency, or the need to make a quick get away in some way, buy a boat, rent a plane, have some work done on his face, he could have any thing that he wanted.

He took the money back to the hospital and sat down at a three legged  table, he checked that there was no-one else on the top floor, he then spread the crisp new bank notes all over the wooden surface, the tiny man sat and stared at the huge amount of stolen cash and he couldn't believe that the money was now his, he neatly folded a few £50 notes and stuffed them in his pocket. Kevin was confident that the holdall would be safe if it was hidden in the lift shaft, because that was that was the only real place that he had to hide the blue holdall. If the lad from down stairs could be believed, then no-one from down there would dare to venture up the concrete stairs to this level, so the cash should be safe enough.

Kevin walked into his home, and as usual Madge was laid down on the bed in her night dress, brown stains from an earlier meal ran in a line from her triple chin and disappeared into the folds of her neck, she looked at her husband and said sarcastically,

"And where have you been, I am starving here, get in the kitchen and cook my tea" Kevin did as he was instructed, and cooked his wife her favourite meal of 8 sausages 4 eggs, 2 pans of chips and half a loaf of thick sliced white bread and thickly spread real butter, as it was going to be her last meal, she may as well enjoy it.

Kevin sat and watched his wife devour everything that he had placed in front of her, he took the used plates into the kitchen and placed them in a bowl of hot soapy water, to allow them to soak. He walked back into the bedroom and looked at the fat lump who now had her eyes closed and was gently snoring. Taking a deep breath he cautiously eased the first of the blanket strips out of his pocket and gently wrapped it around her right ankle, and tied it to the bed post. He then walked silently around the bed, and lifted her left arm and placed it above her head, he gently tied the material around her wrist, and slowly pulled it tight. He went back to her left ankle and secured that in place, when he had all four of her limbs tied to the bed post, she was lay there spreadeagled, and couldn't move any of her limbs.

Kevin went into the kitchen and poured a jug of cold water, he walked back into the bedroom and slowly poured the water over her sleeping fat face. Madge woke up with a start and spluttered something unintelligible, when the jug was empty she glared up at him with bulging eyes, and screamed at the top of her voice,

"What the bloody hell do you think you are doing?" It was at that point that she realised that she was tethered at each corner of the bed, she looked at each of her bonds and pulled as hard as she could, all to no avail.

"Untie me you bastard" she screamed at him. Madge watched him closely as he walked slowly around the bed, and checked that the knots were secure, happy with his handy work he stood at the bottom of the bed smiling down at her, he stared at her with loathing in his eyes. Not having seen him like this before and not quite sure what he was up to, she glared back at him.

"Is this another of your ideas of fun, if it is I am not in the mood for sex or any of your stupid games, so untie me and get in the kitchen and make me a cup of tea". He just stared at her, his eyes full of hate, her fat snarling face making her look even more ugly than normal.

"Well, get on with it then, untie me you weasel!" Kevin walked away and left her ranting and raving, he took the large pair of scissors from the kitchen draw, and walked back into the bedroom, he stepped up onto the bed and straddled her obese body, he stood there looking down at her, staring into her pudgy eyes, for the first time in all of their married life, he saw genuine fear in her eyes,

"What are you doing, Kevin, what are the scissors for?" He bent over and cut her night dress straight up the middle, and folded each side outwards, fully exposing her almost naked body, he then bent further and lifted her stained sanitary pants and cut them from the leg holes upwards, he then pulled the urine stained garment from her body and tossed it across the room, now she was really scared. Madge's mind was racing, she had never seen her husband like this before, and she had to admit, he was scaring the shit out of her. What made things worse was that now, he was just standing there staring down at her, and she could clearly see the hate and loathing, that filled his blue eyes.

Kevin stepped down from the bed, he walked into his room and lifted a pillow from his bed. Back in her bedroom he stood by the side of her bed and just stared down at her trembling body,

Madge's eyes locked on the pillow, and she asked him in a false voice,

"What's that for, Kev love?". He stepped up onto the bed, and this time he flopped down on her chest, landing with a knee either side of her huge flabby body, now she was really terrified, and it showed by the tremor in her bottom lip,

"What are you doing?" she whispered. Kevin spoke for the first time, and said angrily.

"Shut your mouth you hateful bitch, I am going to tell you a few home truths. First I hate and detest you with a vengeance, I loath your fat dirty smelly body, your bad breath and your evil tongue, as for your self satisfying little games of me feeding you cake, chocolate and canned drinks. Well, at first I have to admit that I really enjoyed taking part in those games, but for a long time now I have dreaded even the thought of doing any one of them, and I loathed the thought of seeing you every day when I returned home from work, each day I hoped that you would be dead. I have hated having sex with you for years now, you being so selfish, you would enjoy yourself, and then push me off without a second thought, not caring whether I was finished or not. Well, all that ends here and now. With that he lifted the pillow and pushed it towards her face,

"WAIT" she screamed, now in utter panic,

"I can change, I can lose weight, you can have sex whenever you want it, any way you want it, I will be nice to you from now on, I promise" she pleaded in desperation. "There is no need for all this Kev, love" she smiled at him, but he just stared at her and smiled to himself as her eyes began to grow bigger with fear. With that he pressed the pillow down onto her fat face, she bucked and writhed for all she was worth, all in a desperate attempt to throw him off, but it was all to no avail. He hung onto her using his knees, it was like being on one of those  bucking bronco machines, he clung to her until she was finally still.

The murderer waited about thirty-seconds longer just to make sure that she was indeed dead, when he lifted the pillow from her face, her eyes were wide open and bulging, in her struggle she had bitten her tongue so hard, the bloodied blue tip was almost completely cut through and poked out between her swollen blue lips. He looked into her greying face, smiled and said out loud. "At last I am free of you, you hateful fucking bitch, and I will see you in hell"

# CHAPTER 6

Kevin filled the ruck sack with his wife's chocolate supplies, and anything else that he thought useful that he could fit into the bag, he checked his survival list to make sure that he had a torch and spare batteries, which he placed in his pocket. Finally happy that he had everything he required, he pulled on two warm coats and his bulging back pack, the small man picked up a suitcase that held a change of clothes. Kevin stood at the bottom of the bed, and took one last look at his dead wife who smelled awful, because in her final seconds in this life, she had soiled herself, out of sheer habit of clearing up, he replaced the pillow onto his bed.

With that done he was somehow convinced that, from the TV police shows that he had seen, there was now no way that the murder could be traced back to him, even though he would be their only suspect. They would still have to prove that it was him that had actually murdered her, but in the end he didn't really care either way. Finally ready to leave, he picked up her phone and called the police.

He stood outside the fish and chip shop eating his supper, watching the police as they went about their business, it was getting dark as he watched some of the officers standing in his front garden talking on telephones, as others walked in and out of his house. He had a sudden thought that made him smile. "How would they get the fat cow out of the house?" He would like to stay and see how they would do that, but he wanted to get settled in his hide away, before it became to dark. If he was honest he wasn't really looking forward to entering the hospital at this time of night, but needs must.

Having made his way through the chain link fence into the eerily quiet building, he stood in the shadows and listened to the junkies as they chatted away in their chosen place of residence. Kevin made his way up the dark concrete steps as quietly as he could, each nervous step sounding as if it echoed along the empty corridors. The higher he climbed, the more nervous he became. He would stop and listen at the slightest sound, shining his torch in every doorway and along every corridor, after a while his mind began playing tricks on him and in the darkness he imagined that he could hear voices, children's laughter coming from somewhere above him. Kevin seemed to almost run into his chosen room and close the door behind him, he stacked a few of the mattresses against the door, and sat in the furthest corner, and strained his ears for the slightest sound, the smallest of sounds, scaring the crap out of him.

He sat with the radio on and listened to the local news channel to see if it reported on the death of his wife, but in all reality it was much to soon for that. He was just dropping off to sleep, when here was a loud crash that sounded like it was just outside his door, the hairs on the back of his neck were standing on end, and he had goose bump's all over his body as he frantically searched the dark room with his torch light.

Things stayed quiet for the next couple of hours, and he was just beginning to relax, his eyes were drooping when he heard the handle on the door being tried, he shone the torch onto to the strip of silver metal, just as it returned to its normal position. It was maybe only a minute later that he could have sworn someone right outside his door laughed in a deep voice. Kevin put it down to one of the druggies messing about, saying that, he never slept a single wink all night long, not after that little incident.

# CHAPTER 7

The next morning he was stood looking out of one of the broken windows in the direction of his busy house, a white tent had now been erected around his front door, and people dressed in white paper suits were walking in and out of the tent, police cars were parked everywhere, he turned the radio on and waited.

The newsreader saying that the police were searching for 46 year old Kevin West for the murder of his wife Madge, the reporter went on to describe him and warned the public not to approach him, but to call the police if he was spotted.

Kevin opened the door of his room and looked down the empty corridor, he just happened to look at the floor and the only footsteps that could be seen in the thick dust were his own, so who had it been that had tried to open his door the night before, surely it couldn't be, could it? He decided that it would be prudent to have a proper look around his temporary new home.

All sorts of abandoned furniture lay upturned and broken in nearly every room, he found a nice desk chair with a couple of wheels missing and pushed it back to his room, he then went in search of something to work on and soon returned with a serviceable computer desk. Kevin filled the draws with his supplies and where the wheels on the chair were missing, he had the chair balanced on some discarded wood, he sat at the desk and began to read a book.

He had been reading for maybe an hour when for no particular reason at all, the hairs stood up on the back of his neck again. He strained his ears for the slightest sound, but only heard the normal every day noises from the streets below.

He suddenly stopped reading and held himself completely still, but he just knew that he had to turn around and look behind him, because he could sense that someone or something was in his room with him, watching him.

He turned slowly and caught the glimpse of what seemed to be a small flowing white dress as it disappeared around the frame of the door, the tiny man went to stand up and go take a look when he stopped himself, because he was convinced that he had heard the sound of a young girl giggling as she ran away.

He walked to the door and opened it slowly, he couldn't believe his eyes when he looked down the long empty corridor, he looked at the dust on the floor and again he could only see the footprints that he himself had made the night before, yet he knew that he had seen someone or something leave his room.

# CHAPTER 8

Kevin turned the radio on and listened to the local news, he smiled to himself when he realised that he was still the main news item, the police were bringing in more officers to aid in the search for him. Police were viewing CCTV footage from all the local train and bus stations, warnings were again given out telling the public not to approach him, but if sighted, to call the police immediately.

He would dearly like to sneak out to the shops, because he would love to read the local papers, just to find out what they were saying about him, but he knew that that would have to wait, because deep down he knew that it was still to soon, and people would be looking for him on every street corner.

Kevin searched every room on the top floor, and had collected anything that he thought might be of use, before it had even begun to get dark, he had barricaded the door to his room. That done he turned his makeshift bed so that if he did wake up due to any noise, he would be facing the door. He placed the torch in such a position that it was within easy reach. He lay on his bed and read until it was to dark, he pulled the blanket up to his chin and closed his eyes, it took him an age to finally drift off to sleep, simply because as he lay there, he had been straining his ears for the slightest sound.

Some time in the middle of the night he woke up, shivering with cold, he was suddenly freezing, a sound in his room made him reach for his torch, he turned it on and shone it around the room. He held the torch beam on the swivel chair, because it was slowly turning, around and around. He sat up and pushed himself as far into the corner of the room as could, and just stared at the rotating chair as it continued to move slowly, ever clockwise.

The chair finally stopped moving, he shone the torch around the room and saw nothing, then out of the corner of his eye he caught the slightest glimpse of something white, and then there was that child's laughter again. That was enough for Kevin, he would pack up his belongings in the morning, and get the hell out of there, police or no police.

# CHAPTER 9

The next morning Kevin woke with a start, and immediately looked at the office chair to thankfully find it still, he climbed out of his makeshift bed, walked over to the chair and studied it closely, he turned it this way and then the other, he jumped up and down as he tried the make the chair move in one direction or the other, he then kind of convinced himself that maybe it could have been the wind, or some sort of other vibration. He unblocked the door, went next door and used his porto loo, he then stood and looked out of the window to see that the police were still everywhere, so he decided that there was no way he could leave his hiding place, not just yet.

He was sat reading his book when he heard a noisy commotion from somewhere down below, angry sounding dogs were barking and there were a lot of people shouting. He went to one of the broken windows and looked down to the ground below, and it looked like all the druggies had been lined up, police men were questioning them one by one. The lad that he had seen and spoken to a couple of times when he had first entered the derelict hospital, looked up to where he saw Kevin looking down at him, the lad shook his head, telling Kevin that he hadn't given him away.

He could hear voices on the floor below, and cursed himself for not choosing a hideout with an escape route, he held his breath as he heard footsteps on the stone steps leading up to his floor, the footsteps stopped. He could hear two women police officers talking, they were saying how the whole place was a total shit-hole and the sooner that it was knocked down the better. He then heard this blood curdling scream which scared the crap out of him, the next thing he heard was the sound of two pairs of feet as the police officers ran back down the stone steps.

Kevin breathed a huge sigh of relief, for the moment at least, he was safe. As he sat there pondering his situation, he wondered if the scream had been real or not, if it had been, then had someone been protecting him, guarding his very presence even.

It was late afternoon and Kevin had decided to explore the floor below, just to see if he could find anything useful, he came out of one of the rooms and looked long the corridor to see the druggie lad standing at the top of the stone steps, looking towards him, he lifted his head in greeting and Kevin walked towards him. They stared at each for a few seconds, before Kevin held his hand out and said,

"Thanks for not dropping me in it" the lad shook his hand,

"I know what its like to be on the run Kev, but doing that scream business was bloody clever, them two coppers were almost shitting themselves when they ran out of the building, my names Ed White by the way" Kev nodded,

"Thanks again Ed but it wasn't me who screamed, I think that it was someone protecting me, there have been some strange things going on up here mate I don't mind telling you. If there hadn't been so many coppers about, I would have made a run for it today, but as it was at the moment, I ain't got a choice, I have got to stay up here" Ed nodded and answered, "I did try and warn you about the ghosts up here, I ain't seen any myself but others have, and it scared the shit out of them, this is as high as I have ever been, and its bloody cold up here mate, you must be freezing at night?"

Kev smiled. "I have been too scared to sleep mate, what with the door handle moving, and last night the swivel chair in my room began spinning around all on its own, and when I shone me torch on it, it stopped and I could swear that I just caught sight of something white out of the corner of my eye, as whatever it was left the room" "Bloody hell mate, I would have legged it and handed myself in, and sod the consequences, by the way did you do it like, you know murder your wife and that?" Kev nodded and sat down on the top step, Ed sat down by his side, and waited for his new friend to begin talking,

"She was a fat evil bitch Ed, make no mistake about that and she treated me like a dog, do this, fetch that, feed me this, lick my feet and if we did have any sex, finished or not, she would just push me off like I was nothing, so I tied her up while she was a sleep, cut her clothes from her so that when the police found her, she was open to the world. I took a pillow and smothered the fat cow.

. Oh, don't get me wrong, when she realised that she was going to die, she soon changed her tune, *I can change Kev, we can have sex whenever you want Kev* well I showed the fat bitch, I sat on her chest and hung onto her until she stopped moving, and do you know what Ed [Ed lifted his head for him to carry on} I don't regret it one little bit" Ed sat quiet for a few seconds before saying,

"Sounds like she was a right nightmare mate, I would probably done the same thing. Look Kev, you are safe enough up here for a bit, and if I hear anything I will let you know but I ain't coming up there, I will come this far in the daylight and bang on this metal hand rail three times, and you will have to come down to me, OK. Oh and I am going to the chippy later, if you want anything I will get you some and do the same thing, bang on the rail and leave em on the top step, OK?" Kev nodded and answered happily,

"I would appreciate that, Ed" [he took a twenty pound note out of his pocket and passed it to the young lad} get mine and yours, salt and vinegar for me thanks. Oh and keep the change" Kev smiled and jokingly invited the lad up to his room, but he refused point-blank. "No fucking way mate" he laughed.

# CHAPTER 10

Kevin collected his supper from the top step and was surprised to find £8 sat on the top step beside his dinner. He was relaxing on his bed, listening to the radio while eating his food when he had the feeling that he was being watched again. He looked around the room and a slight movement on the chair sent shivers down his spine. He had never believed in the spirit word until now, but there were too many unexplained events happening around him, for there not to be some truth in it. He asked,

"Who are you?" nothing happened for a few minutes, then a small sound like a wisp of wind seemed to say, "Sarah" He almost shit himself, and the hairs stood up on the back of his neck, he went to speak again, but he caught the glimpse of what looked like white material disappearing through the door. He sat there dumb struck for an hour or more, when he finally came back to reality, he still held his cold fish and chips in his hand. Placing his cold supper to one side he slid down into his bed, curled up and tried to sleep, but he lay there wide awake waiting for the next strange event to happen, because deep down he knew that something most certainly would.

In the orange glow from the street lights below, he studied the shadows, and in the far corner of the room there seemed to be someone or something standing there, staring at him. Well, by someone it looked more like the body shape of a tall man dressed in clothes from a time long ago. Kev stared at the corner and wondered if it was all his imagination, he asked the shadowy figure. "Who are you?" the shape seemed to ripple before it disappeared altogether.

The next morning he was stood with his head resting on his arms, looking out of the window at the quiet streets below when there were three bangs on the banister rail, he walked out to find Ed sat on the top step with two cardboard cups of tea. Kev sat down beside him and taking the hot cup from him, folded his cold hands around the welcoming hot drink, he nodded his thanks, after a few sips."It's true you know, Ed this place is haunted and by more than one ghost, in the middle of the night I saw something small almost like a child, and asked them their name? I was answered by a tiny voice that I swear said something that sounded like, Sarah, I don't mind telling you mate, I almost crapped myself, then later on I saw the shape of a tall man in the corner of the room, as he just stood there watching me. He looked to be wearing some sort of old fashioned army uniform and tall black hat, but when I tried to speak to him, he just sort of disappeared" Ed looked at his new friend. "Are you smoking dope mate, I'm telling you my friend, staying up here will drive you nuts, I wouldn't be living up here for anything, you can always come and stay with us down below, I know the lads would make you welcome?" Kev shook his head and answered,

"it's OK mate thanks, I will stick it out for a bit longer, at least until the coast was clear"


Just for something to do Kev wandered around the empty dusty rooms on both of the top two floors, he was standing in the centre of a room
that had obviously by its sheer size been a four bed treatment area. That was when the sound of two young girls laughing made him turn around, and look at the open door. He just stood there rooted to the spot and strained his ears, the giggling girls were playing some sort of game that involved one of them chasing the other.

He physically jumped when the shapes of two young girls ran past the open door, the sound of eerie laughter following them as they moved down the stone corridor, but when he looked at the dust covered concrete, there was not a single foot print from the running girls.

# CHAPTER 11

As soon as he was awake the following morning Kev took his office chair, and placed it at the end of the corridor, he then sat there and waited to see if anything happened. Nothing happened for at least two hours, when the dust filled suns rays appeared through one of the windows, it cast a bright light into the corridor, in the sunlight he could just make out the faint shapes of the two young girls as they played some sort of board game on the concrete floor. The girls were dressed exactly the same way in white lacy garments, both girls hair seemed to be tied up with a ribbon, he watched the girls who were deeply engrossed in their game. He was shocked when the girl on the right turned to him, lifted her right arm, and seemed to wave to him.

Kev automatically waved back and the girl lifted her head at him, then carried on with the game. Suddenly the sunlight disappeared, just as if someone had flicked a switch, which meant that he couldn't see the girls any more. He stayed where he was for a few more hours, but saw nothing else of interest, but he did hear some faint noises that he could have sworn were voices. He often felt some slight breeze on his face that he couldn't explain, the scent of roses would drift past him, and he automatically breathed in the sweet smell.

Back in his room he sat at his desk and listened to the local radio, and tried to rationalise what he had witnessed so far involving his deceased friends. In all honestly that was the point at the end of the day, they were dead, so what could they possibly do to harm him? The young girl Sarah seemed friendly enough, so maybe he should try and communicate with her, there was nothing to lose at the end of the day, was there?

Sat at his desk in the failing daylight trying to read his book, he sensed that he was again being watched, without turning around he said. "Why don't you come in Sarah, my name is Kevin, I am

not here to harm you in any way" nothing happened for a few minutes, then the wavy shape appeared against the far wall, he turned to face her. "Hello Sarah" she just stood there, her hollow dead eyes staring at him, when she said nothing he carried on talking to her. "I saw you playing with your friend today, what was her name?" the ghostly figure continued to stare at him for an age, before she clearly spoke to him,
"Alice, her name is Alice, and she is my sister" he thought about this,

"Can I meet Alice?" she shook her head. "She is afraid of you and your sort, it was because of a grownup like you that we are here" he went to ask her something else, but she turned her head and looked nervously at the door. "I have to go" and with that she was gone, she just literally vanished into thin air!

Kev woke from a deep sleep, it had been the first good nights sleep that he had had since he had been there, he lay there thinking of Madge and how they would get her huge bulk through the oven doors, at the crematorium? He would have loved to have been there, just to see her going into the oven, but how would she fit through the doors, the fat bitch? He was brought out of his thoughts, by three loud bangs, he climbed out of his bed and went to find Ed, he sat down by the lad and took the paper cup of hot tea from him. Ed asked him how he was doing, the older man told him that he was doing fine, when Ed asked him about the ghost's. Kev looked at him and smiled. "If I told you that I had spoken to a young girl ghost, what would you say?" Ed looked at him and said in all seriousness,

"I would think that you have been on your own too long mate" but Kev was smiling at his young friend, who asked. "You are serious aren't you?" Kev nodded his head. "Sarah, was a young girl dressed in a white dress, and she has a sister that is also a ghost, and they spend their days playing different games. I have seen them playing a chasing game, and a game where they were knelt down on the floor, it was as if they had a some sort of board game laid out between them. I went to where they had been playing and could see nothing, no sign of any marks in the dust, nothing. Sarah came into my room last night, that was when I spoke to her" Ed looked at his friend,

"Do you realise what you have just said mate?" Kev opened his arms and shrugged. "Its Indian tonight if you are paying?" Kev smiled and took another twenty pound note out of his pocket, and passed it to his friend. "Any sort of curry will do, but can you make sure that I have a big naan bread" Ed took the money and bid his friend farewell, saying jokingly,

"Enjoy your day with your young friends" and with that he ran down the steps two at a time, not looking back, but smiling to himself all the way, not believing a word his new friend had said.

# CHAPTER 12

Kev was sat at his table eating a very good chicken curry and rice, and just like the night before he sensed that he was again being watched, without looking around. "Hello Sarah, why don't you come in" he caught a slight movement over to his left, he glanced over to see Sarah, who was holding the hand of a slightly smaller little girl, who he took to be Sarah's sister Alice, when he asked who she was, Sarah said. "This is my sister Alice, she is seven" he looked at a very nervous Alice who was almost transparent,

"Hello Alice, you don't need to be afraid of me, I won't do you any harm" but Alice wouldn't speak to him, she seemed to be nervously hiding her face in her sisters neck, rather than push his luck, he turned his attention back to his supper, the girls ever so slightly moved closer. Kev continued to eat his meal trying hard to ignore the girls, but when he heard the girls giggling, he glanced around to see that Alice had her hand to the ear of her sister, and appeared to be whispering, which in turn was making her sister giggle. "What's so funny, then girls?" He asked. It was Sarah that spoke as usual. "Alice thinks that you look silly and she says that you need a shave and a good wash, our daddy never had a beard and would sing out loudly as he stood at the sink and shaved." The dead girls suddenly looked at one another and just vanished, right in front of his eyes. He sat and looked at the spot where the shapes had been standing, and wondered what or who it was that they were so afraid of?

Kev stood looking out of the windows down into the streets below watching people going about their daily business, when a sharp pain struck him in the back, he gasped in pain and looked around quickly, but saw nothing. Kev ran his hand down his back and when he looked down, his hand was covered in blood, he picked up his shaving mirror and held it behind him, to see a long thin deep scratch down his back. He poured some water onto one of his towels and held it against the wound, it took a while to stop the bleeding, but it did eventually stop, he looked in the mirror and wondered how on earth, it had happened. When he looked at the window, written in the grime in big letters were the words *GET OUT* he knew that the message hadn't been there a few seconds before, so something or someone was trying to get rid of him.

The next morning Ed banged on the rail and Kev went out to his only friend in the world, and sat down gingerly on the step next to the young lad, Ed passed him his coffee and asked. "What's up with you then, mate?" Kev looked at his friend. "What do ya think of this then?" he then pulled his shirt over his head, and turned his back towards the other man,

"What the bloody hell have you done, you will need that seeing to mate" Kev told him what had happened, and again Ed looked sceptical,

"I will get some stuff from the chemist and bring one of the girls up from down stairs to dress it for you" Kev looked at his friend and asked, "before you do anything, please tell me a bit about yourself, it's not that I don't trust you mate but that's just the point, you are the only friend that I have in the world or ever had really, and to be honest, Im not sure I trust anyone" The younger man just sat and studied him. Kevin tried to put him off getting help for him, by suggesting that it wasn't safe for anyone else to know that he was there, but Ed just smiled at him before answering. "And what makes you think that they don't already know you are here, they aren't silly you know. As for myself, well I want you to promise that what I am about to tell you goes no further than the two of us [a nod from the other man was enough] I am from a very wealthy back round, my mother passed away when I was three years old and I don't remember her at all, my father is very well known and has and still was making a fortune in what he calls *Import@Export* whatever that means.

I am not really sure, and do not know in what he deals. All that I do know is that he knows some very influential people all around the world, and basically if he wants something then he gets it, no matter what it is. As for me, well I choose to live like I do simply because I enjoy the life, I enjoy the petty theft, stealing other peoples cars, computers, anything that I see an opportunity in, I take it, even though I know that if I wanted it, my father would get it for me.

I could be working in my fathers company quite easily, simply because I know how it all works and when I am ready or my father wants to retire, or was too ill to carry on, well then I will have to make the decision as to what happens next.

All that my father wants from me at the moment is that I do not get involved in hard drugs, as long as I just stick to weed, then he will support me one hundred percent. To prove this I have to return home randomly twice a month for a shower, a decent meal and a drugs test. If that was the only price that I have to pay to live like do, then fine. So, as you see Kev you can trust me, as I have nothing to gain from you, only friendship, and to be honest with you I am very careful who I make friends with. I have a lot of mates but not many friends" An hour later and Ed returned with a thin young woman with pins and clips all over her pretty looking face, she had a brightly coloured snake tattooed all around her neck. She looked Kev up and down, placed her hands on her hips and smiling, she said out loud.

"He don't look like much of a murderer, does he? But he is kinda cute, in a strange, sexy sort of way. "Ed introduced her as Tina Simmons, she placed a plastic carrier bag on the table. "Let's have a look then?" Kev pulled his sweat shirt over his head and turned his back to her, "Fucking hell mate, how the hell have you done that, it looks like someone has attacked you with a bloody sharp knife?" Kev didn't offer a reply to Tina and Ed defused the situation by saying that Tina used to be a trainee nurse in A&E,

until she was caught sampling the goods, if you know what I mean?" Tina looked up and smiled at Ed, with a giggle, "And still sampling the goods to this day, that is if I can get them"

Tina used a row of butterfly stitches to pull the wound together, Kev watched as she lay a long bandage out on the table and then lay a row of cotton wool along the whole thing, she then poured some brown looking liquid the full length of the cotton wool. Kev watched her every move, and asked nervously. "What is that stuff and will it hurt?" she looked into his eyes and smiled. "Like a bitch Kev, like a bloody bitch". As she lay the bandage along the cut, the stinging made Kev suck his breath in, groan out loud and shout. "Jesus bloody Christ" With that things suddenly went mad, all of Kev's books flew across the room, the table and chairs were suddenly tipped over, a loud ear piercing scream filled the room, forcing everyone to cover their ears. Tina began screaming which added to the confusion, Ed grabbed her hand and quickly led her from the room. As soon as Ed and Tina had vacated the room, the screaming instantly ceased. Kev heard their footsteps as the pair ran down the stairs as fast as they could. Kev looked around the room and said out loud.

"Why did you do that, they were only trying to help me and while we are at it, why did you attack me?" The room became deadly still and silent, he glanced around and could just make out the dead sisters standing in the corner of the room. He stared at the child ghosts and said nothing, after a short while Sarah said very quietly. "We thought the woman was hurting you, we were only trying to protect you" He turned his back to them and said angrily. "Call this protecting me?" Alice seemed to be getting very nervous, because he could see that she was pulling urgently on her sisters hand. Sarah looked at her younger sister and asked her to wait, she then looked at Kev, he heard her whisper. "That was not us that did that, that was John the jailer, in his former life he was jailer to King Edward, he tells us that in all his time in service, he never let one single prisoner escape from his jail" Kev thought about this, and asked. "So why did he do this to me, I have done nothing to him?" the sisters looked at one another, something unsaid passed between them, and then Sarah turned to him,

"He thinks that you are trying to steal his prisoners, you see there are 4 young girls from our time in the end room, and I think they need your help to escape, but I don't know if you will be strong enough to get past John?" Kev was just about to make a comment as the girls looked at the door, and the ghostly sisters were gone in an instant.

The small room suddenly became icily cold and mist filled, Kev picked up his up turned chair, sat down and waited to see what would happen next. Nothing happened for quite a while, then as if by magic the chair that he was sat on, began bouncing back and forth. He gripped the edge of the chair and hung on for dear life, when the chair finally stopped bouncing, Kev looked around the seemingly empty room and called out. "Is that the best that you can do John?" Kev jumped with fright, and ran to one of the corners, because what could only be described as an axe like weapon began to attack his wooden table, blow after vicious blow, crashed into the stained wood, only when every piece of the desk lay shattered in a heap, did the attack stop. Kev was certain that he could hear heavy breathing from the effort of destroying the table. Kev stood dead still, his heart racing and every part of his body was trembling, he tried to speak but his throat was too dry. The room became deathly quiet as the coldness and the mist began to lift, that was when he made the decision to leave, he would go first thing the following morning.

At first light he began to gather his belongings together, he sensed that he was being watched again and turned nervously around, hovering by the door was Sarah, she stood looking at him for an age, before he heard her ask . "What are you doing, you can't leave, who will rescue the young girls in the end room?" Kev shrugged and answered. "What can I do against the jailer?" she seemed to shrink into herself, she whispered so quietly that he had to strain his ears to hear what she was actually saying. "But you have to stay, if you leave who will rescue the girls?" and she then began to cry. He turned and began to stare out of dirty window, trying to think of a way to do what she wanted, when he turned around she was no longer there. Kev opened the door and walked along the long dusty corridor towards the room at the end, he kicked bits of masonry and old drinks cans out of the way, he bent down and picked up thick wooden chair leg. When he reached the room, the door was closed, he pushed down on the handle and using his shoulder he eased the door open. The room was deadly silent and freezing cold, bloody ice cold, he stood in the centre of the room and looked into every nook and cranny. He could sense a presence, but could see nothing, he almost crapped his pants when a deep almost unrecognisable voice said. "Get out of my jail" Kev walked to the door and placed his hand on the handle, but before he opened the door, he turned and looked around the room.

"Don't worry girls, I will think of a way to set you free" he left the room to a deafening, unearthly roar.

Kev found another serviceable table and dragged it into his room, he picked up his books and stacked them on one end. The radio seemed to have been broken, but on closer inspection it was only the batteries that had been knocked out, he soon had the room back to some form of normality. Laid in his sleeping bag, deep in thought, he heard three loud bangs, he opened the door and looked out to see Ed standing on the steps, holding what looked like a bag of fish and chips. Ed passed him the hot brown bag that smelt heavenly of hot vinegar, Ed looked around nervously and asked him if he was OK? Only they had heard a lot of banging and strange noises earlier in the day, and it sounded like it was all coming from up here. Ed looked shocked and began to worry about his friend,

"It was only John the jailor throwing his weight around" Ed

looked questionably at his friend. "Who the bloody hell was John the bloody jailer, another of your friendly ghosts?" Kev sat down on the step, unwrapped his supper and began tucking in. He motioned for the younger man to sit by his side, when Ed was sat down Kev told him the whole story from the beginning, to where he was now,

"I have to find a way to get the girls out of that room and help them" Ed sat there silently looking at his friend, a bemused look on his face. "I think you ought to try some cannabis Kev, it might help you to chill out a little bit, I can get you some in the morning, its good stuff?" Kev shook his head and looked at his friend and asked. "Will you help me free the girls, Ed?" Ed looked shocked, "No bloody way mate, you won't get me up there for love nor money" "£1000 cash money for your help, you did say that they were dead and they couldn't hurt you" he offered. Ed sat deep in thought, as Kev waited for an answer.

# CHAPTER 13

Ed turned up the next morning with a stolen lap top computer, sat on the top step side by side, he asked Kev what type of clothing John the jailer had been wearing? The two men trolled a history site until Kev saw a mannequin, that was sort of dressed in the same sort of clothing that the ghost had been wearing. Kev asked Ed where finding out the information had got them? Ed tapped the side of his nose and teased. "I have a plan, all you will have to do is make it work" Ed tapped away at the computer for the next twenty minutes without saying a word, suddenly he stopped tapping and turned the computer so that Kev could see the screen. On the computer was the picture of King Edward the 4 th, resplendent in a dark red royal gown, on his feet he wore a sort of material shoe and white stockings that reached up to his knees, on his head sat a gold crown. Kev looked at his friend,

"And?" Ed tutted his impatience,

"Use a bit of imagination Kev me old mate, we have a computer and I have some credit cards, so we find an outfit that looks like that king bloke, get it delivered to Dave down on River Street. All you have to do then was walk up to this John the jailer ghost, and order him back into his grave, and see what happens?" Kev looked at his friend and raised his eye brows. "You must be having a laugh mate, it will never work" Ed smiled and spread his arms wide.

"What have you got to lose, Kev, what's the worst that can possibly happen?" The friends sat side by side and Kev watched Ed, as his fingers flashed across the computer keys. When Ed was done, he turned to the older man and smiled.

"All done, delivery in two days, now I want you to do something for me?" When Kevin offered, "Anything" he was then told to smarten himself up as they were going out.

# CHAPTER 14

They stood on the pavement outside the post office, Ed would not tell his friend where they were going, only when a white chauffeur driven Rolls Royce pulled up by the side of them."our transport" smiled Ed. The big car purred along with no effort what so ever, Ed poured them both champagne and they relaxed in the deep leather seats. Kevin could not believe his eyes when the car drove along a long tree lined driveway, cows, sheep and fallow deer roamed freely all around them. The estate house when he saw it took his breath away, the white house was lit up like something you would find in America. Kevin could feel himself trembling with nerves as he walked into the huge house, but he need not have worried because Ed's father Richard White, instantly made him feel at home. Richard who was wearing faded blue jeans and a silk shirt that was open at the top and trainers "Ah, welcome, you must be Kevin, Edward has told me all about you and your problem, come lets go through to dinner and we will discuss it" Kev looked back at his friend, who simply smiled and shrugged his shoulders.

The five course meal was the finest food that Kevin had ever eaten, the wine was the best that he had ever tasted. Some of the conversation between father and son went over Kevin's head, but when the meal was over, Richard lit a huge cigar and sat staring at Kevin, his eyes seemed to be searching every nook and cranny of his face, making Kevin very nervous to the point that he didn't know what to do, stare back or run in fright. Eventually the older man spoke, "Sorry to stare old chap, but I am trying to figure out the best way to help you, and I think I have a plan in mind, excuse for a minute or two, I must make a phone call"

Kevin had been left on his own at the dining table as apparently Ed was off having his drugs test, he physically jumped when Richard came rushing into the room, talking into his mobile as he did so, the older man stopped by the side of Kev and took his photograph from many different angles, and then walked back out of the room. Ed came back and gave Kev the thumbs up, letting him know that he had passed the drugs test. Kev was just about to ask Ed what was going on when smiling Richard came rushing back into the room, Sorry about all that you two but I needed to call Raoul, he's a friend of mine that owes me a huge favour, and I have just called in that favour"

Richard looked at Kev, "As a friend of Edwards, you are a friend of mine and I like to help my friends out whenever I can. Now, Edward has told me all about you problem with your wife and now with the authorities. Well, I can help you there, you see Raoul is a plastic surgeon of world wide renown, if you agree to let me help you, he will arrive at the weekend to start work on you first thing Saturday morning. I have a list of everything that he requires to do the work, and I have already set the wheels in motion. Having looked at your pictures Raoul was confident that with very little work he could change your appearance just enough, which means that there will be not much discomfort on your part. It will mean of course that you will have to remain here for a full seven days to recover, but I will try and make you as comfortable as I can. Now the car will pick you up at the same place at eight am on Friday morning, is that Ok, Kevin?" But before he could say a word, Richard turned his back on him, and then placed his arm around his sons shoulder, and led him out of the room.

Back in the car on the way back to the hospital Kev turned to his friend, and asked him what had just happened, Ed simply shrugged his shoulders and answered "thats how my father works, he knows what the right thing to do is and has the connections to get whatever he needs, when he needs it.

You have to admit that this makeover thing is a great idea and you do realise that this Raoul is the best at what he does, and will be flying in from Zurich just for you. It will be fine mate, and to make things easier I will get Tina to come and look after you while you recover, hows that?" The other man thought about what had just been said and could see the sense in his friends argument, but did he fancy having surgery on his face and how much would it cost?  He nodded his agreement but argued, "Only if I pay for the treatment myself" the other man shook his head and replied, "that was not how big business works my friend, my father obviously has something on Raoul or the good doctor owes my father big time, whichever it was, don't worry about it. You might think that this was about you and changing your looks, but it was probably just a way for my father to recover a debt of favour of some kind, so don't let it bother you. Me and Tina will stay by your side the whole time, more importantly, what we have to worry about first is how to get rid of John the bloody jailer?" This made both men laugh out loud, it looked as if everything was sorted.

Kev was lay on his sleeping bag deep in thought, he had taken his spare clothes out of his bag, and they were hanging up in front of an open window to air, he had lost weight, but was sure that his clothes would still fit OK.  Ed had asked around and the word was that the police were certain that the murderer had fled the country, along with the stolen money, so did he really need this surgery?

All of a sudden he heard a quiet commotion coming from outside his door, he went out into the passage way and saw Sarah and Alice standing in front of John the jailer. The jailer had obviously been on route to see him, but had been halted in his tracks by the two female ghosts, the jailer looked up and waved his fist at Kevin and shouted. "I told you to get out of here, you have until this time tomorrow, if you are still here, I will kill you" with that he turned and disappeared in a cloud of dust.

Sarah seemed to float towards him and hover nervously in front of him, in a shaky quiet voice. "We won't be able to stop him for much longer, we are not strong enough on our own. You will have to leave here soon, or he will kill you" Kevin smiled at the sisters "we have a plan for John, if it works then fine but if not, well we will have to think of something else.

While you are both here, I have to tell you that we, myself Ed and Tina will all be going away for a week and when I get back, I will be looking a little bit different, so please don't be alarmed, will you? Then we will deal with the jailer" It was Sarah as usual who wanted to know if they would definitely be coming back. Kevin made the promise of their return.

# CHAPTER 15

The car Journey back to Richards house on the Friday morning was a very quiet affair, Ed had tried to lift his spirits, but Kev was apprehensive of what was to come. On arrival at the house, Richard was waiting and the house seemed to be full of people, all rushing around in different directions, some on phones, others carrying armfuls off folders. A young blond woman in a white uniform walked up to them and announced that her name was Cilla and the she was Raoul's personal assistant, and that she would be looking after Kevin during his procedure. She took Kevin by the arm and led him away from the others towards one of the back rooms. Ed turned to Tina and asked "fancy some breakfast?" and led her into the dining room. Kevin lay on what looked like a long ironing board with a hole in one end, his hair had been gelled back from his head, his head and shoulders had been sterilised with some thick brown liquid, Cilla looked simply terrifying as she stood there in front of a tray of surgical instruments, dressed in a green gown, complete with face mask and long blue gloves.

The door to the room suddenly bursts open, and a tall thin man dressed all in white marched into the room fully prepared for the surgery, his gloved hands held out in front of him. All Kev could really see were the other mans old grey eyes behind the half glasses. The doctor stood looking at his patient, he hummed some unrecognisable tune as he pushed and pulled Kev's face in every direction possible, He then stopped, looked at Cilla and asked in a deep booming voice,"are we ready to proceed?" She nodded, "yes doctor"

The first injection in Kevin's face made him cringe with the pain, but the anaesthetic soon did its job and within minutes his whole face was numb. The only thing that Kev didn't like was when he saw the scalpel coming towards his face, but to be honest, he didn't feel a single thing, even when the good doctor was working on his nose, which was a weird experience in itself.

After what seemed like hours of pushing and pulling, needles and scalpels, The doctor stopped, looked Kevin in the eyes and uttered these immortal words "there you are young man, you have now turned from an ugly duckling into a beautiful swan. Goodbye" and with that, he was gone.

The recovery period was a lot quicker and less painful than anyone expected, Kevin could not believe the change in his facial features in such a short time, he spent ages looking in the mirror that Tina had bought for him, he had to admit that the good doctor was very good at his job. Tina fussed around her patient like a mother hen, tending his wounds, tenderly rubbing some special cream into his pink scars, feeding him luxury foods which she had requisitioned from the big houses extensive larder. The pair had become very close and the longer that time went on, the closer they became. The first time that Sarah saw his new look she seemed confused at first, it took him quite some time to explain what had happened to him, and the reasons why. It was only a week later when Kev had ventured down to the ground floor looking for his friend, when Ed saw him with his new look, dressed in his clean clothes, the young man walked around him, looked him up and down and commented.

"If I didn't know it was you, I would not have recognised you, me old mate" Kevin smiled. "Fancy a fry-up?" Ed pulled his hood over his head and walked out of the disused hospital, and led the way to the Blue Moon cafe, the pair ate two extra large breakfasts and drank two cups of tea. The pair then spent the morning walking around the shops. Ed did start to get slightly annoyed with his friend, because he would suddenly stop walking when he saw his own reflexion in a shop window, he would study his face as if he was looking at a stranger, but by lunchtime Kev had begun to relax, and enjoyed replenishing his diminished supplies.

Ed had a phone call and smiled at his friend, when he had ended the call he turned to Kev and smiled, "We have a delivery to pick up, have you got a tenner?" After a nod from the older man Ed led the way through the back streets, he stopped and told Kev to wait on the corner, and he would be back in a minute, a short time later Ed walked toward him with two very large light blue plastic carrier bags, he passed one to Kev,

"Let's get back to the hospital, and see what you look like, dressed up as a king?"

In one of the empty rooms on the level four, Ed sat on the floor tapping away on the computer while Kev tried on the new King Edward outfit, when Ed eventually looked up he burst out laughing. "Bloody hell mate you look a right twat" with that he took out his phone, and took his mates picture, he then stood by his friends side and took a selfie of them both. "Thats as close as I am ever going to get to royalty" and the pair began laughing out loud. Ed sat on the floor and looked from the computer screen to the king, and then back again, comparing the two, before adding. "We need a bit of padding, here and there I think, and I will get Tina to come up and do something with that beard, then that should do nicely" Just over an hour later and some padding from one of the old mattresses, Kevin looked a lot like King Edward, Tina stood with her hands on her hips and a broad smile on her face, she looked from the computer screen to the look alike King, and commented. "That ain't that bad, even if I say so myself, the pointed beard just adds the finishing touch, don't ya think so Ed?" Ed smiled,

"Let's hope that its good enough to fool John the jailer?" Tina looked from one to the other with a furrowed brow,

"Who the bloody hell was John the jailer?" The two men sat her down, and told her the whole story from beginning to the end, when they had finished talking, she looked from one to the other, unsure if they were winding her up. When she realised that they were being deadly serious, she asked. "Can I meet this John ghost?" Ed raised hie eyebrows. "Are you bloody mad woman, he was really scary, look what he did to Kev's back?" Tina smiled,

"But, I have always wanted to meet a real ghost, I think I have seen a few, but never actually met one, can I please?" Kev shrugged. "You can if you want, you can come with me now and watch him kill me, if this outfit doesn't work" Ed tried his best to try and talk his young friend out of going with the now look alike King, but she would have none of it, she stood defiantly in front of Kevin. "Come on then your majesty, let's go and get rid of this nasty ghost" Kev walked slowly along level 9 towards the end room, he stood looking at the closed door of the room that held the young female ghosts, he banged on the closed door with his fist and then shouted at the top of his voice. "John the jailer, show yourself" within seconds the door literally flew open and the jailer appeared. Kev heard Tina gasp out aloud, John didn't seem to be shocked at seeing his king standing in front of him, he lowered his head and pushed his right foot forward, he then seemed to bend from the waist and say, "Sire?" Kevin said in his deepest voice,

"John the jailer, you have done your duty well, now return from whence you have come and rest" the jailer didn't even raise his head to look up, but did say.
"Yes, Sire" and with that he just seemed to disintegrate and was gone, gone forever, never to be seen again. Kev seemed to be rooted to the spot, his heart was beating harder than it had ever done before in his life. His thoughts had somehow stopped as if it was some sort of brain freeze, and he was staring into space as if in a some sort of trance, it was only when Tina pulled his arm, and whispered. "He has gone Kev, I don't think he will be back. What do we do now?" Kev slowly turned to her and raised his eyebrows."It really worked Tina, it really did" with that he grabbed her and hugged her hard, she hugged him back, and with

a smile, she tenderly kissed him just under the ear.

# CHAPTER 16

Tina soon became Kev's constant companion, she would go out and collect what ever food and supplies they needed, she trimmed his beard again, this time cut it short and couldn't stop herself from stroking the thick wiry hair. The good doctor had done a good job and Kevin could not believe that he was looking at his own reflection in the mirror, His new look was unbelievable and worth every second of the pain. Tina hung onto him tightly and teased that he could now be her toy boy, as he looked so young and handsome.

There had been no sign of the dead sisters or any other ghosts for that matter, at least not for a few days. In his head he knew that the reason that the girls were staying away, what with his new look and the fact that Tina was now with him all the time now, and until the sisters became a bit more confident with her being there 24 hours a day, he doubted that they would show themselves.
The mismatched couple had somehow become more than just friends, and were now acting like first time young lovers, with hands constantly all over each other, making love at any time, day or night. When things had calmed down a bit and they were sat on his sleeping bag one night, he sensed that they were being watched, he lightly placed his hand over Tina's mouth, and whispered quietly. "Is that you Sarah?" Tina jumped in his arms when a child like voice whispered. "Yes, who is she?" Kev answered the dead girl. "This is my good friend Tina, she has come to help you and Alice, are the girls in the end room ok" nothing happened except that the room became a little bit colder, so he said to the almost empty room. "Are you going to show yourself Sarah, Tina would really like to meet you?" they just about made out the words. "No, I am too scared, I don't know her" and that was that.

The next night the same thing happened, so Tina tried talking to the young girl ghost herself.

"Are you afraid of me Sarah, you don't have to be, I wan't to be your friend and help you" when nothing happened Tina suggested. "Do you want me to go and leave Kevin on his own?" they just about heard the word. "No" so Tina asked. "What about if you and I went into the room next door, that way the two of us can talk on our own?" when nothing happened, Tina whispered into his ear,

"Stay here" with that she stood up and walked into the next room that was filled with the orange glow from the streets below and waited. Tina had been sat there for at least half an hour and still nothing had happened, she asked the seemingly empty room. "If you are there Sarah, let me know or I am going back to the other room to be with Kevin?" "No, please stay" she heard the girl ghost whisper, even though the spoken words were almost inaudible. Tina sat quiet for a while before she looked around the room and whispered. "Show yourself to me Sarah, I want to see you" a few minutes later Tina's heart began thumping as the shimmering shape of what could be the small girl slowly at first, slowly appeared in the far corner of the room, it was a shape that was neither one thing or the other. "All the way Sarah, come closer and talk to me" bit by shimmering bit, Sarah eventually appeared, the hollow looking eyes seemed to bore into Tina.

Tina asked the young girl if she would tell her about herself, and explain to her how she had ended up where she was at such a young age, the young ghost ever so slowly moved along the wall, until she was quite close to Tina. Still nothing came from the young spirit at first, so Tina had to encourage the young girl to speak.

"Do you want to say anything to me Sarah, do you want to ask me anything?" in a very quiet voice, Sarah whispered. " I am very embarrassed about what I really want to ask, but I don't think that I can go on existing without knowing the truth, you see I have watched you and Kev, you know, when you are doing it, and you seem to enjoy it so much, when my uncle Paul used to do it to me, it always hurt me and made me bleed. I had no choice but to put up with what he was doing to me, even though I knew that it was wrong, but by me doing what he wanted, I thought that he would leave Alice alone, he did until I had my first period, then uncle Paul lost interest in me and began to do those bad things to Alice, and it was exactly the same with her, she used to try and scream with the pain, but he would hold his hand over her mouth, he hurt us both so much Tina, so can you see why I am so confused?" Tina smiled at the young ghost and said reassuringly. "It wasn't your fault Sarah, the reason that you didn't enjoy what your uncle was doing to you, was that you didn't want it to happen in the first place, and your body was also not ready for such a thing to happen to it, you were much too young. Tell me, how did you end up here?" Sarah looked away from Tina and lowered head as if she was crying, she again answered in a very quiet voice. " One night when uncle Paul was looking after us, he went into see Alice, I was in her bedroom waiting for him, and I was holding onto the hand of Alice as tightly as I could, I said that if he did it to her again, we were going to tell my father. Uncle Paul went mad and grabbed me and raped me again, right there in front of Alice, he then did the same to her, we both stood there naked and bleeding.

We said that that had been his last chance and we were going to tell, that was when he went mad, he grabbed us and strangled us, hiding our bodies in the graveyard, the one down there by the side of the hospital. He told everyone that someone had broken into the house while he was asleep on the settee, and taken us"

The room had suddenly grown very cold, because Sarah seemed to be sobbing, Tina watched the young ghost for several more minutes, sensing that she was about to leave. Tina asked as softly as she could. "Is uncle Paul still alive Sarah?" the ghost nodded, and said quietly. "Yes, and he has a new victim now, called Molly, but she is so tiny, she is only 7 years old and lives in the house next door to him" Tina frowned. "Where does this uncle Paul live Sarah?" Sarah whispered. "Warner Street, 36 Warner Street" "and what does he look like Sarah?" "He is short, bald, has a limp and he smells, and he always wears a blue and white woolly hat" Tina snarled. "I think that we ought to pay this uncle Paul a visit, leave him to us Sarah, we will take care of him"

# CHAPTER 17

Tina walked back into her boyfriends room and sat down by his side, she had tears running down her cheeks when she took his hand in her own and told him exactly what Sarah had said to her. She looked into his eyes and said angrily. "We ought to sort this fucker out Kev" he sat quietly thinking for a few minutes, and then nodded his agreement. "Let me think about it until the morning" When she woke the next morning she was on her own in the makeshift bed. She was not in the least bit scared as she lay there looking at grey ceiling, that like the walls of the hospital, it to had once been a glossy white, but were now a mass of peeling grey. Now as she walked from room to room of the upper floor in her search for Kev she realised that every room was the same state of disrepair, but in the end she gave up, because she couldn't find her lover anywhere.

So she sat down on the sleeping bag and waited for him to turn up. Kev finally appeared and looked grim, he stood and looked at her before telling her. "We have a plan for uncle Paul, Ed has gone to Warner Street for a look see to see if he can find him. Now you and I need to go shopping". On the high street they ate breakfast, both of them sat deep in thought about the poor dead sisters, and their tragic story. Kev eventually asked her if she was ready and stood to leave, the first item they bought was a pair of very sharp pruning sheers, a marker pen, ball of string and some thin blue nylon rope from an iron mongers shop.

Back in the derelict hospital Kevin made a cardboard sign and tied string to one side, leaving enough of a loop, so that it would fit over the child murderers head when tied to the other side of the cardboard. Ed eventually turned up and dropped heavily into the chair, he opened a can of cider and took a deep swallow of the cold drink, and eventually said without looking at either of them,

"Well, I have located our friend and he don't look much of a problem to me, I followed him for a while and he caught a National Express coach to Derby. According to his elderly neighbour, he had gone to see his mother, but he should be back at the weekend, so we will just have to wait for him to return" Kev nodded, and shrugged his shoulders.

"Well, at least that gives us a bit more time to prepare" Ed continued talking" I have asked around, and he plays darts on a Tuesday night at the Crown pub, so if we are going to do this,Tuesday night would be as good a time as any" Kev looked at his girlfriend who readily nodded her agreement, so he smiled.

"Tuesday it is then" Ed spent a lot of time at the coach depot, waiting for the return of uncle Paul. When Uncle Paul finally stepped down from the coach, he began to laugh out loud as he shared some private joke with the coach driver.

The trio were stood behind a red brick wall at the entrance to the almost dark local park, the dank smelly area in which they waited was situated only a few hundred metres down from the Crown pub. They stood well back in the shadows, Ed waited by the entrance and kept peeking out from behind the wall, so that he could scan the dark street as they waited for their target to show, Ed suddenly whispered. "That looks like him coming along the road now, and he looks a bit pissed" Kev and Tina moved deeper into the shadows at a backward wave from Ed, Ed stood close to a high red bricked wall, he made certain that the streets were empty, and bided his time. Uncle Paul staggered towards him with his hands buried deep in his jacket pockets and his head hanging down, when he was level with Ed, Ed swung a base ball bat and caught him hard on the shins. Uncle Paul dropped to the floor with a grunt, hit his head on the footpath and lay still without a sound.

Ed grabbed him by then jacket collar and quickly dragged the unconscious man deeper into the park, to a place that they had already chosen, in the eery darkness they tied the blue rope around Paul's wrists, Kev and Ed had already thrown the thick blue nylon rope over a sturdy bough of a tree, together they pulled on the rope and literally lifted the unconscious man to his feet. Tina took hold of the end of the rope, pulled the it tight and then tied it to the lower bars of the nearby set of metal swings. Now with his arms stretched high above his head and with a few slaps across his face, uncle Paul slowly regained consciousness, he shook his head and through glazed eyes, looked from face to face, and asked.

"Who are you fuckers then?" Kev stood directly in front of the strung up man and snarled. "We have a message from Sarah, Alice and Molly" uncle Paul's eyes went wide, and his mouth dropped open, he went to speak, but obviously thought better of it, and stayed silent. "Yes, we know all about your perverted little games, you twisted fucker" Paul suddenly realised that his hands had been tied above his head, as he looked skyward. Kev held the home made sign up in front of the murderer, so that he could read it, but with the park being so dark, the drunken man couldn't make out what the words, so Ed flicked his lighter on which allowed the pervert to read it, when he had read the sign Kev hung it around Paul's neck, the sign read. I raped, sexually abused and murdered Sarah and Alice Mauber, I also raped and abused little Molly Smith aged 7 years old.
Paul pleaded with them by saying."Please don't leave me like this, they will kill me"

Kev took out the pruning sheers and held them in front of their prisoner, he flicked the locking clip which exposed the razor sharp blades and flexed the handles. "I was told that these are the sharpest sheers on the market," smiled Kev, uncle Paul who was now completely sober, had suddenly begun to visibly tremble with fear. "Grab his legs" shouted Kev. Tina grips the man's legs as hard as she could with both arms, which allowed Kev and Ed to undo the man's belt and then the button that held his  black jeans together, when Kev started to undo the zipper uncle Paul realise what was about to happen and begun to call out for help. Ed stood up straight and punched the man in the stomach, he hit him so hard that it took all the wind out of the pervert, almost folding him in half. Kev pulled the thick black denim jeans down the man's thin legs, and then did the same to his blue boxers, he burst out laughing at the sight of the perverts small penis and asked his lover what she thought? Tina shone a light onto the man's privates and burst out laughing "I wouldn't even bother with a thing that size" the trio laughed out loud. Kevin gripped the top of the child murderers meat and two veg, with the sharp blades of the sheers.

"Please don't" whispered Uncle Paul and began screaming, Ed moved behind the perverted man and gripped him around the waist, holding him in a vice like grip, Kev looked into Paul's eyes and said.

"Say goodbye to your tackle" before the man could open his mouth to speak, Kev squeezed as hard as he could and simply cut the whole lot off.  Paul let out an ear piercing scream, they had never heard the like of before, the desperate blood curdling screams filled the cold night sky. Lights in nearby houses came on and curtains began opening as tired eyes searched the darkness for the source of the eery screams. Kev picked up the bits that he had snipped from the dying man and placed the whole lot into the almost unconscious man's shirt pocket. Kevin looked down at the thick dark red arterial blood that oozed out of the wound between the man's legs.

"Well, that should stop you, you bastard" commented Kev, his partners in crime both agreed with the statement, with thick dark red, almost black arterial blood running freely down both of the dying man's legs, that was exactly how they left him. They made their way from the park using another entrance, leaving behind them a strange, distant growling noise, and the approaching sound of police sirens filled the night air.

# CHAPTER 18

Back at the doomed hospital the trio of vigilantes were sat on the cold stone steps on level 2, all of them silent as the realisation of what they had just done, suddenly hit them. Tina still trembled as she folded herself into Kev's thin body, and Ed was trying to relax by smoking a thick spliff, all three of them were lost in their own personal thoughts, because if they were caught, they all knew the consequences of the deadly action that they had just taken. The reality of the situation finally sank in after murdering Paul, the child rapist and murderer.

That was when Kev sighed, "I will take the blame for what we have done tonight, as far as the police are concerned you two weren't even there, OK?" his two friends seemed to be somewhat relieved as they both nodded their agreement. Back in their room on the top floor, the lovers silently made love and were lay trembling in each others arms. Tina had not said a word since they had returned to the hospital. Kev didn't turn to look at her, when he asked quietly,

"Do you want to talk about it?" she said nothing for a while,

"I know what we did was right and I know that we did it for the right reasons and that he deserved everything that we did to him, it's just that now that I have had time to think about it, maybe we went a bit too far?" He was just about to speak when Sarah and Alice appeared, the dead girls were standing hand in hand in front of them. Sarah whispered. "We have come to say thank you for what you have done, we briefly saw uncle Paul when his spirit first appeared, but before he could speak to us, he was taken by those horrible growlers, he will be exiled and never see another spirit for ever and ever. When the black demons came for him he was crying, but I didn't feel at all sorry for him, not at all, and now that he has an eternity to think about what he did to the three of us, and thank you again" both sisters smiled and waved as they slowly faded away.

Two days later Kevin was laid all alone, dozing on his sleeping bag, where Tina was he didn't know, but he knew that she wouldn't be too far  away. There were three loud bangs that echoed along the empty corridors, Kev went out to find Ed sat on the steps eating a wonderful smelling bacon butty. Kev sat down by his friend and was handed a hot roll, and a cup of steaming tea, he turned to his friend. "The papers are calling us hero's for what we did to that perv, but the police said that we should have left justice to them" Kev thought about this statement and answered. "But they didn't know what we knew, did they, and if they had known about that shit, while they had been investigating the case, that bastard would still have been messing with little Molly, and we couldn't have that could we?" It was then that Tina turned up, she was also passed a bacon butty and a cup of tea, Thanking him she took over the conversation,

"We need to have a serious talk, I have just been chatting to the other dead young girls, and they are saying that if they are avenged, they themselves may be able to leave this awful place, and then be able to move on to a place where they can then rest in peace forever with family members. So what do you think, in for a penny, in for a pound?" Both men turned and looked at her, she in turn looked from one face to the other and shrugged, Ed stood up and took a couple of steps downwards, and without looking back,

"Count me in". Kev shrugged and nodded his agreement, Tina smiled. "Let me find out some more details about our next target, Sarah and Alice are prepared to remain here for a while, just to help out. It seemed that the other dead girls only want to deal with me, simply because they are still afraid, and have no trust in grown men. They have also told me that some of their stories are to embarrassing to share with adult males." Both men understood and accepted what she was saying, so they decided to leave everything to her.

Tina spent lot's of time talking quietly with the other young girl ghosts, and ever so slowly more and more details of their horrendous stories were told. Sarah and Alice had made it quite clear that they would stay until most of the girls had been avenged, then they would be reunited with their dead relatives, their aunties were already waiting close by to take them to a place where they could be looked after when they were ready. They would then be able to run around for as long as they wanted in the vast parks and play areas that apparently littered the heavens above. They had heard tales of distant schools, specialist children's hospitals, where new born babies and toddlers were allowed to grow to a predetermined age and then educated. Once they had reached the said age, they were then allowed to rest peacefully with their family members, that was until their biological parents passed over, then those adults would be reunited with their offspring.

After a short discussion they decided that the youngest girl Ellie should be the next to be avenged. Ellie was a tiny, 7 year old pretty, petite, blonde haired girl, and after a lot of time spent talking to the older woman. She had eventually told Tina that her daddy was a drug addict, and in a drugged up state one day, he had forced her to take two blue ecstasy tablets, from which she had died a very slow, painful death. But her daddy had lied to the police and blamed her mummy for everything. Somehow the policeman in charge had believed him, and taken her mummy away, to be locked up. Ellie had visited the police station where her mother was being held and witnessed her mummy crying in her small lonely cell, this had made the little girl ghost very sad, she said that she had tried to talk to her mummy, but she didn't know how, because she had not had that lesson yet. Tina snorted,

"This bastard was known as Pecker, because of his beak like nose, and from what I hear he buys his drugs from a bloke called Speck

in the Kiln pub, down on the Walls estate. Kev looked at Ed.
"Your department I think?" Ed nodded. "I will go down to the
pub at opening time and see if he turns up, but I will need a few
quid?" Kev passed him some folded up notes and added. "Why
don't you get something really nasty while you are at it, something
really bad that will teach this bastard a permanent lesson" Ed
nodded and left the lovers sat on the step holding hands, Kev was
again deep in thought, as he made his silent, revengeful plans for
the murdering drug addict.

# CHAPTER 19

Ed had walked miles and asked many discreet questions, in his quest to find the elusive Pecker, but the junkie moved around a lot in his constant search for any free drugs that might be available, sleeping in different squats, on friends floors, cold park benches, all depending on what drugs he could get his hands on. Ed was told that Pecker was stick thin and he couldn't miss him because of his long unwashed brown hair, and a body odour to match, and like his nose, his face also seemed to be pointed, it was as if his head had at some time or other been trapped in a vice. He had red sores all around his mouth, his main feature was his very large pointed beak like nose. Ed was also told that Pecker did on occasion buy his own drugs, but only when really desperate, but if there were anything to be had that was free, he wasn't the sort of scrounger to pass them up.

Ed finally located the murderer outside the local 24 hour shop, and decided to follow him around for a bit, just to see what he got up to. With Ed buying cannabis from different local dealers, he began to find out little bits of interesting information about Pecker, he did this by asking some carefully worded questions. The main thing that he found out was that the target was a selfish bastard, always taking and never giving.

Ed was standing at the bar in the Kiln pub having a quiet drink, waiting and watching, when he over heard two blokes talking at a nearby table about Pecker, and how he had laughed when he had told them how he had set his misses up to take the fall for him, and even boasted about how he had done away with the bitches kid.

"Someone ought to sort that bastard out" one of the men said. Ed found out plenty about Pecker in a few short days, the most interesting thing being that he would walk the short distance down Digby Road from the shit hole that he lived in, to the Kiln pub where and if needed, he would buy his own hard drugs. He normally bought his class A fix, every day around 8 o'clock in the evening.

 As soon as he had his drugs, he would be so desperate for a hit that he didn't even wait until he got home, he usually went straight to the public toilets next to the park, did his thing and would then stagger home sometime later, where he would usually crash out on the settee, completely out of it. Ed sat with his two comrades and told them everything that he had learned about the bastard Pecker, and it didn't take them long to formulate a strategy. The following evening Kev and Ed would be waiting inside the toilets at 8 o'clock, then they would put their plan into action.


The next night the two men were stood together in one of the many graffiti covered cubicles, some of the writings offering sexual liaisons, others were poems that they laughed at as they waited in the stinking toilets, stood there acting like a couple of queers. A few minutes later a scruffy looking geezer walked into the toilets, he wore a mouldy looking green Parka coat, his hair was long and unkempt. When Ed took a peek to make sure that it was their man, Pecker was stood by the sinks. He removed the long coat and just dropped it onto the dirty wet floor in his haste to get his fix, he then rolled up the sleeve of his shirt, they then watched him loosely tie a thin brown plastic belt around his upper left arm. This done he then began cooking his drugs in a dirty desert spoon by using a blue plastic cigarette lighter, just as he was about to draw the drugs into his needle, Ed stepped out of the stall and stood directly behind their intended victim. Pecker looked into the mirror at Ed,

"And what the fuck do you want then?" Pecker shouted. Ed smirked. "I have come with a message from Ellie" Pecker suddenly went white, and stared at Ed,
"What do you know about Ellie, I don't know you?" Ed said

menacingly. "Wash the drugs down the sink, Pecker" the unkempt man smiled. "You ain't got no fucking chance mate, I have been waiting for this all day and a fucking wanker like you ain't going to stop me from having it" with that he turned around with a nasty looking knife in his hand, and shouted angrily. "Now fuck off sonny before you get hurt," Kev stepped out of his cubical with the base ball bat and hit the drug addict hard in the stomach, so hard that Pecker grunted, bent from the waist and dropped to his knees gasping for breath, the spoon and the much needed drugs lying unused in the green piss filled trough.

The two men bound the druggies hands together behind his back with a cable tie, and almost dragged a sobbing Pecker back to the deserted hospital, throughout the whole journey all he did was complain about his drugs being lost, and that he couldn't afford any more. Kev said somewhat sarcastically. "I wouldn't worry to much about that me old son, we have something very special lined up for you" As they dragged him up to the top of the hospital, once there they pushed him into one of the empty rooms. The chosen room had black iron bars at the window, what their original intended use had been, they had no idea. They tied the druggie up by his hands to the steel bars and left him there shouting and cursing, as they walked out of the room and closed the door on him.

With Pecker now secure the two men carried a cheap wooden table into the room, and placed it directly in front of the still moaning drug addict, who stopped complaining and looked at the table quizzically, they left the room just as Tina walked in and studied their prisoner. He looked her up and down and asked sarcastically. "And who's fucking slag are you then?" she smiled at him,
"I might be a slag, but I have never murdered a child" he physically flinched at this and glared at her. "What the fuck do you know about it, eh shit-head?" he asked her nastily. She smiled

and walked out. The two men entered the room again, they were standing at the table looking down at a small clear plastic bag that Ed had placed there, inside were eight oval blue pills, Pecker asked them what they were, and Ed said gloatingly,

"These are new on the market and you me old son are going to be the first person to try them out, they are called back-kick, because they are some sort of high grade horse tranquilliser, it was recommended that when I bought them that you take no more than two pills as they will fuck your brain up, so I thought that eight tabs would just about do the job that we had in mind" Kev nodded his agreement and smiled at Pecker. Tina was in the corridor quietly talking to the child ghosts, trying her best to get Ellie to go into the room, and confront her father. "Without trying to be to rude Ellie, he would literally shit himself if he saw you, so what do you think, eh Ellie love, a chance to get some sort of revenge?" the young girl asked what they were going to do to him? Tina shrugged. "The men have that side of things sorted, they will let me know when it was time and then we will go in, OK Ellie?" the young girl answered. "I will come in with you, but only if all of the other girls will come in with me?"


Pecker watched the two men as they tied his ankles to the bottom of a grey looking radiator with long black cable ties, now tethered spreadeagled the two men took another of the long black plastic cable tie, Ed did his best to hold onto the murderers head, the druggie twisted his head from side to side as he fought Kev as he tried to tie a cable tie around Peckers forehead, and then to the bar that was directly behind his head. Ed suddenly let go of Pecker, he took a step back and punched the man as hard as he could right on the point of the chin. The druggie grunted, as his head fell forward, Ed lifted Peckers head and held it still, Kev pulled the black tie so tight, that it was indented in the man's spotty forehead. They waited until Pecker regained consciousness, he instantly began shouting again. "You can shout as much as you like my friend, no-one is going to hear you and by the way we have a little surprise for you, but we are going to save that for later. Now we want to eat, so if you will excuse us."

Ed went out to the chippy, and the three of them sat at the table in the same room as their prisoner and ate their supper. Ed tormented Pecker a few times by standing in front of him, and offering him a bite of sausage or a few chips, Pecker would open his mouth in anticipation, but Ed would smile broadly, and then pull the food away and smirk as he ate the food himself.

Pecker watched as Ed carried a metre length of clear plastic tubing a blue funnel and some long black cable ties into the room, and placed them onto the table, the tube was big enough in diameter to allow the blue pills to slide through it easily. Tina placed a jug of water and a saucer on the table just in front of Pecker, Kev emptied the blue pills into the saucer and picking up the short length of plastic tubing, and began to swing it around and around, Pecker's eyes locked onto the pills and asked. "What are you going to do to me?" "Never you mind, you will find out soon enough" He then nodded to his lover, so she left the room to fetch the young ghosts, Kev turned to his partner in crime.

"You have always said that you were an unbeliever of sorts, well now you are going to get real proof" Tina returned to the room, she looked at Ed and told him to stand still as the girls hadn't met him before, and that they were still very nervous of strangers. Tina opened the door and whispered to what seemed like an empty corridor, still holding the door open Sarah and Alice seemed to hesitate, they floated in mid air before nervously entering the room, bringing a gasp from both Pecker and Ed, as they were confronted for the first time with something that they had always believed to be a figment of peoples imagination.

The dead sisters looked at the bound man and then nervously at Ed. Sarah placed her hand to her sisters ear and whispered something that only the dead girl heard. Alice seemed to glide from the room, a few seconds later she came slowly back into the room hand in hand with Ellie. Pecker eyes went wide as he was confronted by his dead daughter, Pecker let out a scream that was so loud that it echoed down the corridors of the deserted hospital. "Hello daddy" whispered the dead child, Pecker was now groaning out loud, his eye bulged so much that they looked as if they were standing on stalks, he was now white with fear as a dark stain spread down the front of his dirty jeans, as he literally pissed himself, Ellie asked her father in a tiny unearthly voice,

"Why did you blame mummy for what you did to me, daddy?" the bound mans mouth moved as if he was trying to say something, but no sound came out as he stared into the hollow eyes of his dead daughter. Ellie looked behind her into the doorway and waved, the other dead girls then slowly entered the room. Now all six girls ghosts were in the room, staring with dead eyes at Ellie's evil father, only his terrified eyes moved as Pecker looked from spirit to spirit, he was holding his breath as if his body was going into some sort of shock. Kevin could literally feel Ed physically shaking as he stood by his side. Kev asked Ellie if she had anything else to say to her father. She never removed her eyes from her father as she shook her head. "Then, its time" Kev gripped Ed by the arm and eased him towards the table. Kev picked up a long black cable tie, he then gripped Peckers chin and pulled it down as far as he could, holding the chin as tightly as possible. Kev tied the cable through the metal bars and around Peckers chin, pulling the cable tie tight. Pecker's head was now held so tightly, it was as if his head was trapped in a vice, the white faced murderer was being held there with his mouth forced wide open, his wild blue eyes still staring at his dead daughter.

Kev picked up the first of the blue pills and showed it to Pecker. "You deserve to die through drugs you evil bastard, I just hope that your death will be as painful as your daughters was, are you ready to meet your maker?" Pecker couldn't really speak because of the way that his head was being held. He just stared at the tiny girl that he had murdered. Kevin placed the first of the blue pills onto the back of the man's grey tongue Ed picked up the plastic tube and placed the end into the addicts mouth, he then tipped some water through the tubing using the funnel, he used just enough liquid to allow the man to swallow the pill, they repeated this until all eight pills had been fed to their prisoner. They stood back and watched as he suddenly began to froth at the mouth, he then urinated again, a dark stain spreading even further down his left leg, his body began jerking back and forth, his eyes finally rolled back in their sockets. Pecker then began making a squeaking sound that came from somewhere deep in his chest, then thick black blood that was full of tiny bubbles, oozed out of the side of his mouth. The bound man pushed his body forward as he groaned out loud, then he became silent as his body seemed to literally sag against his bondings, the whole of his bodies weight was now being held by his tethered head, stretching his thin looking neck to what looked like double its original length.

Violent tremors rose up and down his dirty thin body until he finally became still, a few seconds later a lump seemed to expand his stomach, and then a grey cloud emerged as Pecker's spirit appeared outside of his body. The drug addict slowly turned and looked at what had once been him, there came a deep groaning sound that appeared from somewhere under ground, then the growling became even louder, which made them all turn their heads and look into the far corner of the room. The dead girls all seemed to huddle against each-other as they inched away from the unearthly sound, the now low groan slowly but eerily changed to that of an old castle door opening, just as if the hinges had just been used for the first time in many hundreds of years. A loud groan, once-again filled the room as long thin black tentacle shape fingers, simply seemed to just appear out of the solid concrete floor. Peckers spirit began to scream out loud, and his face changed to one of a look of pure terror, as he watched as the long fingers of the many arms of the growlers fold around his now dead body, Pecker was then literally dragged across the room, his dead hands reaching out to them for help, his screams suddenly stopped as his spirit was dragged towards the far corner of the room. Pecker disappeared into the concrete floor to where he would meet and serve his new master, which was just what he deserved.

The room remained deadly quiet for a long time, then Ellie moved to Tina and seemed to fold herself into her, Tina in turn seemed to somehow hold the tiny child ghost, just as a mother would hold a loving child. Everyone else slowly turned and left the room, leaving Tina to comfort the dead child. Ellie eventually pulled away from Tina, the dead girl looked at the open door and smiled, "My nana is coming, she will look after me now, thank the others for what they have done for me, and thank you Tina, I love you". The dead child hugged Tina one last time, on her release she smiled and moved slowly towards the door. An old grey haired woman spirit momentarily entered the room, Ellie called out to her nana, she then floated towards the old woman and after a brief hug, the pair held each others hand and were gone.

# CHAPTER 20

The trio of vigilantes sat on the cold stone steps of the condemned hospital, in the fading light they discussed what had taken place that day, it was Ed that seemed to be more shocked than the others, as he finally had to accept that he now believed in ghosts.

It was Tina that began talking, saying that they ought to stop what they were doing, because she was frightened that the whole thing was getting completely out of hand, and that they would all end up in jail for the rest of their lives. Her lover stared at her for an age as he tried to find the words that he needed, finally he shrugged his shoulders and said, "But we can't stop now, what about the others, they all need to be avenged and there was no-one else to do it but us. Maybe god almighty would punish them one day, but until that day arrived, how many more innocent children would get hurt by these men, if the three of us don't do something about it?" Ed looked from one to the other and again confirmed that he was in for the long haul, he then said that if he was going to prison for what they had already done, then he may as well make it worth while, and finish the job. Tina suggested that they wait and see what happened next with the girl ghost's, and then make their decision.

Nothing happened for a few days which gave them a chance to leave the hospital, and with Kev's new looks, stroll around the shops as if they hadn't got care in the world. But as the days slowly passed, still there was no ghost activity what so ever, it was as if the spirits had simply abandoned them all together.

When the lovers woke one warm sunny morning, Sarah and Alice were hovering by the side of their makeshift bed, looking down at them as if they had been waiting for them to wake up. Kev was now so used to having the dead girls around that he wasn't startled in any way by having the ghosts so close, he just looked from one to the other, and casually said,"Hello you two, we haven't seen you for a few days, is everything ok?" As usual it was Sarah that did the talking, and told them that they had to stay away because, there was a very large lady wandering around up above, and she was searching everywhere for him. She was ranting and raving about taking revenge for what he had done to her. But you are not to worry because there were some very high ranking ghosts in the same area as this fat spirit, these V.I.P.'s had been sent down from the inner cloud to steer her off her in a different direction, so that she could continue her search in a some far of land.

These important spirits are the ones that are in ultimate authority up above, they control everything that happened, and we have it on good authority that they know and appreciate what you had done for us, and they would like you to continue what you are doing. They have also sent a team or security men to keep a very close eye on your dead wife, and they will track her movements. It will be their intention to persuade her to keep looking in a different area, and feed her false information, to make certain that she continues her search somewhere else. They will do this every time she gets anywhere near you, this protection plan will stay in place, and be there all the time that you continue your work. Kev was shocked to hear from Sarah that the fat bitch was even trying to find him in the first place, and he had to admit to himself that he hadn't even considered the fact that she would become a spirit, but what could she do to him if she did ever find him, nothing, right?

Sarah moved slowly forward and looked down at the floor as she asked quietly, "are you going to carry on with the revenge thing, only we heard you talking last night and we wouldn't blame you if you wanted to stop, because we know the risk that you three are taking every time you take action" Kevin smiled his best crooked smile as he realised that the young ghost was communicating with them, in language that was way beyond her years, he wondered how those in charge achieved this?

He reassured the sisters that they were going to continue with their plans, and that they were more than happy to do so. He then asked them which girl was the next that needed their help? Sarah seemed to want to say something, but it was as if she didn't know how. Reading the sign of her nervousness, he instantly took control of the situation, and did his best to reassure the young ghost, by talking quietly to her. Sarah seemed to take hold of her sisters hand, and whispered that they had decided that Steph would be next, but that it may not be as easy as the last two, because there were a lot more people involved, "maybe it would be better if we were to let her tell you her terrible story, we will try our best and bring her to you later, but as before, she will only talk to Tina."

Tina, once she had dressed, waited in the next room for Sarah to bring the nervous young victim to see her. It was some time later that the sisters finally arrived with the tiny shy little girl. The sisters left, leaving the murdered girl standing in the middle of the room with her head bowed as if she had done something wrong. It was as though she was standing outside her head masters door, waiting to be punished for some minor mis deed. Steph finally built up the courage to move to Tina's side, and in a voice that was no more than a whisper, she finally began to tell her the sad story of how she had begun to have piano lessons with a Miss Shelly at her house, "I was almost nine years of age, everything was fine at first and I really enjoyed the lessons and was getting quite good."

It was then that the blond teacher began to do some strange things to me, things that I didn't like or understand. Like after a few lessons she would kiss me on the side of the mouth, just before I left for home, she would hug me to her as she told me how good I had been, and that the kiss was a reward for all my hard work. The next time she kissed me again, but this time it was right on my lips, she kept on kissing me as she rubbed her hands all over me, which made me cry and left me very confused, because I didn't know what was happening to me. When it was time for me to leave, she made me promise that it would be our little secret, and if I told anyone then we would both get into a lot of trouble.

When it was time for me to go to her again for another lesson, I made all sorts of excuses not to go, but my father insisted, saying that it would be an advantage in the future if I could play the piano. Well, as soon as I arrived at the teachers house for my next lesson, the older woman closed the door behind me and pushed me back against it, and then undid her own shirt and revealed her naked breasts, she took my hands and placed them onto her breasts. I tried to tell her to stop, but the older woman just held onto me tightly, and began kissing me on the mouth again, she even tried to push her tongue into my mouth.

[it was at this point that she turned away and almost disappeared] But the young ghost found the courage from somewhere and told Tina that she really tried her best to resist her but she did't know how. Miss Shelly was very strong, too strong for me and she did other things to me that I can't talk about. When it was all over, the blond woman turned my head towards hers, and whispered "that wasn't too bad now was it, and now we have a really big secret that must always stay between us, and you must never tell a living soul what has happened here today, or we will both go to prison, promise?" Well, what could I say, so I just smiled up at her. When the day came for me to go to the teacher for my next lesson, I said that I didn't want to go because I didn't want to learn the piano any more, but my father again insisted that I should go. I cried and held onto my mother, but in the end I had no option but to go. As soon as I arrived at Miss Shelly's house, I knew that something wasn't right, you see she opened the door dressed in a dark blue dressing gown that had a big golden dragon on the back, as soon as I had walked inside, the teacher closed and then locked the door behind her, something that she hadn't done before.

The blond woman removed her dressing gown to reveal her nakedness, I didn't know where to look or what to do. I stood with my back to the door and asked to be let out, and said that I wanted to go home, but the older woman grabbed me by the hand, "But you are a big girl now and we have a big secret, don't we?" I won't tell you what happened next because I am to ashamed, but what I will tell you is this, she removed all my clothes and did these disgusting things to me, and made me do some things to her, things that I really didn't like. After it was all over and she allowed me to get dressed, Miss Shelly sat me down, she then told me that we now had a really big secret, and how if I ever said anything to anyone, they would both end up in prison and I would never see my mother again. "This went on for three weeks, after that it was as soon as I entered the house, I would be stripped naked, she would then take me to her bed, and do these nasty things to me and expect me to do the same things to her." I want you to know that I still wasn't sure what was happening to me, but I did know that what ever it was, it was wrong.

Well, the following week I begged my father to let me stay at home, but he wouldn't hear of it, telling me that education was everything. Miss Shelly had me in her bed again, the first thing that she did was make me open my mouth and close my eyes, I did as I was told and she pushed a pill to the back of my throat, and held my mouth closed until the pill was gone. Almost at once I began to get all hot, and it was as if I couldn't move my arms and legs. Miss Shelly was watching me closely, she then told me "I have a little surprise for you today my special little princess" she then climbed naked from the bed and walked over to a door. When she opened the door two naked dark skinned men walked into the room, I could see their things and everything. I closed my eyes as tightly as I could, the next thing  that I knew was that Miss Shelly grabbed me and placed her hand over my mouth, [the embarrassed ghost hesitated and almost took flight, but she stayed strong and continued to tell her tale] the rest of what happened. Well, I won't tell you about it because it was too horrible to talk about. They did nasty, horrible things to me that really hurt, things that made me bleed, made me scream out loud into Miss Shelly's hand, the whole thing made me feel sick.

When it was all over Miss Shelly put a sanitary towel into my pants and allowed me to get dressed, she then sat me down on the edge of the bed and told me that the secret that we now had, had become a lot bigger, more people were now involved and that they would all go to prison if I said anything to anyone, and I didn't want that, did I?

That night I sat in my room and cried my heart out, my mum and my sister asked me what was wrong, but I couldn't tell them what had happened, could I, or they would all have ended up in prison. I bled for 4 days and my mum thought that I had started my periods early, I didn't know what to do about it, who could I tell? The next week I had to be literally dragged out of my bedroom to go to Miss Shelly's house, she gave me another pill only this time it was even worse, there were four men and they were all doing things to me at the same time, and all the time it was happening, Miss Shelly sat at the side of the bed smoking, one man even, no I can't say what he did, but it made me scream out loud, it hurt me so much, because when he did what he did, well I felt myself split.

When I arrived back home I ran up to my room, locked the door and threw myself onto my bed and cried for hours, it was then that I decided that I had to stop this from ever happening again, so I went into the bathroom and took all the pills out of the medicine cabinet that I could find, I returned to my bedroom and took as many pills as I could. I wrote a note to my father saying simply that it was his fault that I had done what I had done, and that I would never forgive him for making me go to Miss Shelly". And that was my story and that is how I have ended up here, and that is the first time that I have told anyone about this, and if you can stop it happening to any other little girl, then it was all worth while my telling you?"


Tina was crying her heart out at the tiny girls sad story, Sarah and Alice were now hugging the young ghost, as she seemed somehow relieved at having finally told her tale. Tina asked where they could find this Miss Shelly and promised that they would do their utmost to avenge her. With the address of the piano teacher now in her pocket, she sat and told the sad story to the other two vigilantes, both men were very angry but almost in tears at the telling of the sad tale.

Ed said that he would get straight onto it and go take a look see, but Tina stopped him, and said that she wanted to take this one on, she asked Kev for some money to buy some decent clothes and to get her hair done. She would then go and pay this Miss Shelly a visit. Kev gave his lover £200, and told her to spend it all and get whatever she needed.

The second that Tina had left the hospital, the two men began to make plans for Steph's revenge, they came to a joint decision as to how to deal with the abusers, in doing so they chose a large room towards the far end of the corridor that had all of its windows broken and was freezing cold. They took their time and cleared the room of all the broken furniture. Having searched the lower floors they carried 5 serviceable chairs into the empty room and lined them up against the far wall, they cut lengths of rope and secured them to each of the chairs, leaving the bonds hanging down and ready for use, they stood back and admired their handy work, because the first part of their plan, was now in place and ready for use.
Tina had been to the hair dressers and had her hair done, and had spent the afternoon clothes shopping, she had returned to the hospital and retired to the room next door to change, when she

walked back into Kev's room he was aghast, she looked truly stunning, so beautiful, youthful and he fell head over heels in love with her all over again. He made a grab for her, but she darted away from him saying that maybe she would let him catch her on her return, that was if he was very lucky. Tina took a taxi to Miss Shelly's house, she rang the door bell and waited, the woman that opened the door was maybe 5ft 8 inches tall and had a fine trim body, her breasts held high inside a tight fitting white silk shirt, the black trousers that she wore were obviously designer. Miss Shelly asked Tina if she could help her, Tina replied by asking "I understand that you give piano lessons and wondered if you could possibly fit my 10 year old sister, for lets say, 20 lessons?" Miss Shelly invited Tina inside the well furnished house, and told her that she would check her diary. Within a few minutes the lessons had been booked, the first one was to be held in three days time, on Thursday, at 3 o'clock in the afternoon. Tina then said that her little sister Susan, would be dropped off by her two older brothers.

Back at the derelict hospital she told the two men what she had arranged, and what Miss Shelly looked like, and that the rest was now up to them. After a brief chat Kev asked Ed if he could get hold of a nice car? Ed smirked as he looked at his friend and, asked sarcastically "what colour would you like mate?" All three of them chuckled at this. Kev said that he needed to go shopping and would madam care to join him? "only if you get a hair cut and have a shave first?" She replied. So Kev retrieved some of his stolen money and spent the afternoon being pampered as he tidied himself up, he bought new clothes and all of which was chosen by his lover. Even though they lived where and how they did, when dressed in their finest outfits, they would look like a very well to do couple when they were out. Kev had to go to a dodgy electronics shop [that had been recommended by Ed] to get what he required.

With all their shopping requirements finally met, the couple carried the purchases back to the hospital. Ed set up the new cam corder on its tripod, the trio messed about with the new equipment as they learned how to use it, they had a right laugh, first posing one way and then another. When Ed was satisfied that the cameras focus was set correctly, they left the room exactly as it was, ready for their first guest. Kev gave Ed some money and told him to go and buy whatever he needed to pass as a well to do brother to him. Kev shouted down the stairs as Ed went bounding down them two at a time "and get your hair cut while you are at it".

Kev stood on the corner by the bank and waited for Ed to arrive with the promised car, it was Wednesday afternoon at 2.30 and time to pay Miss Shelly a visit. Ed turned up in a brand new black BMW X5, Kev climbed in and looked around at the cream leather seats, "Very nice mate, where did you get it from?" Ed looked at his friend and smirked, "Test drive" as they made their way to Miss Shelly's house, Ed pulled into the short drive outside her house and parked the car, Kev went to the front door and rang the bell, Miss Shelly opened the door with a smile, Kev looked her up and down, she certainly was a good looking woman. Kev pressed the button on the new stun gun that he had bought especially for the occasion, and pushed it hard into the woman's stomach. Miss Shelly went stiff, fell over backwards, hit the back of her head on the slate floor and lay still, the only movement in her whole body was a slight twitch of her left hand. Kev walked past her, reached down, grabbed her right hand and literally dragged her from view and closed the door.

Ed walked into the house and stepped over the prone woman as he began looking around, Ed found a wooden jewellery box and when he opened the box it was full of money, mainly 50s and 20s plus a few expensive looking rings, Ed put the contents into his pockets. Kev raised his eyebrows as he looked at his friend, who smiled "well, she ain't going to need it, where she is going, is she?" Kev shrugged his shoulders, and they carried on searching.

In the bedroom Kev began pulling out drawers, removing books from shelves, after a few minutes of searching, he found what he was looking for, hidden behind a shoe box was a small remote controlled camera. Kev showed Ed what he had found and asked him where he thought the disks might be? Ed said that he would check out her computer, that done the search was on for the hidden disks. Ed found them in a metal cake tin behind the bath panel, each disk was marked with a girls name, her age and the date.

They selected a disk at random, the name on the disk was Amanda, the two men stood and watched the disk on the woman's computer and were disgusted at what they witnessed. The tiny blond girl of maybe 8 years old was being violated by 4 Asian men, who weren't the slightest bit embarrassed by what they were doing to the terrified tiny girl, they were so confident that they would never be found out, they didn't even try to hide their faces. Having seen enough Ed reversed the car up to the front door and opened the boot, a taped up Miss Shelly who was unceremoniously tossed into the boot of the expensive car, and the lid closed on her. Her computer, mobile phone and the disks were also placed into the car.

When the piano teacher regained consciousness she was tied to the middle of the five chairs that had been set out earlier by the boys, she looked at the trio sat opposite her and then tried to free her arms to no avail, she then growled "untie me, what the bloody hell do you think you are doing?" Tina sat in between the two boys and looked from one to the other and back to Miss Shelly, she took the opportunity to speak "well, lets just say that we have a message from a late student of yours, you do remember little Steph don't you, you know the one that you sexually abused so much, that she took her own life?"

Miss Shelly took in a sharp intake of breath and stared at Tina, the teacher went to speak but only stuttered, before she had a chance to finally get a word out Tina began to talk again "I bet you and your Asian friends thought that you had got away with it, you know, when she took her own life, didn't you? Well, I don't know whether you believe in the after life, but it was that poor little girl that told us all about you, and your taxi driver friends, everything that you did to her and what you forced her to do to you and them. Oh and by the way we want their names and phone numbers, because as you can see we have enough chairs for each one of them"

The piano teacher looked to her left and to her right at the empty chairs, and then back at the trio sat before her, in a low voice she growled "are you lot fucking mad or what" they all smiled at her and Kev stood up and left the room, he came back with the teachers computer and placed it on the table facing her, after pressing a few buttons he moved away, the sound of a struggling young Steph, and the sound of laughing adults filled the room. Miss Shelly had suddenly turned very pale as she stared at the computer screen, after a few seconds she whispered "please turn it off" Tina said angrily "no, we won't turn it off, we are going to leave the room now and you will watch the whole disk and when it is finished, we will put it on again and again, until you finally realise what you have done, and how many young lives you have ruined, for what? A bit of self satisfaction, pleasure?"

Well let me tell you lady, what we have planned for you won't be very pleasurable at all, so if I were you I would enjoy the last bit of pleasure that you would ever have" They all rose to their feet and were about to leave the room, when the teacher spoke, "they made me do it, they said that if I didn't do it, then they would spread lies about me, and that would put me out of business, then I would lose my house and everything" not one of the trio said a word as they left the room, Ed glared at her and then snarled, as he closed the door behind them. Once back in Kev's room they all sat down, Kev sighed "let's give it an hour, then we will go

back in and again ask her for the mens names" Ed was sat quietly
flicking through Miss Shelly's phone, when he began clicking his
lips "this may be a lot bigger than we think, there are lot's of
names for taxi's in her phone, the problem was, which are the
ones we want?" Kev stood up "well let's go and ask her?" when
they walked back into the room, Miss Shelly had tears streaming
down her cheeks as the men on the screen were still abusing
Steph.

Tina walked over and stopped the disk, all three stood and looked
at her, she in turn looked from face to face and whispered "I'm so
sorry, I thought that the girls would enjoy it, but now I see that I
was wrong" Kevin said simply "we want those 4 names and we
want them now, if you don't give us what we want, Ed here will
set the disk to replay all night, we will go to bed and leave you to
it" Miss Shelly lowered her head and shook it from side to side.
Ed moved to the computer and did his thing, he turned the
volume up, and the trio left the woman to it.

# CHAPTER 21

Early the next morning Tina entered the room that held Miss Shelly, she stood and looked at the comatose looking piano teacher and it was obvious that she had wet herself sometime during the night. The blond woman's chin now rested heavily on her chest, Tina walked over to the computer and turned it off, as soon as the room fell into silence Miss Shelly lifted her head, and looked at Tina "are you ready to give us the names of the men on the disk?"

Miss Shelly again shook her head slowly from side to side. Tina did no more that walk over to the computer and turn it back on, the sickening sound of child abuse filled the room once-more.

The trio sat and pondered what to do next when Kev turned to Tina, "see if you can contact Sarah and tell her that we need her help" Tina left the room and walked along the upper level, and called out the young ghost's name, it wasn't long before Tina sensed someone following her.Tina stopped and slowly turned, Sarah laughed quietly and moved closer, "You called for me Tina?" Tina told her that they needed her help trying to get some information out of Steph's piano teacher, and could she and her sister come with her and talk to the two men?

Sarah hovered just off the ground as she looked from face to face, as Kevin spoke" Sarah we need your help, do you think that you could persuade Steph to face Miss Shelly, we need to scare the teacher enough, so that she will give up the names of the 4 men that abused her?" Sarah seemed to sit down in the corner of the room for a few seconds before looking at Tina, "Can you put some loose paper and such like in the room, then leave the rest to me and Alice. If perhaps you could just drop a hint or two about ghost's, we will then see what we can do?".

The two men went from room to room finding what discarded

paper they could, in one room they found some really old patient files, so they carried them up the stone steps and placed them in the room with the blond woman, "what are you doing?" the bound woman asked but was ignored, when the last sheets of paper were taken into the room, Kev hinted "I hope you believe in ghost's Miss Shelly, because I know that they get really angry if there was to much paper laying about in one place" he stood still, and looked slowly around the room, he gave a shiver "can you feel them coming?"

They left the teacher on her own in the room that now had its floor littered with loose sheets of paper, they waited out of sight in the silent corridor. They took the occasional peak through the window, nothing happened for quite a while, they saw the odd sheet of paper begin to stir, and then slowly lift up into the air. Miss Shelly watched the thick clouds of dust mixed in with the sheets of paper as they began floating around the room, and for a few seconds convinced herself that it was the wind blowing through the broken windows.

She suddenly became terrified, her eyes standing out on stalks, her jaw had dropped and they could see her visibly shaking, she had turned a very pale colour. The room had become eerily still again, but not for long, the room was suddenly filled with sheets of paper that was flying in all directions, climaxing in a funnel around the stricken woman, so much so that they couldn't even see Miss Shelly, but they could hear her screaming. Just as quickly as the event had begun, the room fell silent again as the paper slowly descended to the floor, to settle all around the piano teacher, the room became eerily still and icy cold, the only thing moving were the piano teachers eyes, as they moved rapidly from side to side. The terrified eyes watched as Sarah floated across the room and hovered by the side of the terror stricken woman. The dead girl looked as if she was whispering into the bound woman's ear, seconds later an ear piercing scream seemed to echo through the whole building. Miss Shelly's head fell forward as she fell into a deep faint, her body so still that she could quite easily have been dead.

Sarah and Alice emerged through the wall to hover next to Tina who smiled "that was pretty cool you two, we might just leave that paper in that room, just in case we need to scare her again" Tina looked at Sarah and asked what she had said to the woman who now trembled uncontrollably, and had a small pool of greenish, smelly urine beneath her chair, a smile seemed to appear on the dead girls face, "I only told her that Steph was going to see her soon"

The trio waited until the teacher lifted her head before they reentered the room, she looked pleadingly from face to face before asking Tina "please let me go to the toilet" Tina looked under the chair, "it seems to be a bit too late for that" the trio all laughed out loud. Kev leaned in close to her and whispered "do you believe in ghosts now Miss Shelly, you see we have been talking to little Steph, you know, the little girl who you abused along with your Asian friends, we want their names, we have your phone and your computer, but there are so many of your contacts identities on both, because of that, we don't know which ones we need to speak to. So either you tell us their names now, or we will let little Steph come in and ask you?"

Miss Shelly slowly shook her head in defeat, as she looked from face to face, she then gave them the four names that they required, now that she was finally beaten, she looked at Tina and asked to use the toilet again. Kev nodded and Ed cut the piano teacher free and Tina took the deflated woman into the room where Kev's toilet was situated, Ed stood outside the door as Tina stayed in the room and watched untrustingly, as the prisoner did her business.

Back in her chair the blonde woman seemed as though the weight of the world had been lifted from her shoulders. Ed sat in front of the computer, he stared intently at the screen and pressed various buttons, when he had located the information that he required, he wrote down each name and its contact details on a writing pad. With names and numbers now in his possession, he led the other two out of the room, leaving the trussed up, teacher all on her own again, to cry floods of big fat tears.

Back in Kev's room Ed looked from face to face "Well, we have the information we needed, now what we need is a plan" Kev answered "we will have to lure them to a quiet place where we will be waiting with the BMW, we will stun them, chuck them in the boot of the car, then drag them up here two at a time, to join their friend.

I have been thinking, why don't we let the girls deal with them, I am pretty certain they must know other ghost's like John the Jailer or similar such spirits that can do whatever needed doing, lets ask them next time we see them?" His partners in crime liked the sound of that idea, and readily agreed with him.

CHAPTER 22

The time was 11-35 pm on a dark windy night and the vigilantes were ready to set the first stage of their plan into action. The first name on the list was Arif Patel, Kev had already dialled his number and was waiting for the taxi to arrive at his location. Kev stood all alone on Decca Street, which was situated down the side of the Odeon cinema and the perfect location for their needs.

Arif had to turn down the dimly lit side street to pick up his fare. Kev turned the stun gun over and over in his pocket, as he nervously waited for the child abuser to arrive. Tina and Ed sat in the BMW, waiting and watching only a few feet away, both of them silent with nervousness, eyes scanning the empty street looking for any prying eyes, but at the same time, knowing that they were most likely being watched from one of the 18 th century terraced houses, each one with its own set of cotswold stone steps, each of the four storey houses had once belonged to someone important, a doctor, lawyer or even a politician.
Each household back then even had its own butler and servants, putting on afternoon tea on Sunday afternoon. But now they would be owned by some foreign corporation and filled to the brim with immigrant families and caring about nothing but profit, the whole area controlled and run by fear.

Whereas the streets here would at one time have seen fine horse drawn carriages trundling noisily over the cobbles. Glowing bright gas lamps on every street corner, always lit to allow the house owner safe passage but now the dark, dangerous streets were littered with broken down cars and piles of rubbish that no one seemed to be bothered about.

This made the street perfect for what they had planned, Ed knew that even if someone was watching their every move, fear would prevent them from calling the police.

Now, both of them were ready to burst into action the second that they were certain their friend had subdued the taxi driver. Kev watched the black cab as it slowly turned the corner, the cab stopped by the side of Kev who opened the rear door and climbed into the rear seat, The driver lifted his head as he waited for his instructions, Kev spoke in a soft voice on purpose so that Arif had to slide the security panel open in order to hear where his fare wanted to go.

Arif turned his head sideways and again indicated with a lift of his head for Kev to state his destination, Kev used this as an excuse to lean slightly forward and press the business end of the stun-gun under the Asian man's ear. The old car lurched forward a few feet as the bearded, middle aged driver slumped down in his seat, totally unconscious.

As soon as Kev climbed from the rear of the cab, his two accomplices stepped out of their car and casually walked the few paces over to the cab, Tina then went to the end of the road and kept watch as the two men unceremoniously dragged their victim out of the front seat of the cab, they picked him up and bundled the thin bearded driver into the boot of the BMW and silently closed the boot lid. Kev took out his phone and dialled the second number on his list, and asked to be picked up at the same location. Ed had moved Arifs cab further down the dark side street, he then removed all the money that he could find, before leaving the black cab parked up, with the keys still in the ignition, just where it was.

The second cab driver Faisal Patel drove a smart looking blue Honda civic, the taxi stopped by the side of a smiling Kev, who climbed into the front seat next to the driver and simply jabbed the stun-gun into the fat drivers brown neck. The car did a bit of Kangaroo jumping, before it stalled, as the man slumped down in his seat Kev unclipped the unconscious mans sat belt. Again Tina ran to the end of the road and looked both ways, with the coast clear she waved her right arm which indicated for them to carry on, and do what they needed to do.

The two men pulled the limp, smelly, beer gutted man aged in his early 40s from the front seat of the car, they then sort of carried the heavy lump of a driver to rear of the BMW. Ed pressed a button on the key fob and the expensive cars boot automatically opened, the first thing that they noticed in the bright light of the boot, was the yellow of the eyes of the first driver, as he stared up at them with a dazed look on his face.

Kev didn't hesitate, he removed the stun-gun from his jacket pocket, and quickly returned the man back into deep unconsciousness. They lifted Faisal and pushed him into the cars boot next to his friend, realising that they had made a fundamental mistake, and should have bound their first prisoners hands together when they had initially captured him. Ed went to the front of the car and took out a bundle of long black cable ties [which he had brought especially for that purpose] from his back pack and between them, they managed to secure the two unconscious mens hands behind their backs.

Ed walked quietly through all the litter and discarded rubbish into the dirty squat to make sure that his druggie friends were all fast asleep, when he was confident that all was well, he walked back to the car and opened the boot, both men were now looking up at him, with eyes filled with fear, confusion and hate. Kev and Tina stood by the rear of the car waiting for Ed to join them, both of the terrified men in the boot begun asking the two white men questions, but Ed smiled and showed them the stun-gun, he then put his finger to his lips to quiet the captured men.

Tina kept watch as her friends helped the struggling men out of the car, it took a lot of effort because they had to almost drag their prisoners up every one of the concrete steps, as they made their way to the top floor. When they had reached the top floor of the hospital, both of the taxi drivers began asking questions of their captors again, but as before they were ignored totally. Both dark skinned men gasped out loud when they were forcibly pushed into the room where the piano teacher was being held prisoner.

The beaten woman sat silent as her friends were dragged forward and pushed down onto one of the wooden chairs, they were positioned one either side of the singing teacher, both men stared at her quizzically, but she would not meet their gaze, she simply shook her head and closed her eyes. The drivers did little to fight their captors as they were bound hand and foot to the chairs. The Asian men began firing questions at the terrified woman, all she did in response was to look from one to the other, close her eyes, shake her head again, and lower her head down onto her chest as she refused to say a word. The two male prisoners stopped shouting at her and began talking to each other in their own language, as they looked back and forth from their captors to the piano teacher. Arif turned his head to look at the two men that were stood in front of them, he went to speak, but Kev smiled and put his finger to his lips, and suggested to Ed that they gag the new prisoners.

The trio of friends retired to Kev's room to make coffee, and form a plan as to where they could lure the other two depraved drivers, Ed knew the area the best and they decided that Shore Street next to The Dockers arms would be as good a place as any, as the side street was always dark, due to the lack of poor street lighting. This row of expensive semi-detached houses were all set well back from the road, each of the houses had high hedges and tall gates, which again made it the perfect place for their needs. So they pulled on their coats and set off on the next stage of their plan.

Kev put on a slightly drunken voice as he rang Suhel Kahn's number and ordered a taxi, Suhel said that he was just around the corner, and that he would be there in a few minutes. Kev watched the black cab turn into Shore Street, the old car slowed down and almost crawled along the dark street, as the driver searched for his fare. Kev stepped into the road and waved his arm, the car stopped by the side of him, and he climbed into the rear seat of the cab. The wife killer spoke quietly and just like before, the fat man in his fifties had to slide the security window open to hear where Kev wanted to go. Kev leant forward and pushed the stun-gun under the drivers left ear, the heavy man slid down in his seat, unconscious as the cab ever so slowly rolled forward and came to a shuddering stop when it collided with a parked car.

As soon as Kev climbed out of the taxi, in a now well practiced routine, Tina climbed out of the car and ran to the end of the road to make sure that the coast was clear, she indicated for them to carry on. Ed ran over to the taxi and helped Kev carry the fat man to the rear of the BMW, once his hands had been secured, they slid the unconscious driver into the boot, Ed pointed out to his friend that the fat man had holes in the bottom of both shoes, and his shiny black suit had seen better days, he obviously wasn't doing very well as a taxi driver. Ed moved the cab further down the road just as before, where he parked it up, making sure that he left the keys in the ignition.

Next came Siad Patesh, Kev rang the number and was told that the taxi would be with him in about five minutes, an old blue Ford came into view and turned the corner into Shore Street, the tyres almost screeching as if it was rallying, when Kev opened the door of the cab the sound of Asian music attacked his hearing. Kev slid into the rear of the saloon car, and before the young driver could even turn around, Kev pushed the stun-gun into the young mans neck, again the driver slumped down in his seat, and the trio followed the same routine as before. With both men now securely bound and safely stowed in the boot of the car, Ed drove back to the hospital, Ed again checked that his druggie friends were all still asleep, happy that they were.

Kev showed the prisoners the stun-gun, told them to be quiet and then escorted the now conscious drivers up the stone steps, all the way to the top floor. Both Asian men gasped out loud when they saw their friends tied to chairs. Within seconds they themselves filled the final two empty chairs, after a quick confused conversation in their native tongue, realising why they were there the newcomers shook their heads in sheer disbelief at being caught out.

# CHAPTER 23

With all five of the abusers now bound and gagged in the cold hospital room, the vigilantes stood looking down at the prisoners, who all stared back at them with hate filled brown eyes, the taxi drivers now realised why they were there, but what they didn't know was what was going to happen to them. Kev turned to Ed "what do you think about stripping them all naked, with the windows already having been broken, maybe chucking a bucket of cold water over them just to make sure that they were really cold. We could then put on one of the disks, set it on permanent play, just to keep them entertained?" because they knew that it was going to be a long scary night for their paedophile guests?

Ed agreed, and having given each one of them in turn the easier option of removing their own clothing, which they all refused. Ed took great pleasure as he used the stun-gun on each prisoner in turn. All their guests were now naked, and because with the cold wind blowing through the broken windows, they all shivered with cold as the wind whistled around the room.

Ed did his thing with the computer, which was now showing all five of them abusing a terrified young brown haired girl, with the volume now turned up high, the trio of vigilantes left the room to find Sarah standing looking at the row of sexual predators through a window, without moving her head she said "Steph is terrified of seeing them again, and I am having difficulty in getting her to face her torturers, but don't worry one of the older ghosts has taking charge of their punishment, as you requested, and she will keep them entertained through out the long night ahead, and from what I can gather, she was waiting for a rather special ghost, and some of her other dead friends to arrive.

When Kev entered the room again, not one of the prisoners was looking at what was taking place on the screen in front of them, when Kev looked at the computer the fat taxi driver had the little blond girls face pushed down into the bed clothes, and was holding the screaming child's body weight with both hands, and was taking great pleasure as he sodomised her. Kev walked over to the fat man, gripped his chin and forced him to watch what he was doing to the screaming child, "WATCH IT YOU FILTHY BASTARD" he screamed, by now there was some blood on the rear of the child's body which made the men all laugh. Kev pulled the man's face around to look at him, and said in a low menacing voice "so you all thought that that was fucking funny, did you? Well, lets see how you like a bit of pain then, shall we?" with that he stormed out of the room, slamming the door behind him.

Kev rushed into his room, filled the kettle to it's fullest and placed it onto his mobile gas stove to heat up, he turned to the others in the room and snarled,"I have just witnessed the full depravity of those sick bastards in there, and seen how they all laughed as they hurt and abused the poor child, well lets see them laugh when I have finished with them" Kev followed by his partners in crime, walked back into their guests room, they were stood looking at the row of prisoners, it was at that precise time that the little girl on the computer, screamed out in agony, which made everyone turn and look at the screen. They all watched as Arif took great pleasure in raping the tiny child.

Miss Shelly was holding the child's mouth open whilst Suhel forced himself into her oral orifice, making the tiny child gag as he tried to force himself down her throat. Kev turned back to the five prisoners and snarled with disgust "you sick load of fucks, well lets see how you like it?" With that he moved to each prisoner in turn, and poured boiling water into each of their laps. Pain filled screams filled the whole floor as blisters instantly appeared on each of the prisoners inner thighs and private parts.

Miss Shelly began whispering hysterically that she was sorry, she didn't mean for it to go as far as it had, and that the men had forced her to do it. Arif who was almost in tears when he snapped his head towards the naked woman that now had big raw looking blisters on her lower stomach and inner thighs, he snapped "who forced you, you lying bitch, you were more than happy to take our money each time it happened"

Miss Shelly began sobbing uncontrollably. Tina touched Kev on the shoulder and nodded to the door, he looked around to see a small group of young ghosts looking through the window. Kev, Ed and Tina walked out of the room to see the corridor filled with ghosts of all ages, dressed in all sorts of different styles of dress, the gathering of ghosts completely filled the full length of the long corridor, Steph chatted quietly to Tina for a few seconds. Tina then took hold of Kev's and Ed's hands, she eased them back against the wall where they stood dead still and looked through the window at the abusers, Kev's lover whispered that the ghosts were ready and would take it from there on in.

Steph held Sarah's hand as she was led nervously into the room, the prisoners all gasped out loud, as they each stared wide eyed at the tiny ghost. Suhel began shouting" No, No this can't be happening, it isn't possible" Kev rushed into the room, and stood in front of the man and whispered menacingly, "Oh it's true all right you perverted fucker, and little Steph was now going to get her revenge, [Kev took a step back and looked along the line of paedophiles] you will each pay the price for what you have done to everyone of your victims" before he could speak, without looking at anyone Arif said sarcastically, "she enjoyed every second of it" Kev moved and stood in front of the naked man, he punched him as hard as he could in the face before he gripped the man's cheeks so hard, he looked like he was about to blow a raspberry. Tina placed her hand on his arm, when he turned to look at her, she shook her head to stop him.

Kev let go of the Asian prisoner and stepped back, Sarah held Steph's hand as they hovered just off the floor, they moved slowly forward until they were directly in front of Arif.

Sarah stared directly into the man's wide terrified eyes, he looked wide eyed into the dead child's hollow eyes, and she said in a quiet, trembling voice "I have seen what you and your friends have done to my friend Steph, and I found it to be truly disgusting, similar things have happened to myself and a lot of our friends. All because of depraved people like yourselves, we have now been forced to live out our existence here in this awful place."

 She turned to look at Steph and then back at the now trembling man, [she then continued] as you can imagine there are a lot of ghosts living here, all of us different ages, lots of them existing here in this very building, because of people like you. A lot of other spirits from different times have come here today, just to see you and your friends punished, some of our friends are from times long, long ago, they are more than willing to do whatever was required of them, just as long as they see you suffer, as you richly deserve.

She stopped talking and looked behind her. As if by some secret signal, the room slowly filled with ghosts from all ages, men and women both young and old, some dressed in black servants attire, some in long flowing dresses, some in simple rags, but each one of them had hollowed eyed.

Ghosts dressed as if ready for battle in first and second world war trench coats, some others even dressed in dark monks habits, looking evil with their hoods draped over their heads, each grey face almost hidden from view. A long ago deceased archbishop in full ceremonial dress and holding a long staff, moved forward and hovered in front of the prisoners. He turned his head first to the right and then to his left as he looked along the row of bound prisoners, his head stopped in front of Miss Shelly, and his dead eyes bored deep into the piano teachers eyes. The holy man began speaking in a deep booming voice "What you and your kind have done to these poor innocent children was beyond comprehension, and I promise that you will be punished more than anyone has ever been punished before. Your four friends here have always been told that when they die, they will go to a better place, where all the women are virgins, but I promise you that where they will end up, will be nothing like that, all that they will know for all eternity will be darkness and loneliness."

"As for you Miss, I think that you are far worse than these doomed men, simply for the way that you supplied these depraved creatures with their poor victims, and you did this without a seconds thought. When all life has left your body, the devil himself will come for you, you will sit by his side and be his and his alone, his to command, to use and abuse for the rest of eternity"' he opened his arms wide, mumbled a few words, made the sign of the cross, and then floated slowly backwards to the rear of the room.

A small grey faced female dressed as can only be described as a mother superior from a time long, long go, she was one of the ghost elders and had come from a place known as the *inner cloud* She moved between the two girls and took their hands in her own and hovered in front of the piano teacher. The old ghost moved forward so that her dead face was as close to the doomed woman's face as could be. She then said in a very soft voice, "myself and all my friends have gathered here today, one by one we will pass through your body, and each one of us will take a handful of your soul, and when you have no soul left, the last spirit that enters your soulless body, will rip out your beating heart, and show it to you the second before you die."

The old ghost looked at the four dark skinned trembling men, one at a time she moved in front of them,"when this evil woman is no longer with us, then the same fate awaits each one of you, except with you, your spirits will be taken from here to a dark place where you will spend all of eternity completely alone." The old woman moved back and released the girls hands. She then floated higher towards the ceiling and held her arms out wide as if she had been crucified, her mouth stretched wide as a high pitched scream came from the ancient ghost. Suddenly a bright ray of yellow light shone out of each eye socket, and as if by magic the rays entered the piano players wide eyes, who reacted as if she had been shot and sat there stiff with her fear, her mouth wide open. The old ghost began to dart around the room like a meteor, she slowly changed shape as she did so, everyone watched fascinated at the magical transformation, the old woman screeched out loud, the living forced to cover their ears as she became elongated like a spear. The old nun suddenly shot forward and entered the piano teachers gaping mouth, and disappeared. Miss Shelly began screaming as she watched ghosts, one after the other change shape and enter her body.

The Asian men began to scream, and tear at their restraints, their eyes almost bulging out of their heads, they were all screaming at the top of their voices as the stream of ghosts moved quicker and quicker, as one by one, they entered the blond woman's jerking body.

Miss Shelly suddenly stopped screaming, all movement and sound in and around her came to a sudden deathly halt, the trail of ghosts slowly gathered on one side of the room after they had stopped entering her now soulless body. Each dead face turned towards the four remaining prisoners as they waited in anticipation, eager to restart their deathly work.

The four trussed up men, all of which were now sat perfectly still as they stared at the holy man that hovered before the dying woman. The archbishop moved his right hand forward and held his upturned fist in front of the teacher. His opened his hand and showed her her blood filled, still beating heart. That was the last thing that she would ever see, that final second before her head dropped forward, so far so that her chin now seemed to be resting between her naked breasts. The silence in the ice cold room was now eerily deafening, as the dead woman that was now a spirit appeared in front of the holy man, she turned to look at the shell that was now her lifeless body.

The room became eerily silent as a deep unearthly growl sounded from somewhere deep below, the piano teachers spirit turned to look into the far corner of the room, from where the guttural growl grew louder and louder, the ghosts all retreated from the room except the small group of dead girls. The growl became even more intense as all the air seemed to have been sucked out of the room, making breathing suddenly difficult. All eyes were staring at the far right hand corner of the room, because that was where the terrifying sound was emanating from, a long black wisp of a hand appeared out of the concrete floor as if by magic, the fingers were long and thin with nails, curved like claws, the rest of the thin arm came upwards into the room as it snaked across the stone floor towards the singing teachers spirit.

The woman's spirit began to scream so high pitched that the trio of live people were forced to place their hands over their ears. A black cloud of a giant shimmering head came slowly into view, the bright red eyes searching each face before the long hand closed around the spirit of the dead woman, and the teachers spirit held it's hands out as if begging for help, but there was nothing that anyone could do. No-one moved as the dead woman's spirit was dragged screaming towards the corner of the room, they all watched as the king of the growlers held her in front of his face, the red eyed devil himself seemed to be staring into her now dead eyes, he licked his black lips with a long flame like tongue, before she was dragged downwards into an unknown world, to exist by his side forever, his servant in hell.

Silence filled the room, as every pair of eyes still stared into the far corner, at the place where the teacher had disappeared. Kev and his two friends left the room and stood looking through the window, as ghost after ghost entered the screaming naked brown bodies, spirits of every kind were happily taking their turn to enter the men's bodies. Screams filled the entire deserted hospital as the four men watched with bulging eyes as the very life was being snatched from them.

Arif was the first to succumb, his spirit hovered and stared at the shell that was once his body. Next was Faisal followed closely by Suhel and finally Siad. When all four spirits were now free from their former bodies, they all looked at one another as if wondering what was happening, that was until low unearthly groans began to fill the room. The spirits searched every corner of the room for the source of the terrifying sound, black shapes rose slowly out of the edges of the room and slowly slithered along the floor, more and more of the black octopus shaped tentacles appeared, each terrifying shape groaning loudly as one by one the four Asian spirits, were dragged screaming into the corners of the room, the same corner as the one that piano teacher had been dragged into.

Soon it was all over, the air was filled with the strange scent of death, distant sounds echoed in the corridors of the hospital as the gathered ghosts made their way back to where that had come from, back to their lives in eternity, ready and willing to do the same thing again at a moments notice, if needed.

# CHAPTER 24

Steph still held Sarah's hand as they stared at the row of now lifeless bodies, an old smartly dressed woman ghost entered the room, she moved to hover in front of the avenged girl, when Steph looked up she softly asked, "is that really you, Nanna?" the old woman held her hands out to the little girl and whispered "yes dear, it is me, I have come too take you away from this awful place, to a place where we can spend our days looking after each other" Steph reached out, took the old woman's hands and with a smile to the sisters, she smiled to each of the vigilantes in turn before she waved, and the old woman holding the tiny girls hand, they simply flew out of the room, to where only the old woman knew the answer to that.

One by one the other ghosts left the room until the only people that remained were the vigilantes, they stood looking at the row of now limp, lifeless perverts, it was Ed that asked what were they going to do with the bodies? Kev stood thinking and to gain a bit of time, he eventually suggested "let's go and get something to eat and then we can talk about it, they ain't going any where" The other two agreed and as Ed began to descend the stairs, Kevin said that he would meet them by the fence.

Kev needed to get rid of Tina for a few seconds so that he could retrieve his money from the lift shaft, and then hide it somewhere else, not that he didn't trust her, but he still had the trusting part of life to learn, never having anyone to trust in his life before, it was going to be a long tough lesson, so he asked his girlfriend if she would go and fetch his jacket. As soon as she walked away, he grabbed the bag full of money from the lift shaft and hid it under a pile of broken desks, it would have to stay there until he could find somewhere just as safe to hide the bag.

He had done this because he had other plans for the lift shaft, plans that he would put to the others over dinner. Kev bought the meals at the Regal cafe, whilst eating he suggested that they hide the dead perverts and Pecker in the lift shaft, and then hopefully when the hospital was eventually demolished, the huge pile of rubble would hide the decaying bodies, even if was just long enough for them to get away from the area.

When the trio returned to the abandoned hospital, the two men lifted each body in turn and dropped them unceremoniously down the lift shaft, they listened as each body landed with a slapping sort of thud, with that done they all retired to Kev's room to discuss what they were going to do next. They knew that there were still abused victims to be avenged, because they had seen them with Sarah, they had stood in a small group as they had watched the five perverts as they got their just-deserts. All they could do was wait until Sarah showed herself again, and then they would plan their next move, if there was one. Meanwhile Kevin went shopping in the small towns precinct, he had a list of things that he needed, a writing pad, large envelopes [both ordinary and padded] brown wrapping paper, sellotape and surgical gloves. With his purchases laid out in front of him on his desk, he set about writing a letter to the police, informing them about Miss Shelly, her enterprise and the names of the dead Asian pedophiles. He wrapped the box of the discovered disks and their secrets, in the brown paper, he then placed them in an extra large padded envelope, that also held the letter, computer, the CD of little Steph being abused, plus the film showing the demise of her attackers.


 He marked the envelope for the attention of the police. The next morning he walked down to the taxi rank, and paid a black cab driver to deliver the parcel to the nearest police station.

# CHAPTER 25

The trio were beginning to get very worried about Sarah and her friends, because they hadn't seen or heard from any of them for over 48 hours, which in itself was very unusual. In an eerie sort of way the hospital seemed strangely vacant without the ghosts constantly being around, and with the intensity of everything that had happened over the last few days, the three of them were suddenly at a loss as to what to do next.

The vigilantes were beginning to relax and spend more time away from the hospital. Kev and Tina had even talked about leaving altogether, before the inevitable happened and they were caught. Even with his changed appearance, someone would eventually recognise Kevin and then they would all be captured.

The lovers had even talked secretly about taking the stolen money and setting up home near the coast somewhere, and when they were settled with new names and identities, they could even start a small business together, then they would send for Ed to join them. Their plans had to be put on hold, because when they returned to the hospital from an afternoon sitting in a sunny park, down by the river, in Stratford, where the three of them had relaxed and ate delicious ice creams. Sarah was waiting for them. She explained that she, Alice and plenty of other ghosts had had a terrible time trying to distract this big fat spirit, that had been searching for Kevin. Because she had heard from some of the other ghosts, all about the good deeds that he had been doing with the children. She had given her watchers the slip, and come here searching for him.

Sarah told them that Alice was with some other young victims that had come forward, each of them in the hope that they could also achieve some sort of revenge. The dead girl told them of a young boy named Robin that had been abused by his grand father, and afterwards drowned in the bath.The grand father was a retired army Major, and the old man believed that he was beyond reproach, and could do whatever he liked, and get away with it. When Robin who was only 7 years old threatened to go to the police, and tell them what the old man had been doing to him, the ex army officer had murdered him without a seconds thought.

Robin had then watched from above as his terrified parents had been instructed by the Major, as to what to say to the police. The couple had no choice in the matter, because they were petrified of the old man and his authoritarian ways. Robin's parents secretly wished that it had been the old man that had died, and not their only child, the old man had scolded Robins mother when she had cried over the death of her loving son, screaming at her to stop crying and to man-up, telling her that dying was part of life's cycle.

Having silently listened to Sarah as she told them about the sad demise of the boy ghost Robin, it was Tina that had said that they needed to teach the old man a severe lesson, a lesson that he would remember as he went down the road to hell. Ed spoke up after a long pause "I have an idea, it is a simple plan, but it might just work, if it doesn't then we can simply take the bastard out. For my plan to work we would need to talk to one of these ghost elders that we had been hearing so much about". The young ghost had told them that she could send a message to the inner cloud, but that it would take time. Sarah told them that she would get back to them, just as soon as she had been contacted by one of the ghost elders.

It was close to thirty six hours before they saw the sisters again, they hovered near the door and as usual it was Sarah that did the talking, "I have been waiting for the elders to get back to me, you see there was a certain area up above that ordinary ghosts like us aren't allowed to go near, it was called *The Inner Cloud * and apparently it was a very special place that is well guarded by the T.I.C.S.S [The Inner cloud security service] Each country has its own so called *Inner Cloud*, and its own set of well respected VIP'S residing in this area, and as in the living world, they have the ability and the specialist resources to help each other if ever needed.

Spirits up above have their own legal system which was really quite simple, the good spirits go above and the evil spirits go below. The justice system was in place for one reason only, and that was to fight those that live down below, and make certain that they stay where they belong. There was in the inner loud a court justice system, set up to settle disputes over the ownership of certain sprits.

I have been told that Ambassadors from both sides would then meet in a neutral place [that only they know about], and that they then thrash out any legal arguments for days on end, weeks even, until both sides had reached an agreement. We always have the S.A.S. on standby, just in case of any attempt at snatching a spirit from those down below was required. These special soldiers have been around all through the history of the world, and have served whichever had been the dominant force of their time, their only duty was to guard and protect the Inner Cloud. From what we have been told, there have also been throughout time disputes over certain unsavoury spirits, arguments which have resulted in those down below sending up snatch squads. These squad members have the ability to appear as ordinary ghosts, they come up from below to try and retrieve spirits that they think belong down there with them, and our squads do the same to them. This place known as the Inner cloud apparently has an impenetrable rolling cloud wall, with only one well guarded entrance and exit.

This rolling cloud was over 250 meters high, and because it continually revolves into itself, it was impossible to breach, but even so, there were security guards stationed at the main entrance. This means that the cloud itself was impossible for an ordinary ghost to get through, so to make a request of some sort it has to be done through one of the cloud elders. With that being the case, just imagine how difficult it would be for a child ghost to make a request like the one you have asked for, it was virtually impossible. That was why the elders have to make a formal request on your behalf, and this has to be done in front of a select committee, These members were in their former lives had been high court judges. We have been very lucky to have been granted an audience with a Lady Mary McPartridge, she has only agreed to do this because she has heard what you three have been doing, and wants to offer any assistance she can".

Lady Mary was a very tall, thin wavy sort of ghost with grey hair, hair that was so tall, from a distance it looked as though a bee hive had been balanced precariously on top of her head. You could just tell just by looking at her, that she was from a time long, long ago, mainly by her full length, flowing grey dress. It was obvious from the way that she held her chin up and looked down her nose at everyone, that she had in her former life been someone of great importance.

She studied the vigilantes from head to toe, and seemed to be fascinated by the piercings in Tina's face,"Does that hurt?" the old ghost asked, Tina smiled sweetly and answered that it only hurt when the studs were first put in. The old woman then moved back to stand by the young girl ghosts, she reached out and took a young hand in each of her own thin wispy hands, she then asked Kevin a very high pitched voice, that sounded as if she, was in-fact singing, what it was that she could do for them?

Kevin told the old ghost the sad story about Robin, all about the Major and what the ex army man had done to his grandson. The little man went on to say that they had a plan to avenge the young boy, but they would need the help of a high ranking army officer, to be able to put their plan into action, and did she know anyone that could help?

Lady Mary looked at each of the living people in turn before she spoke, "no problem at all, I will send Brigadier Taylor-Blythe down to sort the bastard out, you have been granted a direct line to the cloud as from this moment, so just send a message to me via the cloud security, they will in turn let me know as to when and where you would like the Brig to meet you. I will make sure that he will be there in full Military dress" and with that she waved her right hand, turned her head and like a puff of smoke, she simply disappeared.

Kev and Ed walked into the M@S clothes department, and bought smart black suits off the peg, shirts, shoes and ties, they then walked into Smiths and bought a pack of gold embossed invitations.

Back at the hospital Kev wrote out an invitation, inviting the Major to give a talk to a gathering of ex service men, to be held at the local British legion club. On the invitation it stated that if necessary a car would be made available collect him, and then deliver him back home at the end of the evening.

Ed, who was now decked out in his new suit drove the recently valeted, permanently borrowed BMW to the Majors house, he knocked on the door, a timid, beaten down woman with dark, tired eyes answered the door, he asked in his best voice, if it would be possible speak to a Major Carlton-Jones. The nervous woman asked him to wait while she found out if the Major was in, she closed the door and disappeared inside, a few minutes later a tall obviously ex military man opened the door, looked Ed up and down "yes, can I help you?" he asked the smartly dressed Ed. Ed passed the Major the invitation, and said that he was to wait for a reply to take back to the committee. The Major took his horn-rimmed glasses out of his shirt pocket, he opened the invitation with his long thin fingers, and read the neatly hand written card. He then looked at Ed over the top of his glasses with his bright blue eyes, and smiled "yes, I would like that that very much, pick me up at 8 o'clock prompt" Ed nodded "they would like you in full ceremonial dress, if at all possible, Sir" "naturally, I will see you then" he said pompously. With that he turned his back on Ed, walked back into the house and closed the door.

The vigilantes had worked out a plan of sorts, and that it would be best if the Brigadier and young Robin were to meet. There was an old grey foot bridge that Ed knew about, the old structure spanned a tributary that entered the River Thames at Waterloo, and was perfect for their needs. The 200 year old stone bridge had been built over a fast running stream below that joined the mighty river, and the area was more often than not deserted as soon as it became dark, mainly due to the lack of street lighting. It was also a place far enough out of the way of prying eyes to fulfil their needs. For their plan to work, they had to be relatively certain that they would not be disturbed, because they would need solitude to be able to put their deathly plan against the Major, into action.

With everything in place, and with them all knowing what part they were playing. Ed drove the expensive car up to the Majors front door, Ed climbed out of the car, straightened his jacket and rang the doorbell. He could hear the sound of military chimes coming from somewhere deep inside the well maintained Victorian house. He saw the shape of a woman through the frosted glass of the front door, the door opened which the woman [who looked to be standing to attention] held open. The military man came out of the house resplendent in his full dress uniform, made complete by a row of highly polished military medals on the left hand side of his chest.

Ed opened the rear door of the car and the Major eased himself inside, the old man seemed somewhat surprised to see a smiling Kevin already seated there. He was just about to ask who he was, when Kev hit him in the neck with the stun-gun. The response was instant as the old army man flopped forwards and rested his head against the front seat, knocking his green cap from his head, as he did so. Tina, who was sat in the front passenger seat turned and looked at the unconscious officer, and snarled "bastard" Ed started the car and drove the big car to the bridge car park, where they waited in a dark, until the prearranged time. The army man eventually began to come around, and when his eyes regained focus, looked from unknown face to face. With a look of total confusion, he instantly began to struggle against the cable ties that bound not only his wrists, but also at the elbows, which forced his arms to be held straight out in front of him.

The Major began firing questions at his captors, but he was totally ignored, when the old man began shouting at Kev, the wife murderer lost his temper, turned the stun-gun on and held it near the old mans face, and told him to "shut the fuck up". The Major shied away from the crackling sound, he then looked out of the car window and asked in almost in a whisper, where they were, and what they were doing there? Kevin smiled at the old man and said that they had a little surprise for him, one that he had earned and would really appreciate.

 The army man asked question after question, made demand after demand, but each request was ignored. In the end the old man gave up and just sat in the rear of the car, looking up at the bright stars, wondering what the bloody hell was going on?

The fluorescent yellow numbers on the dash board clock finally clicked over to 12 midnight, the trio climbed out of the car without saying a word. With the sound of a nearby church clock chiming and the rustling of the leaves in the nearby willow trees, Ed reached into the rear of the car and grabbed the Major by the arm and dragged him out of his seat. Kevin grabbed the cable tie that bound the old mans wrists and pulled the struggling man away from the car. "What the bloody hell do you think you are doing man, are you mad?" The Major demanded. They dragged the struggling old man to the middle of the old stone bridge and waited, the earthy smell of the fast flowing green water below assailed their noses. Each of the vigilantes began looking skyward as if they were waiting for something, which automatically made the army man look up into the heavens as well. As if by magic a small white cloud seemed to appear out of the clear night sky, and slowly grow in size it drifted towards them. When the shimmering cloud finally reached them, it hovered in front of them for a few seconds, as if watching them.

The Major had a look of sheer abject terror on his now white face, and he began to pull against his restraints in a bid to distance himself from whatever it was that was happening, even though the old man had no clue as to what was going on, but he had no desire to be any part of it. All four of them watched the shimmering cloud as it slowly came to a stop in front of them, but at the same time the grey mist grew in size, and eventually began to change shape, when the ghosts of the Brigadier and young Robin finally appeared. The Major gasped out loud as he stared at his dead grandson, the old mans knees gave out, and he literally sank to the floor. With the help of a few heavy slaps from Ed the retired officer began to rouse himself, he was now being held upright by Kev and Ed, The three men were standing directly in front of the dead senior officer, still resplendent in his full dress uniform.

The Brigadier's dead eyes stared into the majors wide open terrified eyes, as the senior officer began to speak, he lifted his head, "you Major are a fucking disgrace to your uniform, what you have done to this poor young boy was beyond comprehension, and you deserve to be punished to the fullest. For what you are about to receive and deserve, may god have mercy on your soul" Ed stepped forward and placed a strip of silver tape over the terrified man's mouth to stop him calling out, he then bent down and tied a long black cable tie around the Majors ankles, Tina walked forward and placed a 5 kilo kettle weight into both of the Majors uniform pockets.

The suddenly terrified Major realised what they had in store for him and began pleading with them with his wide terrified eyes, urgent mutterings came from behind the tape, but he was ignored by everyone. The ghost of young Robin seemed to raise himself up into the air, until his face was level with his grandfathers ashen face. The hovering young boy stared into the terrified mans eyes and asked in a tiny high voice that was no more than a whisper "why did you do those horrible things to me grandfather, you know that I loved you?"

The old mans eyes just stared at the ghost of his grandson and shook his head in total disbelief. Robin sank back down slowly until it looked as if he was standing besides the Brigadier, the dead senior officer nodded his readiness to the small group of onlookers. The Major, who was still staring at his dead grandson, was roughly grabbed by Kevin and Ed, they turned the struggling army man and simply lifted him up and tossed him over the side of the bridge, into the cold waters, some distance below. The splash when the bound man hit the water was loud in the quiet of the night, it was a few seconds later that they heard the growlers moaning, as they began to appear unseen in the darkness, reaching out of the bowels of the earth, to claim yet another dead evil soul for their own.

An uneasy silence followed the demise of the Major, the ghost Robin seemed to be leaning against the Brigadier, and it appeared that the military man had his wisp of an arm draped around the sad boys shoulder. It looked as if the very old ghost was comforting the young boy in some way, the old army man took the child ghost to one side, he then knelt down and talked quietly to the lost boys spirit.

A few seconds later the Brigadier drifted towards the trio and hovered just off the ground, he looked from face to face, "firstly,

I would like to thank you all for what you are doing, in cleansing the earth of such sick people. Secondly I have spoken to young Robin and he has no-one to look after him where he is going, so he has agreed to come and live out eternity with myself and my wife in the Inner cloud, where we can look after him [once again he looked into each of the vigilantes faces] and finally if you are ever in a situation where you need my help, just send a message to the inner cloud, and I will see what I can do for you".  He smiled at each of them in turn, took hold of the boys hand, turned and in a flurry of cloud like material, the duo simply disappeared into what could only be described as a happy future together, in ever lasting eternity.

# CHAPTER 26

The vigilantes returned to the cold, dark, deserted hospital, no-one had spoken a word on the journey back to their chosen place of residence, they all retired to bed mentally shattered. The last few weeks was finally beginning to take its toll on the trio, all three of them vowing that it was time to take a rest, at least for a week or so.

The lovers made love and slept soundly in each others arms, only to be rudely awaken Ed at the first light of dawn. Standing in the gloom and looking down at them were two of the biggest men dressed all in black, that either of them had ever seen.

Both men shone torches at them, the one standing on the right said in a very assertive voice "get your stuff together and get out, you have one hour, then if you haven't gone by then, you will be forcibly removed. Demolition of this building will begin at lunchtime today, now get moving"

 The two men left the room and began searching the other empty rooms. Kev had dressed and was already packing up his belongings, when an almighty racket broke out in the corridor, just outside their room. When the lovers looked out of their room, they could see the sisters and some of the other child ghosts, apparently attacking the two startled men, who were standing still, shielding their heads with their raised arms as they continued to be assaulted, by something unseen, that they could not protect themselves against. Suddenly the terrified men broke away, and took off running as fast as they could towards the stairs, the sisters giving chase as the men disappeared down the concrete staircase, all the time shouting out a string of obscenities, the like of which the girls had never heard the like of before.

Sarah and Alice hovered in front of their desperately sad friends, the sisters listened as Kev explained to them what was about to happen with the condemned hospital. He asked the dead girls what would happen to them? As usual it was Sarah that spoke, "Please don't worry about us, we will join the elders until you have settled somewhere new, and then we will try and come through to you again.

Maybe we can take up where we left off, because there are more and more victims coming forward every day" Tina became very upset at the thought of leaving the sisters to fend for themselves, but Sarah assured her friend that they would be perfectly well looked after. She promised that they would search for them, and that she was confident that they would eventually find them, where ever they may be.

When the lovers reached the ground floor Ed was waiting for them, taking the items that Tina carried, he then lifted them to the borrowed BMW and stowed the items in the boot of the car. With everything that they owned now safely in the car, the trio took time to stand and gaze up to the uppermost floors, they could clearly see the sisters waving goodbye to them. The trio waved back, but stopped doing so when nearby people began looking skyward, on seeing nothing, they began to wonder what or who they were signalling too, or if it was just a wind up of some sort?

Ed hadn't been driving more than ten minutes when he saw flashing blue lights in the rear view mirrors, "shit!" he exclaimed and began to pull over to the side of the road. Once stopped another two police cars pulled up, one at the side of their car and the other in-front of them, in a bid to block them in and foil any attempt at escape.

Without a single word being spoken each of them were dragged out of the borrowed car by masked armed police men, they were then roughly handcuffed. They were then taken separately to different police cars and driven away, to where only the police drivers knew. The convoy of speeding cars carved through the traffic just like a hot knife through butter, flashing blue lights reflecting in shop windows, and on other slower moving cars, as they sped past. They eventually turned off the main road and made their way up a long shaded tree lined driveway. Kev stared at a large wooden sign that read" Sussex Police Headquarters"

He looked at the16 century red brick country house with it's gothic turrets, the sheer amount of leaded windows showed just how many rooms there were in the old building. If each room housed a high ranking police officer, each of them donned in their dress uniforms and sat with stiff backs, drinking tea and eating biscuits, then there were simply far too many of them. Add to that all the support staff, controllers, drivers, canteen staff and these were obviously well paid civil servants, all of them employed there simply to look after the super elite of the Sussex police force. A quick look at the car park told its own story, each of the shiny new cars were obviously the top end of the market, ranging from brand new BMW's to the latest gleaming Bentley. Just by the sheer number of cars held in their car park, there just had to be at lest 3000 people working in the old building, that had once long ago, been someones much loved family home.

Instead of being delivered to the custody suite as expected, the vehicles were driven to a secluded part at the furthest end of the car park. The dense tree lined space was situated at the rear of the old building. When the cars finally stopped a menacing looking group of armed police officers, some of them with their faces covered with black ski masks, were standing around a dark blue unmarked van, that waited ominously with all of it's doors wide open. The van had its engine running and was obviously waiting for their arrival.

The traffic units pulled up near the waiting van, and the now terrified trio were again dragged out of their respective police vehicles, and made to stand in line, where they had silver duct tape placed over their mouths. Once seated in the rear of the van, hoods were than slipped over each of their heads, to make sure the prisoners could't see the route that they would be taking to their final destination.

# CHAPTER 27

The silent journey seemed to last for hours as the trembling vigilantes contemplated their bleak futures, on and on they travelled, the only noise was the sound of the humming tires as they raced over the black tarmac. The trio had all but fallen asleep when the van eventually slowed, and turned off to the left. The speed of the van was much slower now and bends, lot's of slow bends let them know, that they were close to their journeys end.

The van finally came to a halt, the driver set the hand brake and turned the engine off. Before the driver had even climbed out of his cab, the side doors were violently pulled open and big rough hands grabbed them one by one and pulled them from the van, they were then marched unceremoniously into a silent building of some sort. They were taken into a room and sat down on plastic chairs. They all blinked rapidly as their hoods were removed, they turned and looked at one another with confused looks. Tina smiled with her eyes at Kevin and he did the same in return, as a secret message of intimacy passed from one to the other, at that precise moment, something very deep and meaningful took place between the lovers.

They sat and looked all around the large white sterile looking room, a large space that had rows of silent computer stations, that were positioned at intervals all around its inner walls. On the wall that they were facing were various world maps, five large blank screens, desks full of silent telephones and more built in sleeping computers that stood silent and ready for whatever their purpose might be. An empty desk and a single chair had been positioned in front of them, waiting ominously for whoever it was that was coming to inform them of their fate. Armed officers could be seen through the windows standing guard, some watching them and the others looking in the opposite direction, eyes searching for any possible danger.

They all turned as one and looked in the same direction as they heard the door handle turn, a very tall, thin man, dressed in his best police uniform walked into the silent room, he had a brown leather cane under one arm and a brown briefcase in his right hand, they all stared into the old intelligent eyes, as he walked stiff backed towards them. The old man stood in front of the table, he looked from face to face before placing his briefcase on the floor by the side of his chair, he positioned the leather cane down on the table, and then his new looking officers black hat was set down by the side of the cane. He slowly removed his brown leather gloves to reveal dark liver spots all over the back of his hands. He then held the gloves up and made certain that they were exactly level with each other then he gently placed them into his cap, He sat down stiff backed, steepled his hands on the desk, and rested his chin on his hands as he studied them closely. He again looked from one to the other without speaking.

In turn the trio looked back at the old, obviously ex military man, on the left hand side of his neatly pressed black uniform jacket, the silver buttons were polished as highly as his black shoes. There were three and a half rows of different coloured ribbons, positioned just above the pocket on the left hand side of his jacket, that spoke volumes of the man's seniority. On his shoulders sat three silver pips, that again told of the man's very senior rank. They looked into the old deeply lined, well weathered face, the tired old grey eyes showed his age, he sported a grey military style moustache that sat in a straight line under the bulbous purple nose, his slit like mouth looked just like someone had painted a straight thin line onto the old face. When the man opened his mouth to speak, they were all slightly shocked at the first sight of the man's brilliant white teeth.

He made all three of them physically jump when he picked up his leather cane and slapped it on the table three times, he turned his head and looked at the door as a young blond, well dressed police woman in an immaculate neatly pressed uniform hurriedly walked into the room. She was followed closely by an armed police officer, she marched smartly up to the old man, "Yes sir, what can I do for you?" When he spoke his voice was surprisingly very high pitched, "For a start you can remove that tape" he pointed at Tina with his leather cane. The female officer moved to each of the prisoners in turn, and apologised as she ripped the tape from their mouths. Each of them licked their dry chapped lips. After a much needed drink by the trio, the old man watched as the police woman left the room, he looked from one to the other of the three sat opposite him, and began speaking,"Right, the first thing that you should know is that my name is Commander-in-chief Rupert Mc Phereson, and I have enough on you three to send you to prison for the rest of your lives, for instance I know about the bodies in the lift shaft, I know about the Major that ended up in the river, I also know about your young friends Alice and Sarah" the vigilantes all gasped at this last comment.

Kevin looked at his two accomplices and then back at the old man "but how could you possibly know about the dead girls?" The old man looked back at the door and checked around the room, he confidently whispered "do you think that you are the only ones that have ever had contact with the dead, how do you think I know all I need to about you, and everything that you have done, the people that you have murdered, just as if you were judge and jury?"

Kevin stared at the police officer for a long time before asking "so what is it exactly, that you want from us?" The old man smiled broadly "that my dear friend is really quite simple, I have had a very long successful career in the police force, but certain high profile criminals have evaded capture, some of them on a ridiculously minor technicality, and I vowed to get them, even if it was the last thing I ever did. As I am near retirement, I want you [he opened his arms wide and smiled at the three vigilantes in front of him] well you three, if you agree, to be taken from here to my deceased parents farm house, where you will live quite happily until I contact you with a name and where you can locate that person. You will then do what you do best, and dispose of the said victim, no questions asked. If for some reason you do not agree with my request, you will be taken from here by my special friends outside of this building to the nearest police station, where you will all be charged with multiple, kidnap and murder, do you all understand?

 On the other hand, you will however have everything you require at the farm house to live very comfortably, but be warned you will all be wearing a new type of electronic tag that will transmit a signal to an app on my computer. I will know exactly where you are at any given moment, day or night, and if you try to run or remove the tags, I will also know that instantly and again, you will immediately be arrested, taken to the nearest police station, where you will all face the consequences of your actions, do you all understand?" The large sterile looking room had become deathly silent, and stayed that way for a long time, as the police man waited for a reply, finally Kevin spoke, "It seems that we don't have much of a choice in the matter, does it?" The old man smiled and simply exclaimed, "Excellent" he then banged the table with his leather cane again, and the same young police woman entered the room, followed closely by the same armed police officer. The old man simply nodded "carry on"

They were escorted back out to the van and more or less ordered to get inside, they were then driven to the old police officers family farm [ Mc Phereson's Farm ]. Written under the farms name were the words [Strictly Private, No Entry]. The farm house itself had been well maintained from the look of the outside of the sprawling red brick building. When they entered the house they couldn't quite believe what they were seeing, the decor had been beautifully done, the old oak beams gleamed a shiny black, as if they had just been freshly painted. The furniture was all top end brown leather, the carpets were deep and very luxurious, as they moved from room to room, more and more expensive opulence filled every available space.

The main bedroom held an antique oak four poster bed, the mattress was at least two feet in depth and so soft to the feel that it just had the promise of a perfect nights sleep. The beige carpet was so thick that when you walked upon it, it felt just like walking on a warm sandy beach, if you closed your eyes you could be walking on some far away sun drenched sand. Again the freshly painted oak beams and the antique furniture, had been done to perfection. Tina instantly claimed this room for her and her lover.

Kev walked into the beautifully furnished living room, he was having a casual look around at the ornate furnishings, when he picked up a framed photograph of the commander and a pretty little blond haired girl of about eight years old. There was an inscription written on a brass plate, that had been fixed to the bottom edge of the frame, the simple words read 'Rupert and Molly, in happier times' Having replaced the picture, he saw a large brown padded envelope with his name written on it in flowing bold black letters. He picked up the heavy package and stood there for a full minute deep in thought, he turned the quite heavy envelope over and over in his hands before opening it. He sat down on one of the comfortable brown leather settees, ripped the seal open and looked inside, there were a large bundle of crisp brand new fifty pound notes, a set of various sized keys and on headed paper, a hand written note.

He lifted out the sheet of paper and unfolded it. He was just about to read the note, when he was forced to lay his head back, he closed his eyes and smiled to himself as his girlfriend began singing contentedly, as she worked quite happily in a modern kitchen, a workspace that she had never seen the like of. There had been installed in the perfectly designed work space every mod con that you could possibly think of, and an olive green Aga double oven, that was simply to die for. Tina was so happy at that present time, happier than she had ever been in her short life, that was the reason that she was singing to herself, the joy that she felt as she prepared a proper home cooked meal for her lover and soul mate. She was just grateful to have the opportunity to do this for the very first time, but she knew that it wouldn't be the last.

Kevin lifted up the sheet of paper, the note read..> Kevin. I know that you don't need the money, but it won't hurt to have some ready cash available, just in case of emergencies. The keys are for the house and other out buildings, where you will find some very useful items that will assist you in your quest, also hanging up on the back of the door in the kitchen you will find the keys to my fathers old Jaguar, which has been fully insured for any driver, please be careful with the old car purely, because of its sentimental value. You may have wondered how I know exactly what and how you have dealt with your past victims; well I will tell you. My deceased mother Maud bless her, is still very active in the old farmhouse as you will no-doubt discover, and she will contact you herself when she is good and ready, that is if and when she trusts you all. She will be the one that informs you of the first chosen target, and where you can locate him, she will not tell you the full extent of their crimes, as this is no real concern of yours, but she will give you a clue to help you on your way.

There is also a Range Rover in the garage, you will need this vehicle to dispose of the bodies, in the envelope you will find a small hand drawn map, this map will lead you to a very, very deep specifically dug pit that is full of very thick slurry, all of which was gathered from the now disused cow sheds. If you weigh the bodies down, [you will find what you need in the way of weights, already in the garage] the corpses will sink to the depths and be lost forever, which in my opinion is just what they deserve. I think that is everything, I will see you soon and enjoy the house and everything that it has to offer. Rupert"

Kevin rested his head back, suddenly feeling very tired, he closed his eyes and drifted off to sleep, and was woken when the aromas of roasted Rosemary begun to assail his senses, as they drifted in from the kitchen. Tina proudly carved the perfectly cooked leg of lamb, the whole meal was simply first class, she had even made an apple pie and home made custard for desert. She had learned how to cook when she lived with her grandmother, who had raised her from the age of 9. After they had finished eating, Kev told them about the note from the old copper, and about the cars that were available for their use.

Ed wanted to take the old Jag out for a spin, but was told in no uncertain terms by Tina, that he was to fill the dish washer and switch it on before he did anything else and that she, Kev and a certain four poster bed, that had some urgent unfinished business to attend to.

# CHAPTER 28

After a few days shut away in the farm house, it was decided that they would take the car and go exploring, because they had no idea what so ever where they were. With Ed driving the old green car they reached the end of the farms long drive, Kevin sat in the front passenger seat, they looked both ways along the busy A road. With no indication as to what town if any, lay in either direction. Ed turned left and followed a thin line of traffic, it wasn't long before they saw a sign that read Stratford-upon-Avon, 4 miles. Tina exclaimed excitedly that she had always wanted to visit Stratford, she then asked if they could go to the theatre, and see a play by Shakespeare? Ed laughed out loud, " I will be washing my hair that day" when Kev laughed Tina snapped tartly "I don't know why you are laughing, because you are definitely taking me, and we will be going dressed up in our best clothes, and you will be taking me for a nice meal before we go to the theatre" Kev turned and looked at his lover and answered "if that is what you want my darling, then that is what you will have"

Taking his retort as being slightly sarcastic she poked her tongue out at him. He sank back in the soft brown leather seat and looked out of the old cars wind down window at the passing country side. Fields made up mainly of lush dark green grass, some with black and white cows in them, heads down as they grazed on the lush grass, other fields of wheat that moved like waves on the sea as the warm summer winds stirred the tops of the crops. Acres of perfectly flat brown land that had been recently planted, bordered by rows of neat hedges and large fully leaved trees.

Ed parked the old car in the tree lined car-park that was situated a short walk from the slow flowing River Avon. While they waited for him to pay for the parking ticket, the lovers stood hand in hand, and looked across the green river towards the famous historic town. In front of them was a mainly grassed area, dominated by a large white ferris wheel that seemed to just grow out of the ground, many people filled the glass covered pods that moved forever clockwise at a steady, five miles an hour.

The customers on the wheel were looking down to where people sat on the grass and ate picnics, screaming children ran around, chasing each other, playing games of made up super hero's and villain's. A brass bands musicians dressed in red uniforms, looked resplendent in the cream coloured band stand, as they played gleaming brass instruments,  people relaxed in deck chairs, some dozing, others drinking Pimm's as they listened to the foot tapping military tunes

An old grey stone bridge that had been built hundreds of years before, spanned, the wide river. Tourists from many far away lands and locals alike all dressed in colourful summer clothes, strolled along as they crossed the walk-way in both directions. As the trio walked towards the river they began to see boats of all descriptions, slowly moving up and down the green looking water. Hundreds of ducks, geese and swans, many on the water itself, some waddling around on dry land as they waited to be fed with the seemingly endless supply of bread. A feast being fed to them by parents with young children, photographs being taken for albums, memories to be revisited in years still to come.

The RSC theatre looking resplendent and dominant on the far bank, the old brown building seemed to grow out of the very river itself, a row of shiny silver tables that sparkled in the bright sunlight, set out on a long specifically built balcony that over looked the river, the shiny silver chairs full of customers drinking tea and coffee, some having afternoon teas of crustless sandwiches, miniature cakes and warm scones. The customers looked out over the boat filled, chaotic looking river.  As the trio walked closer to the river, they saw a hand drawn ferry that would take them to the other side of the dark green water.

Once back on dry land, it was just a short walk into the town centre itself. The three left the ferry and climbed the steps into the almost empty park by the old church and headed towards the hub of the old town, passing first the Swan theatre that already had people queuing to buy tickets for that evenings performance. They walked past the imposing looking main theatre, that offered the chance to try on some of the many costumes, costumes worn by many famous artists, who used them to retell tales that had long ago been told within the theatres old buildings brown walls. They stood looking up at the recently built viewing tower, that seemed to fit perfectly to the side of the building, shiny grey-silver steps led up to the main entrance, old brown doors with embossed square panes of glass and brass handles, handles that had had many thousands of expectant hands fold around them over the many years of the theatres long life.

As they strolled along, they glanced over at the hundreds of people that were either sitting on the grass enjoying the warm summer sunshine, or just idling along enjoying a well earned break from whatever it was that had brought them there in the first place. It was then that the smell of freshly cooked fish and chips hit them all at the same time. Not ten minutes later they were sitting on the grass in the park, eating some of the best fish and chips any of them had ever tasted from Barnaby's. The rest of the afternoon was taken up doing all the touristy things that Tina insisted that they do. Kevin made an excuse about the car needing more money putting in the meter, and slipped off to buy tickets to go and see *A Mid Summer Nights Dream*, he would keep the tickets a secret until it was time for them to retire for the night, he knew that once he had given her the tickets, she would be game to try whatever he wanted, he smiled to himself, because he had something very specific in mind for a certain young lady that very evening.

# CHAPTER 29

Nothing changed for the next few weeks except that Tina had discovered an easel and some water paints hidden away in one of the box rooms, saying that she had always wanted to paint, but had never really had the opportunity. Now she spent hours and hours sitting in front of the farmhouse painting away. Ed would find odd jobs to do on the farm, he also walked the farms many tracks, with a shotgun, bringing home the odd duck or pheasant for Tina to prepare and cook. He had located an old Ferguson tractor in the barn, hidden under green tarpaulin. He vowed to himself to get the old machine up and running.

Ed did these things so that the lovers could spend some much needed time together, even on the rare occasion that they had a day out, he would wander around on his own. It was at times like this he enjoyed his own company. He could be standing in the quiet of the copse with a shotgun in the evenings, waiting for wood pigeons to come into roost when Ed would slowly look around the eerily quiet of the surrounding trees, sensing that he was being watched. He would be doing a mundane task like polishing the old tractor, when suddenly the hairs would stand up on the back of his neck for no reason what so ever. He would stop whatever he was doing and look behind him, to see no-one, but he knew that someone or something was indeed watching him. Many times he sat and asked whoever it was to show themselves, he even thought that it might be Sarah and Alice, come back to take up from where they left off, but he could locate no-one.

Ed told the other two about what had been happening to him when he had been on his own, and that he was sure that it was someone from beyond the grave. He also explained that he had tried to get through to whoever it was, but had failed for whatever reason. Tina suggested that she should spend the day on her own around the farm, just in case it was the dead girls, because they were more likely to show themselves to her, rather than Ed. She and the sisters had built up a close bond, especially after all they had all been through, at the now demolished hospital.

Tina immediately felt the unseeing eyes on her as she entered the old barn the next day. She sat down on a straw bale, and looked around the old wooden structure at the suns dust filled rays. Streams of bright light that shone through every crack and hole in the barns outer wall, looking a lot like bright spears that were full of millions of floating dust particles. The old grey tractor that Ed had been working on, one side gleaming, the other dull and covered in dust, just sat there a relic of past times. A row of old rust covered farm equipment, ploughs, harrows and the like all left to slowly rust away, sadly forgotten, never to be used again.

She took a deep breath and began talking to whichever spirit it was that was trying to make contact with them, It took maybe an hour before little things began to happen, a length of twine hanging from one of the rafters of the barn suddenly began swaying from side to side, as if someone or something had breathed on it. The catch on the large black door began rattling, some large blue dust covered plastic sacks that had been stacked upon an old brown oak beam for what must have been years, suddenly began to fall to the ground, one by one. Tina continued to talk as if to no-one, but she knew that she was slowly getting through, it was when she lifted her head and asked if it was Maud that was trying to contact her, that she finally got through. A few seconds later a tiny bright red dot that seemed to be hovering, appeared in the darkest recess of the old barns roof, the dot grew in size until a glowing ball of light began to dart around the upper reaches or the barn.

Tina couldn't take her eyes from the light as it flew from side to side, dodging the old beams as if by magic, the ball of light began to slow down and gradually sink towards her, when the sphere of light suddenly become static, it was exactly at her eye level, it was as if the light was studying her, trying to read her mind in some way, it was as if the strange light was some sort of alien from another planet, a being that had superior powers of some sort.

Tina had been there for a long time without any sustenance, and because of that she had to squeeze her face cheeks hard to enable her to lubricate her dry mouth before she could speak again, when her mouth was just about wet enough, she finally whispered "show yourself to me, Maud, I know who you are, you are Rupert's mother and you are here to help us, but you will need to show yourself to me in order to help us know in which direction we need to go in." Still the ball of light hovered there, just about within touching distance. Tina reached out and tried to take the weight of the hovering ball in the palm of her hand, as her hand neared, the ball darted away, but the red sphere still seemed to be staring at her, unnerving her, making her want to flee, but she was determined to stay and face whatever or whoever it was.

It was as if the shiny orb read her mind about wanting to flee, and to stop her running away a strange high pitched noise slowly began to fill the barn, the pitch so high that she had to place her hands over her ears to block out the sound. It was at this point that the orb began to change its shape, first the orbs outer shine seemed to dissipate, and then the sound in the barn changed to a deeper almost growling noise, as second by second the orb began to grow in size, changing its shape as it did so. The first thing to really appear was the oval head shape, next a long thin body, arms seemed to unfold themselves from the centre of the mass, just as if the grey shape was taking on a human form of some sort.

Finally a face appeared, an old withered grey face with curled grey hair down to her shoulders, the eye sockets were empty, but somehow Tina could still feel the intelligence that had once been there, filtering out to her, as if the ghost of Rupert's mother was trying to reach her by using telepathy. Tina asked the shape, "Are you Rupert's mother, if you are then you need to show yourself completely and talk to me, in the end you will have to talk to all of us, if you don't, then how will we know who it is, that needs to be punished?"

The empty eyes continued to stare at her, Tina physically jumped when a thin, soft trembling voice answered her by saying "yes, I am Rupert's mother, my name is Maud Mc Phereson, I have been over on this side for many long years now, I hated to leave Rupert on his own but what could I do, I have always looked after him as best I could, but there were times in the past when no-one could have helped him, times when I thought that he was insane, like the time that his illegitimate daughter lost her life at such a young age.

 Enough about me, the main reason that the three of you are here to right the many things that the courts got so terribly wrong. I will lead you the best way I know how. I will help you in any way that I can, as much as my abilities will allow. You must have realised from what Rupert has already told you, that I see many things from my position up here, and will therefore be able to guide you as you continue in your quest only if and when my help is required. From what Rupert has told me about his plans, you are to deal with one villain at a time, and you will ask no questions, but be reassured that the chosen victims all deserve whatever fate awaits them."

Tina didn't speak for a few seconds and when she did, it was to ask the old ghost if she intended to show herself to the others. There was a delay in her answer but when it came it shocked Tina. The shadowy figure said, "I would have shown myself sooner but I am not sure about the young man that you have with you, not your amorous lover, I quite like the look of him, even though he has somewhat strange looks, but I trust him completely. I wish that my husband would have had the same ability and imagination that your lover has in that particular department."

The old ghost stopped talking and seemed to be deep in thought, because she didn't speak for a while, when she did, she simply said that she would come to them after they had eaten their evening meal, and with that she simply shot upwards, into the eaves of the barn and was gone.

# CHAPTER 30

After a fine meal of M@S game pie with new potatoes, and with the dish washer doing it's thing, the trio sat drinking bottled beer and nervously waiting for the appearance of the old ghost. It wasn't the fact that she was going to appear, it was more as to how she would show herself. Would she just materialise in a chair, suddenly speak and scare them all to death, or would she show herself as an orb and dart around the room, would she perhaps rise out of the ground, or just walk through the wall even? The three of them sat silently waiting, each one of them nervously looking around the room, waiting expectantly for the inevitable. When the doorbell rang they all jumped. Kevin jumped up and walked to the locked, old scared oak door.

When he opened the heavy door he was surprised to see the commander standing there, without waiting to be invited in, the old man simply pushed past Kevin and walked into the living room, carrying a battered old brief case in his right hand. He removed his black hat and gloves, placed the gloves into the hat and then placed both on top of the briefcase, which he had already laid on the table. He then removed his thick black over coat and folded it neatly, before he draped it over one of the dining room chairs. He turned and looked from one to the other of his house guests, and nodded his head in greeting. Before settling himself down on the settee, he still stayed silent as he waved for Kevin to sit down next to him.

The old man looked at Tina and spoke for the first time "I understand that you have met mummy and had a nice chat with her?" he then looked at Ed "mummy was somewhat concerned about you, she thinks that you aren't reliable and will let everyone down" Before Ed could speak Kevin said, "I would trust Ed with my life, there is no doubt about his commitment." The police man made a snorting noise, and was about to comment but stopped himself. He held his hand up to silence them all "mummy is very close, I will try and encourage her to show herself. "Mummy, Mummy, are you there Mummy, please show yourself, come and join us, we need you here to make plans" they all looked around the room, waiting for some sign that the dead woman was about to join them.

The room suddenly became very cold, so cold that even though there was a fire blazing in the hearth, they all hugged themselves, every breath that left their mouths came out as a small cloud of steam. It was then that what can only be described as a high pitched scream seemed to come out of the blackened beams, beams made out of centuries old oak that supported the very ceiling of the room they sat in. They all looked upwards as the eyeless ghost seemed to appear effortlessly through the painted white ceiling, her grey shadowy form ever so slowly sinking lower and lower until she hovered next to her police man son.

Her sightless head moved from face to face, when she looked at her loving son she appeared to lower her head, to enable her to kiss him lovingly on the cheek, which made him smile, "Hello Mummy, it is so nice to see you again, I understand that you have met Tina. Well, this is Kevin and as you know the other one is Ed. I have it from Kevin that you don't have to worry about Ed, he is loyal to the cause." The dead woman placed her drooping mouth next to her sons ear and seemed to be whispering to him, while her toothless mouth moved next to her sons ear, his hollow eyes slowly turned towards Tina.

When the old ghost had finished whispering to her son, he spoke directly to the young woman "it seems that Mummy will only speak with Tina, and she insisted that you move to the other side of the room, and once you are there, she will join you." The old copper watched Tina as she stood up and walked over to the long oak table, where she sat down on a wooden dining chair.

Maud instantly seemed to simply leave her sons side and glide across the room, until she positioned herself next to her new trusted friend. The tall thin man stood up and removed a blue folder from his briefcase and sat back down on the settee. He sat looking at an coloured A4 photograph of a good looking, clean shaven well nourished white male, aged around 40 years of age. His most dominant features were his bright blue eyes that sparkled and glared out of the picture at you. He had a short stubby nose, a wide mouth out of which you could just about see his brilliantly white teeth, his hair was just showing signs of grey around the edges but he was still a very handsome man, and obviously knew it, the old man passed each of them a copy of the photograph to look at.

 While they each studied the man's facial features, the policeman began to talk again, "This is one Lord Peter Byron-Brown and he is a nasty piece of work, you can look into his eyes and think that butter wouldn't melt in his mouth, but I can assure you that he would kill you just as soon as look at you. He is heavily involved with hard drugs, prostitution and the importation of young innocent girls from Rumania, these poor creatures are aged from 12 to15 years old. The girls are brought in specifically for certain parties that his Lordship hosts once a month in his estate house, and I have it on very good authority [ mummy has attended the parties and tried to help the girls, but it was all in vain, the men seemed to simply ignore her] that he prefers the lower aged girls himself, the younger the better for his lordship.

Once the girls have all been raped, abused and then used repeatedly by his close circle of friends, our wonderful Lord then sells the girls to a certain gentleman, by the name of Gregor, where they are sold to the highest bidder. They will  then spend their lives working in the sex trade. We will get around to dealing with Gregor, at a later date. But for now we will concentrate on Lord Peter. I will meet you all here at 10 o'clock in the morning, where I will show you where his estate is situated, and fill you in about some of his habits. I know about these activities from certain covert operations that were completed about a year ago. It was after that operation that we tried to build a case together against him, but he always seemed to cover his tracks rather well, and having many friends in high places, means that his cases never actually got to court. When you have read his file, you will all agree that he has to be stopped, and the sooner the better" they all nodded their heads in mutual agreement, at what the old man had told them .

The almost retired police man was true to his word and arrived at the farm the following morning, dead on the stroke of ten o'clock. It was a bright summers day with hardly a cloud in the clear blue sky. They took the old green Jaguar with Ed driving and Rupert sat in the front passenger seat. The first thing that the police man commented on was how much he had missed the smell of real leather that he always found whenever he travelled in the old car, saying that it was a fond memory of his dead father, one that he always experienced whenever he sat in the vehicle. Ed easily followed the directions given to him by the old man, Rupert held a photocopied map that had been taken from an official police document, the map showing the boundaries of Lord Peters estate.

When they drove past the main gate, they were watched very closely by three very large, tough looking men, complete with pony tails, motor cycle boots, and long black leather coats, and necks that looked to be thicker than their thighs. "They are all armed to the teeth and not afraid to use their weapons, so be warned. When we get further along the road I will show you the most likely place to get hold of our lordship, and I will explain to you the reasons why".

The Jaguar purred along the country roads with ease, and it was a pleasure just to be sitting in the old car. The old man told Ed to slow down and pull over. Once stopped, they all climbed out of the car and looked along a fairly long, well used bridle path, Kevin used a pair of binoculars to study the wide green track, that ran the whole length of a well cared for, thick copse.

 Rupert laid the map out on the bonnet of the old car he did this so that they could all study the detailed map. The police man explained that his Lordship always rides his black hunter along that very path every Sunday morning, without fail, on his way to completing his circuit of his estate.[halfway along the bridal path there stood a huge golden, almost square structure made out of freshly cut bales of straw] "If you look closely at the map you will see a shape with an X drawn inside, that was the stacked bales of straw, the one that we can see from here, and if you can think of a way to get his Lordship down from his horse, somewhere around there, then I think that as it is close enough to the road, to be the perfect place to kidnap him, then take him back to the farm and do whatever's necessary."

They all walked over to the five bar gate, and lent on the silver painted metal, and studied first the map and then the bridle path, they all agreed with the police man that he was right about this being a perfect place to get hold of his Lordship.

It was at that point that an old battered green land rover drove past them, very slowly, and the four male occupants inside studied them closely. Back at the farm they all sat drinking coffee around the kitchen table, and they talked about the task ahead.

Tina spoke up "if I can go into town again, I think I can maybe tempt his lordship down from his horse, if you two are hidden close by, I will lead him straight to you, the rest would be up to you" The men all pressed her on what she had in mind, but she just smiled, tapped the side of her nose, smiled again, and said, "you will all just have to wait and see"

After a trip to Stratford where Tina had been shopping by herself, she returned to the car with lot's of expensive looking carrier bags, as soon as she was in the car, Ed asked if he could have a look at what she had bought. Tina smiled sweetly and told him once again, that he would have to wait and see.

The young woman was in the bedroom, and she was taking her time getting changed into her new clothes, because she wanted to achieve the correct reaction from the waiting men waiting below. While the three men full of expectation, sat in the living room waiting for the big reveal, they chatted like old friends. It was a good hour later when there was a light tap on the living room door, Tina called out "ready or not, here I come" when she walked into the room all four men gasped out loud, because she could have been very easily been taken for a twelve year old girl. She wore a short red skirt, a white crop top with no bra, a pair of red sandals with white ankle socks, she had tied her hair up in bunches either side of her head, both held in place with a bright red ribbon that had been tied in a bow. Her full make up had been expertly done, and was maybe a tiny bit over the top in colour, but it was the light blue lip stick that did the trick. The men all sat there speechless as she placed her thumb into her mouth, she stood there and seductively swayed from side to side, and when she fluttered her eyelids, the effect was stunning, and she could have easily passed as a prepubescent girl, and she acted the part perfectly.

Kev was so impressed with his lover that he wanted to drag her upstairs, tie her to the four poster bed again and ravish her, just like he had done when he had given her the theatre tickets. What had shocked him most about that particular sexual encounter, was that old Maud the ghost had watched every second, as he had taken a thin willow branch and caned her across the bare buttocks, which she had never had done to her before, but she had enjoyed the experience so much, that she would want it to happen again and very soon indeed. Apparently the old ghost had giggled when she had said to Tina afterwards "I wish Rupert's father had been that adventurous, because I really think that I might have quite enjoyed that, as much as you did" According to

Tina, our Maud had cackled for ages, just at the very thought of such a thing ever happening to her whilst she had been alive.

CHAPTER 31

Kev and Ed reconnoitred the bridle path and came up with a simple plan, they moved a few straw bales around and created an alcove where they could lay in wait for his Lordship. With the plan now in place, all they had to do was wait until the following Sunday morning, and hope that their target did in-fact make an appearance.

When it was time on the Sunday morning to set their plan into motion, Tina donned her enticing outfit and tied her hair up in bunches, when she had finished applying her makeup, she practiced her eye fluttering in the mirror. As she sat in the back seat of the car, Kev made her hold a coat in her lap because she was almost exposing herself, as the tiny red skirt was so short that he could she everything she had. They drove to the location and the two men took up their positions, now all that Tina had to wait for was a message from Maud that their target was on route. Tina physically jumped when Maud appeared by her side and whispered that his Lordship was on his way, Tina went to climb out of the car when the old ghost whispered, "good luck dear, I wish that it was me doing what you are doing, it's really is so exciting" Tina began her slow walk along the bridal path. Just for effect she was sucking one of those round lollies on a stick, she saw the huge white horse heading in her direction, she knew where the boys were hiding and had to speed up slightly so that the encounter would take place in the right spot.

When his Lordship was close enough, she looked straight at him, spread her feet and began to sway her hips. She watched as the man stood up in his stirrups as he spotted her, he stopped his snorting white stallion just in front of her, looked her up and down and literally licked his lips at the thoughts of pleasures to come. He looked around before asking "where have you appeared from little girl?" Tina answered in a tiny voice "my parents are cooking breakfast in the camper van, just up the lane there, I was bored and decided to take a walk, sort of an adventure if you like" she swayed her hips from side to side, and she could clearly see that he was becoming sexually aroused "and what sort of adventure are you looking for?" she swayed some more and shrugged her shoulders. he looked all around again "this is private property you know, I might have to punish you for trespassing" she simply smiled and said, "go on then"

His lordship lifted his right leg over the back of the horse and dropped to the ground, he tethered the horse to a nearby branch and walked over to her. He took hold of her hands and held them wide as he examined her, "oh yes, I am definitely going to have to punish you" she looked at the bulge in his riding breeches, he looked to where she was looking, "undo my breeches and take it out if you want" so she did, when he was fully exposed she held onto his erection and almost dragged him to where the boys were waiting.

As soon as he stepped behind the bales, Kev hit him with the stun-gun, the handsome man dropped to the floor without a sound, the trio stood looking at their victim whose erection had quickly disappeared, "fetch the car Ed" Kev said, Ed ran down the bridle path towards the old car, he reversed to where the others were waiting, they placed the unconscious and bound man into the boot of the car.

 Tina untied the horse, turned it around, slapped it hard on its rump, and sent it running back in the direction that it had originally come from. That done, they then made their way back to the farm.

When his Lordship regained consciousness, he found himself bound to some horse rings that had been set in the old stone wall of the garage, he was all alone and scared, he called out for help, but no-one came. The vigilantes were all seated in the living room drinking beers and waiting for Rupert to arrive, because when

Kevin had phoned him and told him that they had his Lordship in captivity. Rupert had said not to do anything to him until he arrived. They walked outside when they heard a car approaching.

Tina had carefully hung her new clothes in her wardrobe, she would save them for some later fun and games with her lover, but she still had her hair up and her lipstick on. When the old policeman climbed out of the shiny new car, he asked what they had done with his Lordship and they led him to the garage where the good-looking man was tethered. The old man walked over and stood right in front of the prisoner who glared at the police man and snarled "so it's you that's behind all this, then. Well Gregor will find you and I pity you when he does"
Without taking his hate filled eyes from the Lord, the old man whispered to the others "this heap of shite used my mother to try and intimidate me when we had him in custody on the charges of the importation of drugs, and when I refused to back down, he sent me a video of him holding a gun at her head, so I had the charges dropped. The next morning a car drove up to the farmhouse, the back door of the car flew open and they pushed my mothers dead body out of the car as if she was nothing, well today we will have our revenge"

The old man lifted his head and looked into the roof of the garage, held his arms wide and asked "are you there mummy, please show yourself mummy" his Lordship began laughing out loud and began shouting "yeh, c'mon you cantankerous old bitch, I enjoyed putting you out of your misery, watching you squirm as the very life left your wrinkled old body" His Lordship suddenly stopped shouting when a bright red ball of light appeared in the rafters, all eyes were locked onto the glowing sphere as it slowly descended to hover by the side of the old police man. Rupert still held his arms spread wide, he opened the palm of his right hand and the ball of light seemed to settle in the palm of his hand. His Lordship began stuttering "What sort of fucking trickery is this then?" When they looked at the bound man it was as if his eyes were standing on stalks, as he stared at the bright light.

Rupert smiled his best smile "My Lordship, may I introduce you to my mother" the ball of light lifted from his hand and moved to be near Tina, ever so slowly the light faded as the old ghost slowly revealed herself. She shimmered as she hovered, and then began to glide slowly across the garage space, until she hovered right in front of the bound man. With her empty eye sockets, she stared into the now bulging eyes of her killer "this can't be happening, it's impossible" he muttered. "Oh, it is very real sir, she has come to take her revenge on you. Mother has come to take your life, you hateful piece of shit, you have raped and murdered dozens of those poor young girls, many others you have forced into a life of prostitution, and for what, just for your own selfish monetary gain. Each one of them faces an existence where they will be further abused, by sick bastards like you. Well, today my friend, I have to tell you, it all ends for you and when I get there, I will see you in hell" with that the old man took a few steps backwards.

The bound man stared at the ghost and shouted "what can she do to me, she's dead for fucks sake" and he then began laughing hysterically. The vigilantes all moved back out of the way and stood against the rear wall, they remained silent as a very high pitched sound began softly at first, a sound that they had first heard a few weeks earlier, the first time that they had first encountered the dead woman.

Maud now had her mouth wide open, just as if singing a high note, and the high pitched screaming sound that came out of her now oblong shaped mouth was quite remarkable. The old woman seemed to stretch and become elongated and thinner, until she had become almost arrow shaped, she began to slowly glide around the garage space, moving faster and faster until she had a terrifying elongated facial expression, she eventually looked just like a dart in mid flight, she weaved in between them, moving faster and even faster, his Lordship began to scream louder and louder as his eyes followed the old ghost. While his mouth was forced wide open in mid scream, Maud took the opportunity to fly like a dart straight into the villains gaping mouth, her whole long grey dart like shape rushed head first into his body.

If it was at all possible his eyes bulged even further as his very body was being invaded by the old ghost. He could feel her twisting around inside his stomach, over and over she rolled inside him, tearing his insides to shreds as she did so, suddenly and without warning, she exploded from his stomach with a spray of tiny droplets of blood. His Lordship continued to scream as the dead old woman hovered in front of her murderer, she held her right hand out to him and sitting there right in the palm of her hand, was his still beating purple heart.

His Lordship stared at his own heart for a split second, until his head dropped forward to rest on his chest. He was gone, dead, the man had died a terrible death, but one that he had earned, and richly deserved. Maud turned her head and looked into the far corner of the garage, and in a flash, she flew towards the roof of the small building, she hovered for a few seconds, and then was gone.

A deep, low rumbling sound filled the garage space, as the growlers came to claim yet another disciple, the dead man had just enough time to leave his old body as a spirit, look back to what had once been himself. That was when a long black hand with fingers many feet long, came out of the garage floor and stretched towards the new spirit. The black hand was followed closely by the growlers terrifying, most evil black head, that had bright fluorescent green eyes, then another growler came out of the concrete floor to assist the first, as they both slithered towards the dead man's terrified spirit, to claim yet another evil recruit.

When it was all over they released the Lordships body from the wall, and simply let the empty corpse drop on the cold grey concrete. Ed reversed the old black range rover to where the body lay, they lifted the dead man into the rear of the 4x4 vehicle. Ed picked up something that suspiciously looked like a black grease covered engine block, and lifted it into the back of the land Rover. They then drove down the bumpy farm track towards the slurry pit. The two men stood and looked all around, just to make sure that they were not being observed. Happy that they were on their own, they lifted the dead man out of the four wheel drive vehicle and lay him on the grass by the edge of the rank smelling hole. They tied the engine block to his ankles and slid the lot into the thick smelly dark green cow shit.

His body seemed to right its self like a fishing float does when it first entered the water, before the whole lot slid under the sun dried surface. What would always stay with them for ever, was the look of hatred in the dead man's eyes, eyes that seemed to stare at them, as the sockets  filled with the thick green slurry, just before he finally disappeared out of sight forever.

# CHAPTER 32

The two men returned to the farm house and parked the car in the garage. They walked back to the farmhouse, Tina and the old police man were sat at the dining table studying a wad of papers that had been spread allover the antique tables surface. "What's this lot then?" asked Ed. The old man looked over the top of his glasses and replied "this is our next target, his name is Edward Reardon, he is an Australian national and one of the biggest importers of heroin to this country that we know about. Teddy as he likes to be known was another nasty piece of work, and just like his Lordship, we have always known of his involvement and guilt, but he has never served one single day behind bars.

I was personally involved in a water tight case against our Teddy, but when it came to the trial date, well, all the evidence against him had somehow mysteriously disappeared from the evidence room, and yet again our Teddy walked free.

He arrives at Heathrow in two days time, on the 23rd and you Ed will be there waiting to meet him, you will be at the arrivals entrance and have a card with his name written on it. If he asks, you will tell him that you are to take him to Lord Peters residence, and that a special party had been arranged in his honour, OK?" Ed nodded and copied the flight arrival times down on a pocket note book, "When I arrive back here, do you want me to drive straight into the garage or bring him into the house?" Kev suggested "we will hear you coming down the drive, I will wait for you in the garage, you get out of the car and open the rear door, and I will do the rest." They all agreed to the simple plan and that was that. For the moment at least they could relax, and talk some more about that days events.

Having heard what the Australian's traded in, Kev sent Ed to score some Heroin and pick up some syringes, they would give

Teddy a taste of his own medicine, and see how he liked it.

Ed picked up the drug dealer at the airport without any problems, the Aussie slept all the way back to the farm house. Once back at the farm Ed climbed out of the car and opened the rear door, Teddy had one foot on the floor and was lifting himself out of the car when Kevin stepped forward, and pushed the stun-gun into the man's neck. Teddy flopped down onto the grey gravel and lay still, the two men lifted him up and dragged him into the garage, and tied him to the horse rings where Ed covered the man's mouth with some silver duct tape.

They stood looking at the unconscious man and Ed said casually, "He don't look much does he?" Teddy was of slight build, maybe five feet four inches tall, a handsome face but he was a ginger, and Kevin for some unknown reason had always disliked gingers. They checked that he was securely tied, turned the light off, and left him there with only the spiders for company.

When they opened the garage door the following morning the stench of stale piss was overwhelming, Teddy had pissed himself and his trousers were soaking wet. Kevin waved his hand under his nose as he looked at the red faced man, who was trying to say something from behind the tape, all four of them stood looking at the drug baron and Kevin nodded to Ed, "get the hose pipe mate, wash him down and try and get rid of that stink" Ed had great fun soaking the drug dealer who writhed and made deadly mumbled threats from behind the tape, threats that none of them understood.

Not a word was said as they made their preparations, the two young men carried a table into the garage and set it down in front of Teddy, just for fun they then spread out various work tools that they found in the garage, in a bid to scare him. Ed took a sharp looking flick knife out of his pocket, exposed the blade and laid it down on the brown surface, he then took out the heroin and syringes, then lay them down by the side of the knife. Teddy's eyes scanned the tools of torture, he then looked from face to face with pleading eyes, still no-one said a word as they all trooped out of the garage, and left the soaking wet man to his even more confused thoughts.

Having eaten a fine lunch and desert cooked by Tina, they all returned to the garage, to find that Teddy had pissed himself yet again, but he was past caring, he looked from face to face and shook his head at the old copper. Ed took some long black cable ties from the table and joining two together and bound Teddies ankles together. Kevin dragged one of the engine blocks over and between them they tied Teddies ankles to the heavy lump of metal, they then dragged it away from the wall, therefore stretching Teddy torso outwards so that all of his weight was now on his wrists.

Ed picked up his flick knife and turned to Teddy, the drug dealers eyes went big as Ed slit the man's sleeve of his shirt from wrist to shoulder, he then took a neck tie out of his pocket [which he had taken especially for the job] and tied that around the man's upper arm, that done it made all the veins in his arms swell and stand proud. The young man smiled, picked up the heroin and showed it to the Aussie prisoner. Knowing what was coming, he began to shake his head and plead with his eyes. Ed reached behind his back and took a desert spoon out of his back pocket, he then tipped the heroin into the spoon. He then lit his cigarette lighter and held it underneath the bowl, until the pale powder turned to a sort of thick brown liquid and began to bubble. Ed then drew the thick brown substance into the plastic syringe.

When he had sucked up all of the warm drug, he pointed the needle into the air and pushed the thick brown substance upwards, until it began to ooze out of the tip of the needle. Ed nodded at Kev who moved forward and grabbed hold of the drug dealer around the waist in a bid to keep him still, but the Aussie struggled for all he was worth, so much so that Tina had to add her weight to hold the surprisingly strong man still, finally being held motionless, Ed pushed the needle into Teddie's exposed swollen vein, and sent the warm evil drug into his body. Ed smiled at the Australian as he undid the tie that released the neat heroin into Teddies circulation, "Let's see how you like it, you arse hole"

They watched his reaction as the drugs coursed through his body, and when his eyes rolled back in his head and his body slumped against his restraints, the tiny man became completely limp. They left him in the darkness to his pleasant, but very uneasy dreams.

Late in the evening the old man left them and headed home, the trio walked back to the garage to find the Australian almost back to normal, Ed grabbed hold of the prisoner this time, but there was no need for any rough stuff because the Aussie hardly put up any fight at all, and when Kev pushed the needle into his vein again, the tethered man almost welcomed the brown liquid. A smile appeared on the man's mouth as the heroin sent him once-again into a state of complete oblivion. The next morning when they entered the garage Edward Reardon seemed almost glad to see them, he watched closely as Ed prepared the heroin, and they were certain that if his mouth hadn't been taped closed, he would have licked his lips in anticipation. What he hadn't noticed was that Ed had prepared a second syringe full of the brown stuff, Kev didn't even have to hold the Aussie still this time, he watched closely as Ed pushed the needle into his vein, but instead of pushing the heroin into his vein.

Ed turned to look into the desperate man's eyes "before I give you this little lot, I want you to take a few minutes and think about all the families that you have helped to ruin, all the people that have suffered, because of the stuff you have brought into this country. I want you to have a thought for the people that have over dosed on your product, and I want you to imagine what it must feel like to die such a slow, horrible death, because my Australian friend, you are about to find out exactly what it was like" with that he released the drugs into his system, followed closely by the second fatal syringe full.

The Aussie suffered immeasurably, he shat himself as his body jerked and twisted against his restraints. It took Teddy a few hours to actually stop breathing, but only seconds for the growlers to make an appearance, the long arms came once-more to claim yet another of their evil workers.

Ed removed the dead man's Rolex watch and fixed it onto his own wrist and then emptied the dead man's pockets of anything valuable. That done the two men then placed the body and his luggage into the boot of the Land Rover and  drove him to the slurry pit. They stood and watched as the weight of the engine parts took the body down into the green darkness, to a place where the worms and bugs would feast on his small body, until there was nothing left but a few green cow shit stained bones.

# CHAPTER 33

Nothing was seen of Rupert or his dead mother for close to 5 weeks, it was as if the trio had been totally forgotten. They were all in bed one night, it was the early hours of the morning when Tina woke with a start. She screamed out loud, because Maud was pulling at her night dress with one long wisp of a hand, with the other hand she held a long thin finger to her mouth, in a bid to quiet her. She then moved forward and whispered,"someone was outside searching the out buildings, there were two of them dressed in dark clothing"  Maud turned away and disappeared through the outside wall to keep watch on the unwanted visitors, Kevin was sat up in bed by now, looking at his lover, "what's wrong?" She whispered what Maud had told her, he jumped out of bed and pulled his jeans on, he then ran out of the bedroom and woke Ed, the two men ran down stairs and opened the gun cabinet, they both loaded a shotgun and picked up a torch, and headed outside into the silent darkness.

Rather than split up, they walked side by side with their guns cocked and ready, it was as they turned around the side of the garage that they saw two dark figures scurrying away, running into the security of the open fields. Kev and Ed fired both barrels at the fleeing intruders, a startled yelp from one of the fleeing men made the two vigilantes smile, as they made their way back to the farm house. Just to make sure of their safety, they checked every window and door was securely locked before they returned to bed. When Kevin walked into the master bedroom he found Tina almost in tears, because she had heard the gun shots, but didn't know who had fired them.

The next day was going to be very special for Tina, because this was the day that she was going to the theatre to see *A Midsummers Nights Dream*, she had been out and bought a complete new outfit, and had booked a meal at the *Vintners

Restaurant*, which had a first class reputation for fine dining. Kevin, much to his annoyance had also been out and bought new clothes, he did this just to keep his lover happy.

They were dressed in all their finery and standing in front of the farm house, waiting for Ed to bring the recently waxed car around. He was doing his chauffeur bit, by driving them to the theatre and bringing them home again. That was when the lovers saw three black cars coming down the driveway at great speed, the cars screeched to a halt, ten men climbed out of the cars, and spread out in a fan shape all around them, each one of the men stood still and glared at the lovers. A very broad shouldered man with long greasy hair tied in a ponytail, dead green eyes, a broken nose, dressed in black just like the rest of them, stood out amongst the rest of the hard looking men.

When he spoke, they thought that his accent sounded Romanian, but it could have been from anywhere near there, he said slowly "you may have heard of me, my name is Gregor, myself and my comrades, we look after security on Lord Peters estate and we seem to have lost our benefactor, also a very important Australian gentleman friend or ours, has gone missing. Now we, as a team have been wondering why you have been taking so much interest in the estate? You see that old green Jaguar of yours, [he pointed to the old car with Ed sat in the drivers seat] it is very rare and quite distinctive, it has been seen at various points on the estate, by my men, which makes me think that you have something to do with our problem.

So we have taken it upon ourselves to come and have a look around your property, with your permission of course" the big man smiled, and that was when all the guns came into view. No-one said a word as two of the armed men took up positions either side of their boss, the rest of the men simply walked into the farm house and other out buildings, they searched everywhere from top to bottom. A few minutes later the men came out of the farmhouse, the man in charge of the search party shook his head at his boss, telling him that they had found nothing.

Gregor was still smiling as he said "we are sorry to have troubled you, but I know that you had something to do with the our problem, and when I can prove it, we will return and next time you will not get off so lightly!" The big man stared at Kevin for a long time before he nodded his head, that was the signal for the hard men to climb back into their vehicles and leave.

The trio of vigilantes just stood there unable to move, they were rooted to the spot with sheer terror, Ed moved first and walked back to the car, he opened the rear door and the handsome couple climbed silently inside. It had taken a good few minutes before Tina spoke, she simply asked "what are we going to do, I don't know about you but they scared the shit out of me" neither man answered her, but Kevin was deep in thought as they headed towards Stratford.

The evening had been ruined before it had even begun, but the lovers still went through the motions, and made the best of a bad thing. When they climbed back into the car at the end of the evening, Ed drove off but kept checking the rear view mirror, Kevin asked, "is everything OK Ed?" The younger man answered "I went for a walk round Stratford tonight, and I am pretty certain that I was followed every step of the way, and now I think that we are again, being followed?" The lovers both turned their heads to look at the following car, as they did so, it dropped back, when they turned into the entrance to the farm, the other car slowed right down, as it drove past the entrance.

Kevin walked into the farmhouse to find the whole place had been trashed, furniture had been torn apart, the full walled book case had been emptied with its contents strewn everywhere, pictures had been slashed and ruined, anything that could be damaged, had been, every room in the big house was exactly the same. Kev took out his mobile phone and called the commander.

The old man walked into the trashed farm house almost trance like, without saying a single word he began to wander around the invaded house. When he had finished looking in every room, the old man sat down heavily on the righted settee, he eventually looked into the eyes of the three standing in front of him, "Mummy tried her best to stop them, but there were just to many of them, she told me that they were very angry about their missing friends.

She also said that the one in charge has vowed to get his revenge, he intends to set the farmhouse on fire, he said that he will do it one night when you are all asleep" Kevin walked over to the window and stood looking out, he finally asked the old man, "what are we going to do about it, commander?" The old man stood up wearily and walked over and stood next to Kevin, and said quietly, "I am not without friends you know Kevin, I will make a phone call to a certain army officer friend of mine first thing in the morning, and between us, we will come up with a solution. You say that these men were definitely armed?"

Kevin looked the old man in the eyes, "Most definitely commander, we all saw the guns, and I don't think that they would have any problems using them" Rupert rubbed his pointed chin, "so they could be classed as terrorists, armed terrorists at that, hmm, yes that may be enough to get my friend interested. I will call the insurance company straight away and get them to send someone out to look at the damage, until then I suggest that you stay alert and keep a loaded gun nearby" with that the commander left them to prepare for a long, sleepless night.

Although they stayed awake all night, nothing untoward happened. Tina had gone to bed at first light, leaving the two men still stood looking out of the windows, watching, searching for anything out of the ordinary. The commander rang the farmhouse just after nine o'clock the following morning and spoke to Kevin for quite some time, before hanging up.

 Kevin placed the phone back down in its cradle, and said to his friend "the insurance people are on the way, and should be here any minute, we are to let them into the house, when they have finished doing their thing, we have to go out. The commander says to leave the farm unguarded. Apparently the armed attack on the farmhouse yesterday was being classed as a terrorist incident, and because of the commanders involvement, steps were being taken to put an end to the problem, once and for all.

We have a critical part to play, and must get the timing's just right, but that was for later. I will go and wake Tina, you get one of the shotguns and put in the boot of the car with a few cartridges. We will meet you outside in a while, OK Ed?" OK, boss " he smiled excitedly and was gone in a flash to get the car ready.

# CHAPTER 34

The insurance people arrived and it took a whole day to make a complete assessment, they then left with a promise that there would be no problem with the claim, as the damage had been an obvious break in. The trio spent the day in Cheltenham, mainly shopping. Kevin had slipped away to do a personal bit of business. He rejoined his friends where they passed the time in the busy tree lined park on the edge of the town, where Kevin sat down and told his partners in crime of the commanders plan to put a stop to Gregor and his men. For everything to work out as it should, their timing would need to be crucial. Until then they could all relax as they waited for the appointed time to arrive. That was when they needed to return to the farmhouse.

The time eventually came for them to make their way back to the farm. When they were driving along a country road near Lord Peters estate, Kevin asked Ed to pull over somewhere quiet. When they had stopped he climbed out of the car, removed the shotgun from the boot and loaded it with two cartridges, he then climbed back into the rear of the car and wound the window down.

They waited until dead on the stroke of six o'clock, which was the time that the commander had told Kevin to drive past the main gate of the estate, and fire both barrels towards whoever was stood there. And then high tail it back to the farm house, as quickly as they could and then hide somewhere safe.

Ed drove past the front gates of the estate very slowly, the two huge men on guard duty stood either side of the gate, and stared at them with hate filled eyes. Kevin pushed the twin black barrels of the shotgun out of the cars window, and fired both barrels into the air, the men dressed all in black instinctively dived onto to the ground, they both drew black hand guns and began firing at the old car, as it sped away. Tina and Kevin were crouched down as low in the back seat of the car as they could get. Tina was screaming at the top of her voice, at the same time she held her hands over her ears, because the sound of the shotgun being fired in the close confines of the car, had been truly deafening.

Ed drove up to the farmhouse, they all jumped out of the car, ran into the house and locked the doors and windows behind them. They stood looking out of the front windows and wondered where the commander was. Kevin ran from room to room in the hope of finding the old policeman, but the house was completely empty, he ran back to his friends, "I have a bad feeling about this, we will have to arm ourselves the best we can and hope for the best" Kevin made his lover hide in the downstairs bathroom, while he and Ed raided the gun cabinet, both armed with shotguns and a full box of cartridges each, they went to the front windows of the house, they opened the windows, said a silent prayer, and waited for Gregor and his friends to arrive.

It was maybe half an hour later that the convoy of black cars began to make their way down the farms drive, the intimidating cars screeched to a halt at the end of the drive. The army of men all dressed in long black leather coats climbed out of their vehicles and followed their leader until they were stood in an arc facing the farm house. And just like before Gregor stood in the centre of his men. He had the same confident smile on his face simply because of the sheer weight of numbers, the big man looked at the shiny gun barrels that were pointing out of the windows, and smirked "my friends, there was no need for all this, why did you shoot at my men?

They have done nothing to you" Kev shouted "What about our house? I don't suppose that was your men that did all that damage?" Gregor shrugged "I think that they maybe became a tiny bit over enthusiastic, what did you expect after you shot one of their friends, now look at those silly little guns you have, we have much better ones" he waved his hand, some of the huge men pulled out small black machine guns, the others pulled out long black AK 47s from under their long leather coats, and cocked them menacingly. "I will give you until the count of ten to come out, after that my men will come in. If that happens, then your woman will have to entertain each of my men until they tire of her, and then they will slit her throat" shouted Gregor.

He began counting very slowly, when he reached eight, as if by magic his head simply exploded into a thousand pieces, it was just like a ripe tomato erupting. His lifeless body then dropped stiffly to it knees and then fell forwards to lay there still on the gravelled drive, and was most certainly dead. There had been no sound of a shot, the only sound was the thwack as the bullet struck the big man's head, the rest of Gregor's men swung their machine guns from side to side, as they searched in every direction for a target to shoot at, then silently, one by one they died, some were thrown backward's as the copper bullets slammed into their heads and bodies.

In a matter of seconds it was all over, the front of the house looked like a battle field as twisted bloodied bodies lay strewn everywhere, some on their backs and the others crumpled on their fronts, and yet the two stunned men still couldn't see where the fatal shots had come from.

The friends walked out of the front of the house and stood looking at the mass of twisted bodies, that was when the groaners began to appear from all directions, the pair moved back to stand in the doorway, within seconds it looked as if a million blow flies had settled on the bodies, the groaners eventually slid back from where they had come from, armed with a small army of new disciple's.

The two men smiled to one another as a black car came along the farm track and pulled up besides them, the commander climbed out of the rear of the car, dressed in civilian clothes for a change, out of the other door climbed a man dressed in camouflaged clothing. The army man looked at the bodies and then spoke into a tiny hand held radio, within seconds two large black vans drove along the driveway of the farm, followed by a highly polished black range rover.

The range rover stopped half way along the driveway, the driver climbed out of the powerful car and opened each of the cars doors, also the boot, he stood by the side of the car and spoke into a radio that he held in his right hand. As if by some kind of magic four shapes that were obviously army snipers, seemed to simply rise out of the stubbled ground, each of then carried a long black rifle, complete with a long telescopic sight fixed to its top.

Each man shook their camouflage netting from their backs, and let it fall to the stubbled earth, they then casually walked to the land rover and stowed their made safe rifles into the boot of the big powerful car, they each climbed into the car, and were driven away. Eight large men dressed in green overalls and black army boots stepped down from the big van, each of them wore a white mask over their mouths, and began to silently load the dead into the rear of the vans, they then collected all the discarded weapons made them safe and placed them into the rear of the vans along with the bodies.

Three of the men took a seat in the black cars of the dead, When it was all over, the commander shook hands with the army officer who climbed back into his car. He was then driven away from the farm, followed closely by the black cars of the dead, all trace of the security men and their vehicles from Lord Peter estate, was gone forever .

The commander turned and looked at the two men that were under his control, rubbed his hands together and smiled "well, that should put an end to that little problem then?" He turned to Ed, "Will you please drive me home young man?" Ed took great

pleasure in driving the senior police man home. When Ed
returned to the farmhouse, it was obvious that something was
going on, he could tell by the worried look on the his  friends
faces, the young man looked at his concerned looking best friend,
and asked"What's up?"

# CHAPTER 35

Tina whispered into his ear "we need to go somewhere soon, we have urgent things to discuss" Ed looked from one to the other, something unsaid passed between the three of them. Ed took the hint "Shall we go into town, for fish and chips maybe?" He suggested, the other two nodded their agreement, they wasted no time as they all climbed into the old car, Ed drove towards Stratford, where they made a beeline for Barnaby's chippy.

Sat on the grass in the park, it was Ed who spoke first, "c/mon then you two, spit it out?" Tina looked around making sure that they couldn't be overheard, and said in a very low voice "You know when I was hiding in the bathroom when everything was kicking off out front? Well, I had a visitor, Lady Mary came to see me, and she was very troubled about something that she had heard, it was to do with the commander, she said that she couldn't stay for long as Maud was not only spying on the three of them, she was also keeping all other ghosts away from her son, especially Sarah and Alice.

Mary said that she had been asking discreet questions amongst the other ghosts, and apparently there's a very dark family secret to do with the commander, but no-one was saying what it was. She said that she will keep trying to find out what she could, and when she did have more information, she would let them know what she has found out, that is if she could? She also suggested that I start going for walks in the evening, somewhere out towards the slurry pit, then if it was safe, she or Sarah would come to me?" The two men sat looking at her for a few seconds before Ed asked "what could it be, we all have secrets, but the commander, it was very hard to believe that he could be involved with anything the least bit dodgy" Kevin shrugged and added "Well, Lady Mary has no reason to lie has she, and I don't think that she would know how to tell a lie anyhow, so all we can do now, is to watch this space and see what, if anything transpires"

Tina took to walking the lonely lanes every evening, no matter what the weather, knowing that sooner or later one the ghosts would arrive and make contact with her. Late one sunny evening as Tina had just reached the slurry pit area, a tiny voice told her to walk just a little further towards the small copse. Tina did as she was instructed and when she arrived at the small group of trees, she could see that Sarah was waiting for her just inside the trees, so she smiled broadly, waved and quickened her pace. Sarah genuinely seemed so happy to see her friend, her ghostly form seemed to move forward and wrap itself around her and give her a hug, when she eventually moved away, Sarah hovered and moved her head as she looked in all directions, making certain that the old ghost Maud was nowhere near.

The dead girl began talking, and said in all sincerity,"Oh, Tina we have missed you all so much, I miss you terribly, but I have to tell you that there was a lot of disappointment amongst the some of the young children when you left, many more victims have come forward, all in the hope that one day they would get revenge against their abusers, do you think that you will ever be able to take up where you left off?"

[Tina shrugged her shoulders and told the truth when she said, she honestly didn't know what was going to happen in the future] Sarah took up the conversation and after another look around whispered "I have found out a little bit more about the commander and his dead mother.

From what we have been told that Maud has apparently caused no end of problems in our world, she has done this just by using her army of friends whom she has bullied and cajoled, all this just to strengthen her position in the inner cloud, and to reinforce her sheer, brutal dominance. By doing this she has managed to almost permanently bury the families dark sorrowful secret. Apparently the commander had a pretty little eight year old daughter named

Molly, whom he doted on, and had complete custody of after a very messy divorce. Since she passed over to our side, Molly has been hidden away, out of reach of anyone that knows the family. She is kept hidden away somewhere in the depths of the inner cloud. Maud has spent a lot of time scaring the other spirits that are looking after her into silence, simply by using her strong influence. The old ghost managed to have Molly taken there by a very high ranking politician, who just happened to be some distant relative of hers, this was done under the strict instruction that Molly sees no adult ghosts, and to keep her happy, other dead girls of her same age were sometimes brought in from the outside of the inner cloud, just to play with her.

 A young girl named Annabel was her favourite playmate, and I have been talking to her, it seems that the commander wasn't all he was made out to be, and the family secret that they were doing their utmost to keep hidden, was that the commander himself, had sexually abused and murdered little Molly. The story goes that one day everything simply went to far, and after he had crept into her bedroom and abused her, she had said that she knew that what he was doing to her was wrong, and it was dirty, and that she was going to tell her teacher the next day when she went back to school. Well, the commander couldn't allow that to happen, because of his position as one or the highest ranking officers in the British police force. So he took the terrified girl from her bedroom and tried to strangle her with a length of rope in the garage.

Thinking that she was dead, the crazed old man left her laid on the cold concrete floor with the ligature still around her neck. When she finally regained consciousness and tried to stand up, an unknown force grabbed the ends of the ropes, pulled them tight and held on for a fair while, just to make certain that she was dead. When little Molly arrived over on our side, she eventually told Annabel that she had seen the dead old woman that had murdered her, and it was the commanders mother, Maud.

That was the reason why Molly had been hidden away for so long, it was just to keep her away from you three, and if they could manage this, then they would manage to keep the families dirty secret and the commander safe."

Tina was quiet for a long while as she contemplated what the young ghost had told her, she eventually told the dead girl that she would go and tell the others what she had told her, and that she was not to worry. Tina then asked Sarah, when the time comes to deal with the old man, if she thought that she could get Molly to come to the garage to confront the commander?

Sarah thought about this for a few seconds "I don't know if we could get the young girl out of the inner cloud and past Maud, she protects her grand daughter at all times, and if she ever found what was going on she would do her utmost to stop us, and she wouldn't want all this coming out, would she?" Tina told the young ghost that she would discuss it with the other two, and that she would return the following evening at the same time, at the same place and let her know if they had a plan.

Tina returned to the farmhouse and told the others that she needed to go into town to do some personal shopping, and would they care to join her? Just the sheer look of concern on her face was enough for the two men to understand that what she wanted to discuss, was very urgent. Ed walked into the garage, collected the car and drove them into Stratford without question. Sitting on the grass in the park again, she retold the complete story that Sarah had relayed to her.

Having listened to his lover, Kevin lay back on the grass, closed his eyes, thought about the commander and tried to figure out why, if he had such a dark secret, would he knowingly get them involved. Surely the old man must have realised that he would eventually get found out. Maybe that was the point, he did want to get found out. That being the case, he wondered what they were going to do about it, there was no doubt that he had to be punished, but how to do it with the old ghost protecting him all the time, was a different matter.

After laying there on the cool grass with his eyes closed for a good while, Kevin eventually spoke, "Do you remember when we were told that the growlers could if they wanted to, transform themselves into ghosts, you know, to come up from below for trials and disagreements, snatch squads, things like that. Well, couldn't we arrange for one of the growlers to meet up with us and Sarah, somewhere quiet, like down by the slurry pit, that way we could inform him about Maud, let him know what she had done to Molly, and that the old woman belonged down below with all of the other murderers. That way we just might be able to get her out of the way, and we could then deal with the commander." Tina said that she would put it to the dead girl later that evening, and get her to contact Lady Mary, she would know how to contact the growlers .

# CHAPTER 36

Tina was sat in the long grass not far away from the smelly slurry pit waiting for Sarah to arrive, luckily she was down wind as the smell was awful in the hot sun, she looked up and saw the dead sisters waving as they drifting towards her, they stopped close by, but they seemed to be very nervous about being seen, especially by the old ghost Maud. The dead girls sat either side of her, and it seemed that Alice had her head resting on Tina's shoulder. Alice whispered "I have missed you so much Tina, I miss you more than I miss my mummy" Tina turned to face the dead spirit. "You should never say things like that Alice, Im sure that she loved you very much." When Alice said nothing else, Tina looked at Sarah and told her what Kevin had suggested, only to be told that what she was asking was virtually impossible, but if she could get a message to Lady Mc Partridge. Maybe she could then contact the Brigadier, and between them they might be able to make a strong enough case to take to those in ultimate control. He did say, that if we ever needed his help, to simply send a message.

Tina walked the lonely farm tracks every evening for a week after that and she saw no-one, it was on the following clear sunny day, whilst she was sitting in the long grass, that she saw three wispy figures floating towards her. From what she could see, the one in the centre of the trio was a lot taller, and older than the other two. When the figures became more defined, she could clearly see that it was in fact the Brigadier, in between the dead sisters, she could also tell that the tall man seemed to be holding each girls hand. The trio of ghosts hovered in front of her, the tall man smiled, "I never for a minute thought that I would be seeing you again, especially so soon Tina. The girls have told me of your problem, and what you need from me, I can't see a problem setting up the meeting, except that it would have to happen, away from the farm, as Maud would not allow such a meeting, if she ever found out about it"

Tina suggested holding the meeting by the main gates of Lord Peters estate, all the army man would then have to do, was to get a message to her, let her know the time, date and they would all be there.

It was getting on for two weeks later before any further contact was made, and when it came, it was from a completely different unexpected quarter. As usual Tina was waiting somewhere near the slurry pit, and was very surprised when Lady Mary Partridge made her way towards her, the old ghost seemed to sit by her side, and reached out as if to touch Tina affectionately on the arm.

Lady Partridge turned her hollow eyes to the young woman, "It is so nice to see you again dear, I rather hoped that I would. This problem of yours has caused quite a stir in the legal systems of the inner cloud.There have been all sorts of arguments from both sides, the growlers say one thing and the inner cloud then say another. Basically it boils down to the fact that the growlers refuse point-blank to meet with you and your friends, but they have agreed to meet with the inner clouds leaders to discuss the problem of Maud Mc Phereson.

It appeared that the growlers had tried to take the old woman at the time that she murdered little Molly, but she managed to make her escape before the black fiends could get there. They had tried on numerous occasion since that day to take the old ghost, but she somehow always seemed to find out that they were coming. What she didn't know was that the Flea squad {T.I.C.S.S. The Inner Cloud Security Service] were putting a plan together as we speak to arrest her, and then take her to the inner cloud for questioning, regarding the death of her granddaughter.

It was a forgone conclusion really, but both sides had to follow certain procedure's. When she is eventually found guilty of all charges, which she would be, she would then be handed over to the growlers for them to do with as they saw fit. There is no doubt that when you have dealt with her son, the same thing would happen to him.

When the commander is in-fact dead, mother and son obviously believe that they will happily spend eternity together, which I have no doubt would suite them both, but in fact the exact opposite will happen. When the Flea men have taken her, I will come again to see you and hopefully bring the sisters with me.
They would have come this time, but they are having to deal with this huge woman, this female seemed to be quite deranged as she searched for her husband, she has vowed terrible revenge on him, when she does eventually catch up with him. But tell Kevin not to worry to much, we know all about her and we are dealing with that particular problem. Well, I will have to get back and see what was happening back up there, all this tooing and frowing, well it is really quite exciting you know dear, I haven't had so much fun in years. I will see you soon" With that she made as if to kiss Tina on the cheek, before she smiled and simply floated away from her, waving as she did so.

Three days later there was a loud knocking on the door at what seemed to be the middle of the night, but it was in-fact almost dawn. Kevin ran down the stairs and opened the door, a distraught Rupert was standing there, he seemed to have suddenly aged ten years since Kevin had last seen him, which had only been a few days before. The commander pushed himself past Kevin and immediately began blabbering "mummy, mummy, is mummy here?

Have you seen her, please tell me that she is here?" Kevin took the old man's arm and led him inside, and sat him down on the settee, went to the kitchen, and made them both a cup of tea.

When he walked back into the living room, the police man was on his knees by the wall, his hands stretched upward and pressed flat against the cold plaster, his finger nails began scratching paint from the old brick work "Where are you mummy, please don't leave me, I need you so much." Then the old man sank back on his heels, held his head in his hands, and began sobbing his heart out, big fat tears running down his face as his bottom lip began to tremble.

 Kevin eased the commander to his feet and then led him back to the settee, he lay the old man down and lifting a throw from the back of the settee, he covered the distraught man. When Kevin stood back and looked down at the man it was obvious he was having some sort of mental breakdown. The policeman lay there, sucking his thumb like a baby.

Tina came down the stairs and entered the living room, she took one hateful look at the child murderer, and seeing the state he was in, went to him out of sheer pity. And took his hand in hers. The old man instantly relaxed. "There you are mummy, I knew you wouldn't abandon me" Tina looked at her lover and shrugged as if to ask, "what am I supposed to do?" ·

 Ed walked into the room looking as though he had been up all night, he took one look at the commander and growled "what's up with that murdering twat?" his friend smirked and said sarcastically "he seems to be missing his mummy, which could mean that she has been arrested. If that is the case, she won't be coming back any time soon" Ed smiled and answered his friend,"so does that mean that we can deal with him, because I have a rather suitable plan for our dear old commander" Kevin shook his head "I think that we need to make certain that the old woman is no longer here, and then we need to ask the commander some very awkward questions first, don't you think?"

It took Tina most of the day to get the old man back to some sort of normality, she did this by using plenty of brandy and paracetamol, the mixture of both seemed to do the trick. Rupert still trembled as he sat up on the settee holding a mug of tea. The trio of vigilantes sat opposite him. And Kevin was just about to begin asking him some leading questions when Tina grabbed his hand and looked across the room.

Lady Mary Partridge hovered in the far corner, she waved a shaky hand that seemed to be beckoning Tina to her, the young woman stood up and walked over to the old ghost, her two friends sat and watched as Tina and Lady Mary had a quiet conversation. Tina nodded her agreement at what had been said, and the old woman simply faded away, leaving Tina standing there all on her own.

When she returned and sat down next to her lover, he immediately tried to ask her what was going on, but she silenced him with a stern look. She turned her attention back to the old man, and coughed to get his attention, "commander, I have it on good authority that your mother has been arrested by the TIC'SS squad, and is being held on a charge of murdering your daughter Molly, [the old man just shook his head from side to side in some sort of denial] and I also know that the devils disciple's were doing their best to take her down below as one of their own. Unfortunately it seems that you are more to blame than your mother, because it was you that was sexually abusing your own daughter, and when she said that she was going to tell her teacher, you panicked and tried to kill her yourself. Unlike the two very young girls before Molly, you just couldn't go through with it this time, and your mother had to step in and finish the job by taking her own granddaughters life, just to protect you. Well, it appears from what your own mother has said at her trial, that you have always been troubled in that way, but it was only when you got older, that you acted out your sick sexual fantasies.

So commander, we as vigilantes have been instructed to deal with you as soon as possible, because there is a certain red eyed devil waiting to welcome you into his fold, where, once there, you will never have a days peace for the rest of eternity, and as for your mother, a woman and spirit who has devoted her life to protecting you, wrapping you in cotton wool, doing her best to cover up for dreadful crimes. Maud will be punished by being sent to a far remote universe, where she will exist completely on her on for the rest of eternity, where she will never see another spirit, just darkness, loneliness and be powerless". The old mans face had turned completely grey, his head shook slowly from side to side as if he had suddenly developed Parkinson's disease, he began to mumble. It was just loud enough for them to understand what he was saying, "I'm so sorry, I couldn't stop myself, I tried, I really did, but something inside me just took over, she was just so young, so perfect and so like her mother. I just had to have her all for myself.

Mummy tried her best to stop me, she talked to me for hours, it was as if she knew what I was thinking, even when I was doing things to young Molly, Mummy was trying to pull me away, trying to save me from myself, but I was too strong for her. That was the first time I have ever heard mummy cry, that first time with Molly, the other two young girls didn't seem to bother Mummy at all, but young Molly was different. I'm sorry for what I have done, I am ready to face my punishment, whatever it may be" Kevin whispered, "we would normally tie your hands with cable ties, but in your case I don't think that it will be necessary, will it commander? You do promise not to try and run away, don't you?" the old man nodded his head "I have longed for this day to arrive, that was the main reason that I got you three involved in the first pace, because I knew that you would find out about Molly one day, and then do what has to be done.

Many times I have tried to kill myself, maybe out of guilt or regret, but mummy has always stopped me, telling me that she would take care of everything. Now that she has gone, I have nothing left to live for. You will find in my brief case my last will and testament, I have left everything that I own to be shared equally between the three of you. I have had the papers drawn up and they have all been signed, so everything that I own is now yours. I have no other family or friends, and the work that you are doing deserves to be rewarded, so take the farm and everything else that I own as your reward, and enjoy what I have left you" The commander seemed to suddenly collapse into himself with the effort of having made such a long statement, and it was clear to the others that he had finally given up on life, the sooner that he was dealt with the better. As he sank back into the leather settee, the old man closed his eyes, whether to shut out the world or to try and sleep, no-one, not even the man himself knew.

By early the next morning Ed had prepared the garage for the commander, he had thrown a length of the blue nylon rope over one of the rafters and tied one end to the tow bar on the land rover, in the other end of the rope, he had tied a menacing looking noose. The oval shaped ring of nylon, more than big enough to fit easily over the old man's head. Directly underneath the noose stood a wooden garden chair. Ed climbed onto the chair to make certain that he had his measurements about right, he pulled on the noose to make sure that it would take the old man's weight. He climbed down from the chair, and was about to return to the house, when he turned around to see Lady Mary hovering by the garage door.

When Ed never spoke to her, the old ghost said in a quavering voice "what you have planned is a very fitting end for the commander, I have persuaded Molly to join me here today, she is very nervous and waiting outside with the sisters. When you bring the commander into the garage, I will bring in the girls" the old grey ghost seemed to smile at Ed, before she simply turned her head, and disappeared through the old stone wall, to rejoin the waiting girls.

The commander walked untethered towards the garage to meet his much welcomed fate, as they walked through the green metal door, the old man stopped and looked up at the nylon rope, his old grey eyes followed the rope from end to end and back again. The police man walked to the chair and was about to step upwards with his left leg, when Lady Mary stopped him, "Wait Commander, you really didn't think that ending your life would be so easy, dId you? You deserve to suffer just like you made that poor innocent child suffer. The old ghost turned and disappeared through the garage wall, seconds later she reappeared hovering behind Molly. The matriarch looked to have her old grey hands resting on the poor girls narrow shoulders, as if in an act of reassurance. The commander gasped out loud as he looked into his dead daughters empty eye sockets, he sat down heavily on the wooden chair and without looking up he asked everyone in the garage "does she really have to be here to witness my demise, please do the decent thing and take her away" Kev took a step forward to stand directly in front of the old man "I think she deserves to be here to see you punished for what you have done to her, we have explained what will happen to you, and about the growlers" When no-one else spoke, little Molly moved to hover in front of her father, she reached out and placed a long wispy grey arm around the old mans shoulders, when she moved her head forward and appeared to kiss the old man on the left cheek, that was when the condemned man broke down, and began to cry.

He sobbed his heart out for quite some minutes, floods of tears dropping from his chin onto his neatly pressed black uniform trousers, the dead girl whispered "please don't cry daddy, you didn't have to hurt me, I would never have told my teacher about our little secret, I only said that to try and make you stop hurting me. Every time you did things to me, I cried for hours afterwards, because I thought that if you could hurt me so much, then how could you possibly love me, I only ever wanted you to love me, as much as I loved you" The old man turned his head and looked into the dead empty eyes,"that was the problem Molly, I loved you too much, I worshiped you because you looked so much like your mother. I am so sorry for all the bad things that I did to you, and the awful things that I made you do to me, I hated myself, I just couldn't control myself. I wish that we could be together when this is all over, I would look after you forever"

The dead girl moved away from her desperate father, as she hovered just out of reach of the old man, her answer when it came surprised everyone "I wouldn't want that father, you may begin touching me again, and I would hate to live out eternity going through all that again. So I think that it is better that you are going with the growlers, that way they will stop you ever doing those bad things to anyone else. Because of that I am glad that I will never see you ever again" The old man nodded his head, because he knew that his daughter was right in what she had said, he looked from face to face before standing up, he turned around and climbed onto the chair, he took hold of the nylon noose and placed it over his head. He reached to the side of his neck and tightened the noose, he took one last look at his dead daughter, lifted his arms in the air and held them wide, he then looked into the roof of the garage and began shouting "I'm coming mummy, are you there mummy? We will soon be together forever, then we can sleep in the same bed again, just like we did when I was growing up, when you use to hold me so tight and tell me that you loved me" With that he simply took a step forward and stepped from the chair, there was a slight crack from somewhere in the old neck, he kicked his legs a few times as the noose tightened. They all watched as his face turned red and then a bluish colour, his swollen blue tongue began to slowly appear as his jaw began to relax, and then it was all over, the old man was dead.

They all watched as the spirit of the police man stepped out of his now lifeless body, he looked at his daughter and smiled at her, he went to reach his arms out to her as if to pick her up, but she moved away from him and folded herself into the old ghost for protection. It was then that the deep growling noise began, he turned to face the growlers, he held his arms wide again and began shouting "come my friends, I am ready to join you, take me

to my mother, are you there mummy, where are you mummy"
The long black arms stretched out of every crack in the concrete
floor, the old man stood silent as what seemed like hundreds of
long black tentacles folded around the old man. Rupert never
made another sound as his evil spirit was dragged down into the
cracks of the garage floor.

Out of respect for the old man, rather than dispose of him in the
slurry pit, they buried him in an unmarked grave in the copse.
Tina placed some freshly cut sweet peas on his grave that same
day, but that was the one and only time that she did so.

One year later.

CHAPTER 37

How life could change in one long year, Tina had given birth to a beautiful baby daughter who they had named Samantha, uncle Ed was completely smitten with the child, and had volunteered to baby sit whenever needed. Tina had also learned to drive which had been very useful over the last few months. Ed had managed to renovate the old tractor and had begun repairs on the other farm machinery, the now very wealthy young man had finally found himself a girl friend name Mandy, who worked at Mc Donald's, she was a petite blond girl of nineteen, and had the bluest eyes that any of them had ever seen.

Mandy only had one fault that they knew of and that was that she would sleep walk naked, and she did this almost every night that she slept over at the farm, they had all almost choked on their Sunday lunch one day when they were all sat around the table eating, because only the night before the young woman had walked naked into the master bedroom. What made them laugh so much was Kevin, in all seriousness said, "It would have been OK if I could have found my bloody glasses, before I did, Tina had taken her back to bed" which made them all laugh out loud.

Kevin spent his days working on the very large portfolio that the commander had left them, Rupert's father had been a very astute business man almost a hundred years before, because he had bought all the land that he that could, most of it, in and around Stratford. Some of the biggest stores in the thriving town paid them ridicules amounts of rent every month, whole streets of houses, hotels, car-parks, B@Bs by the score were all resting nicely upon their land.
Rupert had followed in his fathers footsteps and bought houses, one after the other, and rented them out through a letting agent, and there were dozens of them dotted all over the town. Two nearby farms also belonged to them, and when Kevin looked deeper into the paper work, the old copper had been very shrewd,

and had been granted planning permission to build over a hundred houses on nearby Pear tree farm.

The other farm was going to have a much needed hospital, hotel and a shopping precinct eventually built on it's land. They all laughed one evening whilst eating their evening meal, when Kevin announced "No-matter how you look at it, no matter what we do, we will never be able to spend all the money that we now have at our disposal, there was simply too much, and the total just gets bigger every day" With that being the case and with them each being that well off financially, they had both been told that they could do whatever they wanted, buy whatever they fancied with the new credit cards that Kevin had just given them. The first thing that Ed did was look on the internet and search for a company to take on the renovation of the barn and all the old machinery inside, two days later a convoy of low loaders arrived and removed all the antique rusty machinery.

Once the old wooden barn was almost empty, it was dismantled and burned, plans had already been passed by the local council for a huge modern Dutch barn to replace the old building. The plans were passed to a local builder, and not long after that, the first Yellow digger arrived on site to begin the work.

It had been decided over dinner one night because of the problem with Gregor and his men they would step up the farms security. A local security company was called in and work began immediately to install state of the art burglar alarms for the house, and the three main entrances to the farm. Part of the hedge row had to be taken out at each entrance, and that was to allow for brick walls to be built, the high walls would then hold the new electronically controlled gates. The steel gates had cameras situated high above them, on top of tall grey metal poles. The gates would be controlled from a new office that had been created inside the farmhouse, and stay on and keep watch, twenty-four hours a day. A simple call from the gates intercom system from any visitor, would be answered by any one of the three. A simple push of a red button was enough to open the gates and allow entrance to the caller, if they so wished. If any of them were out in one of the cars, on their return to the farm, the gates opened automatically on their approach.

Tina walked the farms tracks with baby Sam at all hours of the day and night, sometimes simply to get the child to sleep, other times it was to see the dead sisters. She would be strolling along singing sweetly to baby Sam, and when she looked up, the sisters would be either side of her as if they too had been enjoying the walk. It was on such a day as that that Sarah told Tina that Lady Mary was coming to see her, apparently the old ghost had some very interesting news to tell her, plus she was also desperate to see baby Sam for the first time. Early one evening two days later Lady Mary arrived at the farmhouse, rather than just appear in front of them and scare them, she rattled a few items of furniture, blew some papers from the table onto the floor. It was Tina who asked whoever it was to show themselves, the old woman floated down from the ceiling and settled by the side of Kevin, she looked at each person in turn before she began to speak,"the good news that I have to share involves mainly you Kevin. For a long time now there had been a legal tussle going on between the inner cloud and the growlers, the argument has been over your deceased wife Madge.

The problem being that both sides thought that she belonged with them, the ambassadors and their teams have argued back and forth, the case flowed first one way and then the other. Two days ago one of the growlers researchers discovered a vital piece of hidden information, and that was that Madge had already been wedded before she married you Kevin, and from the information brought forward from old police records, she had abused her first husband who was named George, in exactly the same way that she did you. Only she went too far one day and stabbed him 24 times, then hid his body in a compost heap at the bottom of the garden. She did this in the vague hope that it would eventually break down and disappear. She moved up to Scotland soon afterwards, and changed her name. She did that just before she moved back down south and married you, which in law was deemed illegal. So our Madge was taken kicking and screaming down below by the growlers, which means that you are now not only free of her legally, but your personal safety was now almost guaranteed"

Having made such a long speech, all the old woman wanted next was to see baby Samantha, as soon as they had left the room to go and see the child. Kevin sighed a huge sigh of relief, because he never thought that this day would ever come. He had always been concerned in the back of his mind, that when he did pass over to the other side, Madge would be waiting for him, and take terrible revenge on his spirit, but at last he could rest easily. But before the old ghost left them and returned up above he needed to have a quiet word with her, he needed a favour.

Ed was driving the old tractor down the lane towards the slurry pit late one summers evening, when out of the corner of his eye he saw movement off to his right, he stopped the tractor and sat watching the area behind some old buildings. There was a pile of old rusty children's play equipment. A slide, climbing frame and what looked like another twisted climbing frame, old bent and twisted swings were stacked against the stone wall of the old cow sheds.
When the sun went behind a cloud and the equipment went into shadow, he could clearly see the dead sisters taking it in turns on the slide. He climbed down from the tractor and ambled over towards them "how are you girls?" he asked, they both waved and hovered over towards him, they stopped in front of him. He asked them how often they played on the slide.

Sarah answered "every day now Ed, we have been granted special dispensation, and we more or less live down here on the farm with you and the others, some of our friends have asked if they can come down and play too, but we had to say no, because we only have the slide to play on. We do sometimes go into the woods and play hide and seek, but best of all, we like to sit and watch baby Samantha when she is asleep" Ed, fetched the old tractor, and attached a rope to the front end of the old machine and pulled the climbing frame away from the wall, he straightened the old metal bars out as best he could and the sisters begun climbing in and out of them. He looked at the pile of twisted metal that used to be a set of swings and decided that they were not worth trying to save.

Ed left the girls to their game and walked back to the house in search of his best friend, Kevin was deep in concentration on his book work, so rather than disturb him he went in search of Tina. The young mother was in the kitchen, happily making some sort of pie on the work surface, standing in front of the kitchen window, baby Sam was fast asleep in her carry cot by the open back door. Ed told her about seeing the girls playing on the old equipment, and suggested that they buy them some new play things. She told him that she had seen the sisters playing chase in the empty field behind the house a few times.

Ed took Tina by the hand and led her out of the back door, they both stood looking at the empty field and Ed suggested "why don't we get them some new play equipment, plenty of different things, then they can then bring their friends down to play" Tina smiled at the idea, "I will make some drawings in the morning, and we will talk about it tomorrow evening over dinner. I'm sure Kevin won't mind?"

The drawing for the play equipment that Tina did was amazing, Tina had taken her time and drawn the whole lay out in fine pencil. The play area when finished would be better equipped than any park in any town, she had even penciled in the sisters going down the huge slide. The trio looked over the drawing that had been laid out on the dining room table, some bits were added and others taken away, within half an hour the final decision had been made, and Ed went on the computer and ordered everything that they required.

With delivery in 10 days time, the young man set about preparing the field for the equipments imminent arrival. Ed carried the drawing around with him as he marked out which piece of equipment went where. Contractors were brought in to lay the concrete bases where needed. Pleased with his finished preparation work, all he had to do now was wait for everything to arrive.

The workers never stopped as they erected swings, slides, climbing frames, see-saws, sand pits, bouncing castles, you name it and it was there. The trio sat in the evening sun looking at their very own ghost park, it didn't take long before they saw the two ghostly sisters, as they used the new slide. Sarah sat in front, and Alice hung onto her sister as they slid down the huge slide, screaming with delight. They sat and watched the sisters try out every piece of equipment, before the girls seemed to run across the field to stand in front of their live friends. Sarah said excitedly "Thank you for everything that you have done for us, we have never seen anything like it before, we like the bouncing castle the best, because we can play on it together. Would you mind if we brought a few friends with us next time, so that way we can all play together?" Kevin looked from sister to sister "you can bring as many friends as you like, we did this for all of you, nothing would give us greater pleasure than sitting here watching you all enjoying everything, and when Sam was old enough, she can play with you as well." The sisters hugged each other excitedly, before they skipped away. The trio watched as the sisters simply faded into the late evening shadows.

The following day there must have been at least ten child ghosts enjoying themselves on the new play area, they made it difficult to count as they seemed to be running everywhere all at the same time. The following day there could have been anything up to fifty boy and girl ghosts, some of them had their deceased parents sitting on the grass watching them play. Tina walked over and tried to talk to some of them, but they simply vanished if she went anywhere near. The following day there were even more ghost children running everywhere, and even more dead adults sitting on the grass watching the dead children enjoying themselves. The Brigadier and Lady Mary could be seen coming out of the shadows, they would stop and stare at the different games that were being played,  no-one spoke as the dead couple sat down on the grass by the side of Tina, happy to just sit and watch the hoard of dead children at play. It was the Brigadier that spoke first,"you do realise that some of these children have never played with other kids their own age before, because of their upbringing, they just never had the opportunity.

I used to feel really sad for the young ones that came up to join us, simply because a majority of them have only ever known mistrust, pain and suffering in their lives, but when you see them at play like this, you have to realise that they will remain like this forever, what could be better for them but to be able to play with their friends everyday and for always to remain, young at heart. This, this[the old ghost opened his arms wide as if taking in the whole field] was just what the doctor ordered you know, well done all of you." The old woman sat next to him began giggling, "We only came down to see what all the fuss was about, this new play area was on the lips of everyone up there, it really was quite strange not seeing any children messing about and being naughty up there. When they have all gone back up, do you think that the Brig and I could have a little go ourselves?" Ed spoke up first "you are more than welcome to have a go on anything that you like" it looked as if the old woman ghost was stamping her feet and clapping her hands in excitement, as she relished the thought of getting the old man on some of the new play equipment.

One morning in early November Ed walked down the stairs to see a red light flashing on the computer from one of the security camera's, he logged on immediately and began to scroll through the previous nights footage. At three, ten am, two big men with torches, in long black coats could clearly be seen trying the gates to see just how strong they were, one of the men shone his torch on the grey pole, on seeing the camera on the top pointing down at them, both men walked quickly away with their heads down.

For the next few weeks things began to get a little bit weird, it was as if all of them thought that they were being watched, even followed, be it in the car or walking around the nearby town, there always seemed to be someone watching. Kevin asked the Brigadier if he could arrange for someone to keep an eye on Tina when she was out in the car, or walking the farms tracks. The old soldier said that it would be done at once, he asked Kevin why he wanted Tina protected? Kevin explained what had been going on over the last few weeks, and the feeling of being followed every where they went.

The dead army officer said that he would get some of his security men to look into it straight away, and if they saw anything out of the ordinary, he would report back to him. If on the other hand it was something that they could deal with themselves, then it would be dealt it.

CHAPTER 38

Tina was in the house on her own doing some house work, when the buzzer rang for the main gate, she walked into the office and looked at the computer screen, standing there smoking a cigarette was the most beautiful woman that she had ever seen, she was tall and slim, with long blond hair that hung down almost to her waist, she was leaning against her red sports car in her white trouser suite, looking up and obviously posing for the security-camera. When Tina asked "yes, can I help you?" over the intercom, the voice that came back was low and very sultry, and very, very sexy indeed, Tina had never been into women in that way, but she was instantly in love with this mystery woman. "I'm looking for the owner of the farm, please?" when Tina said that she was one of the joint owners, the blond woman asked if she could come in for a chat? Tina pressed the button that opened the electric gates, and told the unknown woman to follow the drive up to the farm house.

Tina for some strange reason ran up stairs to change into one of her best outfits, she sprayed herself with her most expensive perfume, pulled a comb through her hair and ran back down the stairs, she walked into the kitchen, and with shaking hands switched the kettle on.

The blond woman tapped the old oak door and simply walked inside calling out "hello", When Tina walked into the living room she shocked herself when she had thoughts about this beautiful woman, that she did not really understand, the tall woman had removed her white jacket and tossed it casually over her right shoulder, not that she would normally look, but Tina could clearly see the woman's erect nipples through her very thin, almost see through silk shirt, and her own body reacted accordingly. The blond woman draped her jacket over the settee and walked confidently forward towards Tina, who automatically thought that her guest would hold her hand out to be shaken but no, she walked forward and folded herself around Tina, as if she was an old friend and kissed her on the cheek, as both women took in the others scent.

The tall stranger whispered sexually "hi I'm Petra, Peters sister and the new keeper of the estate next door" her voice close up was pure honey, just the sheer sweet sound of her voice, took Tina to a place that she had never been to before, but she would want to go there again, very soon. The two women sat at the kitchen table like old friends. Petra told Tina that she had been forced to return from Paris by her father, where she had lived for the last six years, she had come back to take over the running of the estate since her brothers unfortunate disappearance [the tall woman casually placed her hand onto Tina's arm, she looked deep into Tina's eyes and said] If I am really honest, it doesn't surprise me at all that something had happened to him, what with his drug dealing and strange male only parties.

 The people that he was involved with were real nasty, dangerous foreigners. I have even had some of them trying to harass me over the last few days, this big man with a strange accent was going on about my missing brother. He told me that his brother used to run the security on the estate, he even suggested that he should have the same deal with me, that was if, I was to continue with my brother's nefarious businesses, which I am not. I ask you, the bloody cheek of the man" they sat silent for a minute or two before Petra smiled, "So tell me about yourself, Tina?" Tina told her story of living on the streets, from her life on drugs to riches beyond anything she could ever have dreamt of, about Kevin, Ed and baby Samantha. Petra seemed a little disappointed at the mentioned of Kevin and the baby, but the second that she saw baby Samantha asleep in her cot, she was as smitten as everyone else that had seen her.

The two women stood side by side as they smiled at the sleeping blond haired baby, somehow as if it was the most natural thing in the world, they slipped their hands together, folding their fingers in-between each others. They stayed like this until they heard Kevin walking up the stairs, they quickly freed their hands, and glanced at each other guiltily. Tina whispered for him to be quiet because of the baby, before he had even set eyes on Petra he asked his girlfriend "who's was that red sports car out front?" When Petra stepped out from behind the bedroom door, he physically jumped and exclaimed "where did you come from and who are you?" the blond woman instantly took control of the situation and again explained her reason for being there, and about the strange man enquiring about his missing brother, and her brothers businesses. He suggested that he send a security firm over to the estate to make the house safe, then as least she would be able to sleep easily at night.

Tina almost fell to the floor when Petra suggested quite casually "I was hoping that I might be able to borrow Tina here for a few nights, so that I can have some company until I can get things sorted out, Im sure you understand, I mean it is such a big house to be all alone in, especially at night. I get so scared, it would only be for a little while, I'm sure that you two men can look after the baby, can't you?" What could he say when she had put her argument so eloquently, he stammered that it would be fine. As soon as he had finished speaking, Petra turned to Tina "go and throw a few things in a bag and we will be off."

Tina felt like a queen riding in the open top sports car as they sped towards the estates main gates, when the blond woman drove past the estate entrance, Tina turned and looked at the smiling driver, who smiled, "Lets me and you have a day out, do a bit of shopping," Petra drove the fast car with confidence, she parked in the local railway station flicked a switch, and the soft top automatically slid silently into place.

They climbed out of the car without saying a word, Petra slid her hand into Tina's hand, and they walked into the station, the blond woman bought two 1st class returns to London. Tina went to speak but the tall woman placed her fingers over the other woman lips, "There are certain items that we need, and we cant get around here, but I know just the place that we can get exactly what we need" by this time Tina was already a lost soul, she was in love and would follow this beautiful woman to the end of the earth, if she wanted her to. Unabashed they held hands all the way to Paddington station, Petra knew exactly where she was going, they jumped into a black cab and headed into London town, the cab darted down back streets, pushed its way through junctions, tried its best to beat every red light in London as it raced to who knows where.

The black cab pulled up outside an ordinary looking building in a busy street, somewhere in Soho, Petra told the driver to wait, as she then pulled Tina out of the cab. They walked up the stone steps at the front of the building, where Petra spoke into the silver intercom. A few seconds later there was a loud click and the door opened just a fraction, Petra placed her hand in the small of Tina's back, and eased her through the highly polished door.

Tina walked into what turned out to be a shop that on first sight made Tina gasp out loud, because if you could imagine a ladies only shop that was as big as any high street shop, and sold everything that a modern woman of a certain persuasion could ever need. Not only to make her feel good about herself, but if she had a partner of the same persuasion, then there was everything on display to satisfy every female desire, in every way possible, then this was it. Petra picked up two pink plastic baskets and passed one to Tina, "Choose what you like, and whatever you think that I would enjoy" Petra smiled at Tina [who blushed a dark crimson at the thought of buying such items] and gave her a quick kiss on the lips, before she turned away and strolled between the aisles without a care in the world, where she began filling her basket with sex toys of all description.

Tina on the other hand was totally embarrassed at just being there, and hid herself away in between two racks of clothing, not really knowing what to make of it all, while she watched a confident Petra in a large mirror as she continues to shop. When Petra came back to find Tina, she just smiled and took her soon to be lover, by the hand and led her around the shop, she selected all manner of things that Tina had only heard about, but never actually seen before, and dropped them into Tina's basket.

With two full baskets they walked to the counter to pay for their purchases, Petra took out of her pocket a roll of crisp 50 pound notes and paid the young woman behind the counter. With two almost full brown paper bags, they climbed back into the cab, and Petra instructed the driver to take them to the Dorchester hotel, she smiled at Tina and casually placed her hand on her thigh. "a spot of lunch before we go back, don't you think".

The day out in London had been perfect in every way, as soon as they were back in the trains first class carriage and underway, Petra drew the curtains and locked the door, and for the next hour Petra introduced a willing Tina to womanly love. After that first hour of perfect love making, Tina made her mind up that she would never need a real man in her life, ever again. The new lovers made love to each other all night that first night, and very soon became inseparable, and only after two full days together Tina ended her relationship with a devastated Kevin.

She shocked him further when she said that she as going to move in with Petra permanently, and that she was leaving baby Sam with him and Ed, at least for the foreseeable future, until she had sorted herself out.

# CHAPTER 39

The two men soon settled into the new routine without Tina. As they saw it, it was Tina's loss that baby Sam had taken her first steps and her mother had not been there to witness the event. Tina did make the effort occasionally and walked across the fields to see her daughter, on one such occasion she mentioned that Petra had been receiving renewed threats from the Albanians about some missing drugs, and that almost a millions pounds in cash had gone missing, and they wanted it back.

This new man Igor, who was now in charge of the Albanian gang and lived in the gate house with his men, wanted to take over security on the estate. He also claimed to be Gregors brother and wanted to know what had happened to him, his men, the drugs and the cash that had all gone missing. Tina told Kevin that she had heard them arguing, and this Igor was getting really angry, because he had people that needed paying and he wanted the missing money to pay them. Igor was very angry with her and said that he was going to pay you and Ed a visit, because if he believed that Petra had not got the drugs and money, then it was obvious that you and Ed must have them.

He desperately wanted the items back, and was prepared to do anything to anyone to get them. Tina also told Kevin that she had seen this Igor and his gang of thugs, and they were simply terrifying to look at, they were all big hard looking men that wore long black leather coats, and every one of them carried a gun of some sort, and that they were just like the last lot that had been there.

Igor had told Petra that Gregor had told him all about what had been going on on the estate, he knew all about the men only parties and the missing Australian drug lord, and everything about Lord Peter. She also told him that this Igor bloke, had laughed out loud when she had mentioned that Kev and Ed could be murderers and thieves.

Igor had laughed out loud as he said, "These two little men are no match for us and our ways, we will soon make them tell us what we want to know, if they do not, then we will kill them both, and then burn the farm to the ground." Kevin explained to Ed what Tina had told him while they were eating their evening meal, and Ed had simply answered, "Where is the commander when we need him?" Kev sat and thought about the problem, "I think we aught to ask Lady Mary McPherson if she can get some of her ghost friends to go and have a look see at our Albanian friends, and maybe find out what their plans were. At least that way we can prepare, although I don't know what we can do against all those guns?" Ed simply shrugged  "we sure could use some help, lets take baby Sam for a walk and see if we can find the sisters, we can then get them to contact Lady Mary"

As soon as the two men walked out of the back door of the old farm house, the sisters drifted towards them, they listened to what Kevin had to say, and it was Sarah that said that they would leave straight away, and send a message to the old woman, and get her to contact them as a matter of urgency. The old ghost appeared that evening and listened to  Kevin as he explained all about their problem, she told them not to worry and said reassuringly that she would contact the Brigadier at once, and get him on the case, because he would know exactly what to do to help them.

At lunchtime the next day the sisters brought the old soldier to see them, he looked at the two men with his hollow dead eyes, the dead army man told them that he had sent two of his best men to spy on the group of men, and that he would soon know what their plans were. As soon as he knew anything, then they would know.

Tina lay on the soft bed literally squirming, her young body fully alive after a night of perfect love making, Petra walked naked into the bedroom, "You had better get dressed lover, we are taking a trip in London today, can you be ready in an hour?" Tina nodded that she would be ready, but at the same time wiggled her fingers at her lover, and tried her best to entice the woman back to bed. But, the she was having none of it, and said that she would make a start on breakfast, she then walked out of the bedroom and left a very disappointed Tina behind.

Petra carried a heavy looking leather holdall out to the sports car, and stowed it in the cars boot, she then slipped into the drivers seat, placed a post code into the cars sat nav system, and set off towards London. Following the instructions given out by the well spoken unknown woman. Petra drove the car with confidence as she weaved her way through the back streets of Hendon. Tina was a bit surprised when her lover stopped the car outside a run down looking building. She looked up the flight of broken brick steps that led to a large double door that looked as if it was made out of steel. Standing on guard outside the door, looking mean and menacing in a long black letter coat, was a huge black man with a shaved head. His brown eyes never leaving Petra as she walked up the steps carrying the leather holdall, when she reached the metal door, the black man opened it without a word. A confidant Petra stepped into the old building.

Tina waited patiently in the car for her lover, she watched the huge black man as his eyes constantly searched the surrounding streets for any threat. When the door finally opened another man, equally as large as the doorman, carried a large green holdall that looked very heavy, down to the car, and placed the it into the boot. A few minutes later Petra walked down the steps, climbed Into the car, started the engine and drove away without a word. Petra drove confidently through the back streets of the capital, but her eyes kept a close watch on the rear view mirror, it was as if she was looking to see if they were being followed. Petra parked the car outside the Berners hotel which was seconds from Oxford Street, Tina watched as her lover approached the doorman at the hotel, she said a few words pointed to the car and slipped the man a crisp fifty pound note. Petra locked the car and the lovers walked the short distance to one of the most famous shopping streets in the world. Petra spent money as if it meant nothing to her, they bought shoes and clothes just for the sake of buying them, neither of them really needed the items.

They carried the shopping bags back to the car and stowed them in the boot next to the holdall, the two women then entered the 4 star Berners hotel for a leisurely lunch that lasted for two hours. Tina did mention the holdall and its contents, but Petra just smiled, shrugged her shoulders and said, that it was to do with her father, and that was all that was said about the whole affair.

CHAPTER 40

The brigadier hovered in front of the two men, and said worryingly that the Albanians were making plans to search the main estate house for the missing drugs and money, because they did not believe what Petra had told them. It also appeared that this Petra woman was trying her best to put the blame onto Kev and Ed, by saying things like "where do you think a pair of little farmers, that never really do any farming, get their money from, and they do seem to have an awful lot of money, and, another thing, from what we can tell the last anyone knows about Gregor and his men, is that they were heading for the farm to have a chat with the farmers, and were never seen or heard of again. The old soldier then went on to tell them that his men were making a discreet search of not only the gate house, but also the main house as well, and that he would let them know if his men found out anything of interest.

It was two days later that the Brigadier reappeared at the farmhouse, he told the two men that the Albanians were making plans to kidnap one of them, and that they had cleared out a room in the basement of the gate house in preparations for their victim. The Brigs men had also found out that the foreign men had a large cache of guns. Small hand guns and some long rifles. As for the main house, his men had found a substantial amount of large denomination currency in a locked chest. This chest was hidden away in one of the spare rooms, and in the same chest were some brown parcels, the contents of the packages was unknown, but they did look very suspicious. The dead army man warned the two men to be on their guard, and that Lady Mary was at that precise moment talking to the war council, and trying to put together some protection of her own. She was doing this as a sort of reward for all the happiness that they had brought for the young child ghosts, in creating the play area.

All was eerily quiet for a few days until Petra pulled up at the main gate of the farm, and was frantically pressing the intercom button, when Ed asked the blond woman if he could help her, she was in floods of tears as she asked him if Tina was there, because she had set out on foot that morning to come to the farm to see baby Sam, and now she can't get hold of her, she was not answering her phone or anything. Ed told the blond woman that they had not seen or heard from Tina in a few days, but he would go and find Kev and they would drive around the farm to see if they could find her, just in case she had fallen over or hurt herself in some way. He told Petra to go back to the estate house, and that they would ring her if they found out anything.

Ed rushed off and found Kev, he told him what Petra had said. They immediately went out to the child ghosts, and asked them for help, for them to spread out and search the farms land for Tina. Sarah gathered all the other child ghosts that had been playing on the play equipment around her, and organised everything. Soon there were child ghosts gliding off in all directions. When the news came back that Tina was nowhere to be found on the farm, or the estates vast grounds, Kevin asked Sarah to contact the Brigadier, and tell him that they needed help and quickly. It was obvious to Kevin that the Albanians had takenTina, and it was up to them to try and rescue her, but first they wanted to know where she was being held, and then they would formulate a plan.

Tina was sitting on the cold slate floor shivering, she had been grabbed by two of Igor's men as she walked down a lane that led from the estate to the farm. She had only wanted to see her daughter, but here she was now, trapped in this cold room with only a single lightbulb and a steel bucket for company. There were no windows in the room and only one way out, and that was through the locked heavy oak door. Tina had tried the door only to find it firmly locked, she listened at the solid oak door and heard nothing, she walked around the small room one more time, moved into one of the corners, sank to the floor, closed her eyes and for the first time in a very long time, she began to pray.

One of the Albanians eventually opened the old oak door, passed her a Tesco carrier bag, without uttering a single word he closed and locked the door again. Tina looked in the bag and found some tuna sandwiches and two bottles of water. She opened one of the sandwiches and was just about to take a bite when she sensed that there was someone from the other side in the room with her, she looked around the room and asked "who's there, show yourself, is that you Sarah?" The sisters gradually materialised, Sarah looked at Tina and asked if she was ok? Tina had tears running down her cheeks at the sight of the dead girls and uttered excitedly, "Oh, I am so glad to see you two, is baby Samantha ok, you must go and tell the others where I am, and ask them to call the police, tell them to come and rescue me." Sarah looked nervously at the door, and said they already knew where she was and that plans were being made to rescue her, she just had to be patient and stop worrying.

Sarah looked behind her, whispered "someones coming" and just like that, they were gone. Tina's heart raced when she heard muffled voices coming from behind the door, but relaxed again when no-one entered her prison. She sat staring at the slate floor for ages as she thought about her situation, she would be very lucky to survive this and she knew it. It was then that she spotted a slight step in the slab of slate in front of her. When she looked closer she could see that there was a hollow underneath the step, she worked away at the gap with her finger nails and gradually made it slightly bigger. Tina had broken all of her nails as she worked at the gap. She stamped on the slate as hard as she could, she did this until both of her ankles hurt, she needed something harder, a nail, a screw or something made out of metal that she could use to lever up the slate step, if she could achieve this, she may just have a weapon of sorts. Tina walked around the room as she looked over the walls to see if she could find anything that she could use, but as much as she searched, there was nothing. She tried stamping on the hard slate again, all to no avail, she sat there looking at the grey stone, and then smiled to herself, she quickly removed all of her top clothing, dropping her bra onto the floor and quickly dressed again.

Once reclothed she picked up the bra and tried to force the under wire from out of the thin material with her fingers, she soon gave up and began to rub the thin cloth across the floor, and tried to wear the fabric away. It only took minutes before she smiled to herself as she held the under wire in her hand. She straightened the piece of metal and pushed it into the crack of the slate and tried to prise the slate upwards, but the single bra wire was not strong enough, so she picked up the ruined bra and rubbed away at the other wire. Now with two wires pushed into the gap in the slate, Tina pulled with all of her might, she changed the angle of her body as she tried with every ounce of her strength, all of a sudden there was a sharp cracking noise, and she fell over backwards as the slate finally gave way. Tina sat up and looked all around her until she spotted the thin, hand sized flat piece of slate. On closer examination she could clearly see that the thinner edge of the slate was very sharp indeed.

The young woman held the shard in her hand, and decided that if the correct circumstances presented themselves, then she would have a chance of escape. Tina sat and planned, she tried the sharp edge of the slate against the material of the ruins bra and with the lightest of touches, the soft cloth parted, leaving a smile on the young woman face. Back at the farmhouse things were moving along quite quickly, the Brigadier and Lady Mary were hovering in the kitchen, while Kev and Ed sat at the table cleaning shotguns, and filling cartridge belts with red cartridges. Lady Mary was just about to speak when she suddenly turned and looked away, The old ghost turned back and said excitedly," Petra is in bad trouble, the Albanians have her tied to a chair and are torturing her, they think that she has the missing money and drugs, they are trying to get her to talk, she has been badly beaten, and has broken fingers and toes.

The Albanians have found a locked room and are trying to break into it as we speak. Tina is still being held in the gate house, and there is only one man guarding her, so now would be a good tine to try and rescue her". The old dead couple had a quick conversation, and Lady Mary turned back to Kevin,"The Brigadier suggests that you send baby Samantha somewhere safe with Ed, meanwhile he and the Tic's men will do their best to help Petra, and he wanted you Kev to go to the gate house to try and save Tina. Word has already gone out to the police and they were on their way, but he does not think that they will be here soon enough to save either of the two women" Kevin looked at Ed and asked for his opinion, the younger man made it obvious that he wanted to go with Kev to the gate house, but his best friend soon persuaded him to take Samantha, into Stratford and to a place of safety.

Kev kissed his daughter before Ed placed her into the car seat, and drove the old car away. Kev picked up the two loaded shotguns and mounted the farms quad bike, he then headed across the fields towards the gate house, in a bid to rescue his ex lover.

Tina had a plan of sorts, it wasn't much of one, but it was the best that she could come up with, she undid her jacket and all the buttons on her blouse, she stood by the door and listened for any approaching footsteps, hearing nothing at all, she began thumping the old door with her hands and shouting at the top of her voice. It took an age before she finally heard the heavy boots on the stone steps, she walked across the room and lay down on the floor, she pulled her clothing open, therefore exposing her naked breasts, she lay there with her eyes wide open, and her right hand that held the slither of slate was positioned just above her head. She heard the key in the lock and held her breath, The big Albanian pushed the door open with his left hand, in his right hand he held a black pistol, he saw Tina lying on the floor and rushed to her side, he knelt down by her, he placed the gun on the floor and began feeling around her neck for any sign of life. It was when the big man lowered his right ear towards her chest to listen for a heartbeat, then the young woman struck. Tina lashed out with all of her might as she brought the sharp edge of the slate down on the big mans exposed neck, over and over she slashed, warm, dark blood began to spray out of the gashes in the man's neck and land all over Tina, she tried her best to cover her face with her hands as warm blood sprayed everywhere. The big man screamed in terror as he jumped up in fright, he grabbed at his damaged neck with both hands, thick black arterial blood stained the walls, and the unstoppable flow, oozed through the fat fingers of the Albanian.

He turned to look at her as he sank down to his knees, his eyes were already glazing over as he flopped forward onto his face, dead. A large pool of dark red blood began to spread around the dead mans head as the first sounds of the growlers could be heard. As the black devils made their approach, Tina moved back against the wall as the devils workers came out of the floor, and took yet another evil spirit down below, another poor soul to serve their red eyed master.

Tina reached for the discarded hand gun as she heard more footsteps on the stone steps of the staircase, she pointed the gun at the open door with shaking hands as whoever it was drew ever closer. The young woman was terrified, and wanted to scream out loud as the long barrels of a shotgun came into view. It seemed to take forever before the newcomers foot came into view, now the gun was really shaking as she closed her forefinger around the steel trigger, she saw a shape appear in the doorway, closed her eyes and pulled the trigger over and over. BANG, BANG, BANG, BANG, BANG, BANG. Tina kept pulling the trigger even though the gun had stopped firing, the noise of the shots in the tiny stone room had temporarily made her deaf. She looked through the cloud of blue smoke to see a man laying still in the doorway, she dropped the gun, then sank down to her knees and began crying. It was then that she heard the sound of the dead ghosts as they began screaming, not one, not two but lots of them were screaming, she heard the sound of the growlers as they approached the cold room.

She watched as the spirit left the still body by the door, then she began screaming herself, as the spirit of her child's father stood there looking at her, they both turned and looked into the far corner of the room as the growlers made their approach. Kevin turned back to look at Tina, "Look after Samantha, take good care of her" that was when the first of the long black fingers came out of the slate floor, and slithered across the floor towards him. The long black fingers were inches away from the murdered man when many long grey wispy hands came from down the stone stairway, they wrapped themselves around the dead mans spirit and dragged it out through the doorway, and up the stone stairs. The sound from the growlers grew louder and louder, as Kevin's spirit became further and further out of their reach Tina looked on horrified as the fingers stretched out ever longer, as they went through the doorway and headed up the stone steps.

Everything suddenly became silent as two silver round canisters bounced down the stairs and rolled into the room, she stood there mesmerised as she stared at the smoking objects, the flash when it came was blinding, and the noise from the explosion drove her into deep unconsciousness.

The next thing that Tina knew was when she woke up in hospital, she looked around the sterile room at the array of bleeping monitors and she could see an armed police man standing on guard outside of her door. When she could finally focus correctly, she could see the dead sisters standing in the corner of the room holding hands, staring at her with their dead eyes. Neither spoke as Tina tried her best to remember everything that had happened.

When things finally began to come back to her, she looked at Sarah and with one word she asked "Petra?" Sarah shook her head, and said that the growlers had taken her down below with all the others from that room. Sarah went on to explain that the armed police had entered the house, and on locating the Albanians in one of the upper bedrooms, they had tossed in some stun grenades before storming the room.

All the Albanians except Igor had been killed quickly with small arms fire, the leader of the gang sat in the middle of the room with a large knife held at Petra's throat. The armed police gave him ample chances to give himself up, but he had just laughed at them and drew the razor sharp blade across Petra's throat, killing her instantly. With that the police opened fire and killed the leader of the Albanians stone dead.

When the police had eventually searched the bedroom they found almost two million pounds in cash, and six kilo's of pure heroin locked in the old chest. Tina had said nothing of her dead lover as she asked the dead girls if Samantha was safe, Sarah moved to the side of the bed, and tried to place her hand into the injured woman's hand. Tina looked down at the transparent hand and closed her hand as if gripping the dead girls tiny fingers, she lifted her eyes to look in the empty eyes of the dead girl, who seemed to be even sadder than usual. Tina frowned "Are you ok, Sarah?" The dead girl lowered her head and whispered,"you do know that Kev is dead, don't you Tina?" Tina gasped out loud and just stared at the dead girl for a long while, because the hidden memory of what she had done, suddenly came flooding back to her.

Huge tears ran down the young woman's face, as she remembered seeing the spirit of her babies father, as it was unceremoniously dragged up the staircase only seconds before it was to be taken by the growlers. She had killed the man that she had once loved, shot him dead as he tried to save her, how would she ever explain to Samantha how her father had died, how would she ever forgive herself for being the one that had killed him?

# CHAPTER 41

Kevin just could not accept that he was in-fact dead, his main problem was that Tina, Ed and baby Samantha could all still see him, talk to him and in the babies eyes, still play with him. Tina had moved back into the farm and had taken to being a mother again, she had suddenly become very over protective of her child, it was as if she blamed herself for everything that had happened. If Petra had not turned up at the farm that day, then the blond woman and Kevin would still be alive. Samantha would still have a father, and Ed would still have a best friend. Ed was devoting all his time in looking after Tina, and her daughter, he would sit and hold Tina as she sat and cried her eyes out at the memory of what she had done, at how her selfishness had ruined everything for everyone.

Ed now had some much needed help on the farm, it was in the form of two brothers John and Tom Forest, John to run the farm and Tom's main job was to take over Kev's duties, and look after all the finances. Ed had no concerns about Tom fiddling the books, because he was convinced that Kevin would be around somewhere, looking over his shoulder, just to keep an eye on things were done, right and proper.

Tina was standing by the sink holding a steaming cup of coffee, and seemed to be staring into space, when Ed walked over and stood by her side, she asked without looking at him, "Why don't the children come and play anymore, Ed?" Ed looked out of the window and could see the gentle breeze stirring the long grass, and making the empty swings move gently back and forth. He answered, "the sisters blame themselves for what has happened to Kev, they seem to think that if they had gone into that room first, then you would not have fired that gun and killed him, they think that they could have stopped you somehow, and Kev would still be alive" Tina stayed quiet for a good two minutes "I best talk to them, make them understand that it was not their fault, if it was anyones fault then we have to blame Petra. If she had not taken the drugs and money in the first place, then the Albanians would not have gone looking for it, would they?" When he did not answer her, she placed her cup down onto the draining board "Maybe I will take Sam for a walk up the lane and see if I can locate the sisters, and maybe have a chat with them to try and put their minds at ease?"

Tina did walk up the lane towards the slurry pit that day, but it was not the sisters that she found, it was Lady Mary. The old ghost asked Tina to sit, when the sad woman was seated on the grass, the old ghost positioned herself by her side, and tried her best to explain that everything that had happened was not her fault, and that she had to stop blaming herself for Samantha's sake, if not her own. When Tina asked why Kevin had not been to see her, the old ghost explained that her dead lover was in a safe place for the time being, because the growlers had snatch squads out trying to locate him.  Because they believe that he belongs down below with them, and they will keep searching until they find him. There would be an investigation by the tic's squad, and most likely a trial that would be attended by both parties, but she told Tina that she was not to worry, because they had right on their side.


Lady Mary and all the other ghosts attended Kevin's funeral, Kevin stood in the back ground when the service took place, he watched his beautiful innocent daughter, who was totally oblivious to what was happening. Ed cradled the child in one arm, and held onto Tina with his other arm. There were not many living mourners, simply because they had kept themselves to themselves, and had gone out of their way not to make friends, mainly because of the ghosts, and the complications that that association would bring, they had found and accepted that life was just easier that way.

Kev didn't go to the wake, he was whisked away by the tic's squad for his own safety, mainly because one of the tic's sensed that the growlers were close by. Kevin had begun spending a lot of time with the dead sisters, and the more time that he spent with them, the more that they opened up to him about what had actually happened to them leading up to their death's. He was appalled that someone, a grown man could do such terrible things to a child, listening to the sad tales of some of the other dead girls made him wish that he was still alive, because after listening to them, he would have taken up the gauntlet once more, and sorted out more of the sick bastards.

He sat deep in thought, and wondered if maybe there was still a way that he could help other children, both dead and alive, maybe he would have a chat to the Brigadier, and see what he thought, maybe there just might be a way?

# CHAPTER 42

Life on the farm soon settled into a new routine after the death of Kevin. Ed and Tina had become very close, mainly because Tina still blamed herself for everything that had happened, and now Ed spent almost all of his spare time with her, walking the lonely lanes of the farm for hours on end, constantly talking to her, reassuring her that Kevin's death was not her fault. Tina could not get the sight of Kevin's spirit as it left his body, out of her mind, after all, she had been the one that had actually pulled the trigger on the gun that had killed him.

As they sat on the grass watching Samantha having fun on the playground equipment, they were almost touching, but not quite. Tina turned her head and looked at Ed, he turned his head and returned the look, she leaned over and rested her head on his chest, and asked him to hold her. Ed lifted his arm and draped his arm around her shoulders, as she began to cry once more, Ed talked quietly to her and did his best to reassure her for the thousandth time. When he turned to her, she lifted her lips to his, it seemed the most natural thing to do. From that first kiss their relationship quickly deepened, the death of their partner had somehow changed them both into responsible adults, made them grow up in some way, maybe it was because they had become that little bit older.

Gradually life for the couple soon became perfect as they lived life on the farm, they had joined some local farming association, Tina had formed a local artist group. On certain days, they allowed the participants onto the farm to paint. For the first time in their adult life, they had people their own age other than just the three of them, that they could rely on. They now had friends from the local community that they regularly invited to the farm for meals. This change in their circumstances did Tina the world of good as she began to drive into town on a regular basis, mainly to meet her new mates for coffee. Baby Samantha was at the age where she had begun going to pre school, and this brought yet another new group of friends. Ed was walking the lane of the farm one day when he sensed that he was not alone, he sat down on the grass and looked around, even though he saw no-one, he knew that someone was close.

"Is that you Kev mate, if it is, please come and have a chat, I miss you so much" the grass stirred by his side and ever so slowly the ghost of his best friend began to materialise, When the dead eyes just seemed to stare at him, Ed lowered his head "I am so sorry for what has happened to you me old mate, you didn't deserve it. You do know that Tina still blames herself for what happened to you, I have tried my best to get her to believe that it was nothing but an unfortunate accident, but the whole thing with Petra and her death as well, well to be honest mate, it has broken her. Tina has grown up now, she has finally begun to take her life seriously, you do know that we are together now, as a couple, don't you?" The dead empty eyes just stared at Ed as the spirit seemed to be analysing every thing that he had just heard. Ed physically jumped when the ghost of his best friend began to talk to him, "I am sorry that I haven't been to see you sooner, but there have been certain problems up above that were beyond my control. I am pleased for you and Tina, you are much more suited as a couple then ever we were, in-fact I could never see what she saw in me in the first place.[it was a few minutes before Kev spoke again] I have been spending a lot of time with the sisters Ed, I have learned a great deal more about what actually happened to them, and I only wish that I was still alive to deal with even more of those people. I know that the sisters and the other child ghosts have stayed away from the play area, I have not asked them why they stopped going, but I think it was because, they believe that with them being there, it would simply remind Tina of what happened on that awful day.

The dead sisters may only be young but they are wise beyond their years and clever enough to know when someone was troubled, and in need of help. We can see a lot from up there Ed, I can tell that for the first time, you are really happy and contented with your life now. You have everything that you ever dreamed about. I want you to try and enjoy your life and live it to the fullest" Ed just sat and stared into the dead eyes as he analysed what his once living friend, had just said to him, "Please tell the sisters to come back and play, we miss them, Samantha misses them".

I will get Tina to talk to them, she will make it right. As for me mate, well life is pretty perfect, and now that I can still talk to you, I have everything that I need. I still look over my shoulder at times when I hear a car approaching, I think it's mainly because of all the things we did to all those people, but each and every one of them deserved what they got, and I don't regret any of it." Kevin assured his friend that he had nothing to worry about, those up above were more than happy. As for the growlers well, they were now sort of happy, and as far as he could tell, the police had given up looking into any of the old cases. Kevin seemed to stare at his once best friend as if he wanted to say something more but didn't know how, so Ed had to prompt him. "Spit it out mate." His dead best friend eventually spoke, "a while back I asked for some help from Lady Mary in finding someone, I asked her if it was possible to locate your mother, I hope that I have done the right thing mate, but she is here, she is staying hidden just in case you don't want to talk to her " [tears were running down the other mans cheeks] he didn't speak he just nodded his head in acceptance.

When Kev left his best friend, his mothers spirit was lovingly wrapping herself around her son, and Ed held his arms out as if he was holding his mother in his arms, as his shoulders heaved, he cried millions of long held back tears, not only for his mother, but also for the loss of his best friend.

The very next day, Kevin looked like the Pied Piper as he came into view followed closely by the dead sisters, who were followed by a hoard of excited young ghosts. Within seconds every piece of play equipment was again in use. Ed, Tina and Samantha walked out of the kitchen door and just stood there hand in hand, smiling broadly as they watched the return of the dead children. The sisters stopped playing and waved at the trio, the three of them all waved back. After a brief discussion between the sisters, they turned and floated towards the trio and without saying a word, they each seemed to take a hold of Samantha's hands, the little girl ran off quite happily with her dead friends towards the bouncy castle. As Tina watched her daughter running off with the child ghosts, she suddenly realised that one day soon she was going to have to sit her daughter down, and try and explain about the dead sisters, and that was one conversation that she wasn't looking forward to having.

Kevin was sat on the grass watching the children at play, he had finally accepted his death and his new existence as a spirit, although some of the rules up above took a bit of getting used too, like different dead people had different amounts of powers, some could move objects down below, some could make noise, some like himself could talk to the living, as though they were still alive. Others could give warnings about forth coming dangers, letting their living relatives know that they were still there, to watch over them and protect them when needed.

From what information he had gathered in the short time that he had been up above, these different powers were distributed from higher ranking spirits that reside deep inside a place called the* Inner cloud*. He had also been informed by Lady Mary, that there were different levels of existence up above, and there were various time limits as to how long each ghost was allowed to stay as they were, and whether or not they could keep the various powers that had been granted. If the said spirit had used their powers to wrongly intimidate an innocent party, then they would lose their powers and be punished. The strength of the punishment was based on how each spirit had used its given powers. In the worse case the said spirit could be banished to some far off universe.

Naturally, there was always the case as to each spirits usefulness to the system up there, which always helped. What usually happened was that, when the last of each spirits generation arrived up above, that particular families spirits were then moved on to the next level of existence, and so on until that generations spirits ended up living his or her existence, with their extended family, in a place where they wanted for nothing.

These spirit families then stayed together on that particular last level, left to happily wander the universe, to discover new things, new beings, spirits of long dead heroes that they could chat with like old friends, they would be happy and contented for ever more.

Kev lay back on the soft grass, and lost himself in his thoughts about all the famous people that he would eventually meet, when he finally reached that highest level. If he could choose one ghost that he would really like to meet and talk to, it would be Einstein. Just imagine the conversations that you could have with a spirit like that, hours and hours of intellectual chit chat. The main thing that Kevin couldn't get used to, was how sterile everything looked up above. Whatever it was they seemed to walk on, that looked like a white landscape with large white constructions in the far distance, parks and people but you never seemed to be able to get there, because there appeared to be no roads or paths as such, nothing up there was solid, real.

Whatever direction you looked there white and grey trees, bushes, marked trails and tracks. Huge swirling pillars that rose out of the lower layer of whatever it was the they wondered around on, and those same twisting pillars reached all the way up to and disappeared into the upper layers of whatever it was that was up there, each of these pillars looked as if they were some sort of static tornado.

Spirits after death always rematerialised in a time when they had been most happiest in their lives. Dead married couples walked hand in hand as if they were a young again and deeply in love, their dead children[if they had any] playing chase amongst the trees and bushes as if they were on a family day out, even though in reality the parents could have been in their seventies of eighties and their children in their thirties, the happier times always prevailed. Other spirits looked as you wanted them to look, not the way that they actually were when they had died, no longer, old, damaged, burned and broken.

Some spirits even tried to form new relationships, just for the sake of companionship, which in principle was fine. What if in your eyes the other sprit was a beautiful young man/woman, when in fact that spirit could be a hundred years old and wrinkled from another time many hundreds of years before. Kev thought that life down below was complicated enough, but up there it was even harder, and much more confusing.

# CHAPTER 43

Kev was brought out of his thoughts by the sudden arrival of Lady Mary, she hovered nervously in front of him, her head moving from side to side as if looking for someone. Kev finally asked the old spirit what she wanted? "I need you to come with me, Kevin. We have to go and meet some very important spirits, and they are waiting for us as we speak" she said all this as she continued to look around. Kev went to speak, but she shushed him with her hand, she then turned to leave, and with a wave of her right hand she beckoned for him to follow her. Kev followed the flowing grey dress of the old spirit without question, to where only she knew the destination.

Lady Mary, led Kev to the entrance of the inner cloud, the guards did not even try and stop them as they approached. Once inside the upper sanctum Kevin could see the difference as to how the more important spirits existed. Looking down from where they now were, the landscape was basically as you imagined it would be, and wherever you looked you could see spirits walking around, some of them on their own wandering aimlessly, like robots as if deep in thought, some chatting away with family members, all happy and contented, other spirits stood around in small groups, probably talking about their past lives. Here inside the inner cloud there were clearer paths, some secluded, some not so, but where these pathways ended up, he had no idea. There were seats, benches that had been placed just inside the high rolling outer wall. Most of the seats were filled with spirits of different nationalities, all dressed in their traditional dress, and they all seemed to be deep in conversation. Spirits of higher rank nodded at Lady Mary as she drifted by, they seemed to be going higher into an unknown world. They passed by what looked like many half moon shaped rooms, all created out of clouds, with rolling steps that moved ever upwards, towards a pair of large darker clouds, made to look and operate like huge  doors.

Standing in front of these doors blocking their way, was a female spirit that had  been some sort of doctor in her former life, she wore a white coat and had a stethoscope draped around her neck, and she made it quite obvious that she was in-fact awaiting their arrival. The pair stopped in front of the woman spirit when she held her right hand up to stop them going any further, the doctor looked from one to the other, "My name was doctor Leslie and when I worked down below, I used to be a paediatrician. I have been instructed to work with you, but first I have something to show you, now, if you would follow the pathway please" Lady Mary and Kev made their way along the fluffy white path until they came upon a large enclosed space, in the centre of the area was a small group of child spirits that appeared to be sitting down on cushions made of clouds. They are listening to a young female spirit named Lisa Wood, who held their attention as she told them the age old story of Hansel and Gretel.

The three of them stood and listened to the well practiced young woman as she told her story to the child spirits, all of whom were aged between four and ten years old. The doctor turned to her visitors and very quietly said, "These poor children have suffered the most terrible abuse in their short lives, they are all from the same area of the North East and were repeatedly raped, abused and finally murdered by the same man, who's details you will be given when you go inside. This man used his position, and his wealth as a way of gaining access to these children, and I personally want to see him severely punished for what he has done. Now, if you would like to make your way back down the lane to the double doors, the Major will be waiting for you."

The pair nodded their thanks, took a final look at the children, and silently made their way back along the lane to find the Major waiting for them in front of the doors. The Army man simply asked them to follow him, he then turned and made his way through the already open doors. Once inside the inner sanctum of the inner cloud, the whole atmosphere changed. The Major led

Kev into the centre of the room and left him there on his own.

There was a sudden stillness, a silence the like of which he had never felt before. Sat around the outer wall of the round room in little alcoves, were twelve long since dead, high ranking court judges, each of them resplendent in their official red gowns and wigs. As Kevin looked from dead face to dead face, a huge spirit that almost filled his alcove with his sheer bulk coughed loudly to draw all eyes to him. Now that he had everyones attention, he began to speak. He said in a deep booming voice, that echoed around the room,"My name is Kenneth Wattage, and down below I was a Lord Chief Justice, and today we have asked you to appear before us, because we need your help.

We have all heard of your endeavours down below, and we are all very grateful for what you have achieved, especially what you did for the children. As you have just seen for yourself, we have a very similar problem before us now, with our young victims. We are doing our very best to get the children to regain their confidence. W are doing this by getting them to interact with the other dead children, like the ones that go down below and play with the sisters on what we up here have named *the play farm* but, we know that if we do not act fast, there will soon be other victims. That being the case we would like you to go and do what you do best, and that is to go down below and sort the buggers out, before any more of these poor helpless children suffer needlessly.

The main offender and financier of the whole scheme is one Lord Cecil Watson-Brown. Lord Cecil provided the up-front money for the Nalmond Brothers, Arthur and Neal to become loan sharks, and the biggest supplier of drugs in the North East, and by the explicit instructions of his Lordship, they were to lend money to anyone, but they were only allowed to give drugs on credit to mothers with young children, they were to lend those same mothers, as much money and credit as they wanted, until they were in so much debt, that they had no other option, but to give up their child.

You might think that most normal mothers would never do that under any circumstances, but the Nalmond's ran their business on fear and intimidation, they have a reputation for extreme violence even on occasion, permanently maiming non payers. As you have already noticed in your short time with us, there are many levels of capability up here, different spirits have certain capabilities all of which are distributed from this very room, but you personally will have every one of the said capabilities available to you, you will have every tool that you will require to complete your task. You will also be assigned two other spirits, both of them especially selected from the tic's squad, and they will obey your every command.

Your main targets will be those three men, and we would like them to be dealt with as soon as possible please". Kevin looked at the judge for a long time before stating "I will do as you ask, on one condition, I would like the mothers of the dead children to be given the chance to see their dead child one last time if it is possible, this will be done simply to let these mothers know that their offspring spirit were being well looked after. Because, I think that they deserve that chance after what they have been through, none of which was any fault of their own".

The judge announced in his deep voice,"This sort of thing has never been achieved successfully before and we will agree with your demand, but only If you complete your task satisfactorily. On the successful completion of this task, you will personally be rewarded, but we will leave that until everything has been done and dusted. When you leave us, you will be met outside by your two helpers, these spirits will have exactly the same powers as yourself, so do-not be afraid to use them, these ex-soldiers know where to find your targets, and they will take you there immediately.

That is all for now Mr West, good luck and good hunting" before Kev could even open his mouth to speak, each of the judges simply faded away, suddenly he was left standing in the silent rotating room, all on his own. Kev walked out of the inner cloud to find two big spirits dressed in green army fatigues waiting for him, as he approached them, both men stood to attention, the bigger of the two saluted "Sir, my name is Joe Smith and this here is Andy Taylor". Kev looked from one to the other, signalled for them to follow him, turned and made his way to the benches that he had seen earlier.

Kev sat down, but the two dead soldiers still stood stiffly in front of him, Kev shook his head, "look lads, if we are going to work together, this army stuff ends here, just relax, now where can we find these Nalmond brothers, I think that we ought to have bit of a look at them first, and then we will deal with Lord Cecil, so lead on"

# CHAPTER 44

The three dead men appeared in an office that was full of stacked cardboard boxes, that were quite obviously full of illicitly obtained goods. In the centre of the room stood a very large desk that was cluttered with dirty cups and littered papers, behind the desk sat a big white man that had a scarred fat ugly face, it was the older Nalmond brother Arthur. He was scruffily dressed in a cheap blue suit, he had his feet up on his desk as he talked on the telephone. He ended the conversation, and looked across the desk to another big man who was his younger brother, but this man was huge, very handsome with newly trimmed back hair. His clothes were immaculate, he wore a grey designer suit that was obviously very expensive, a clean shirt and tie, highly polished shoes that had been hand made. The elder brother who they took to be Arthur spoke, "You had better go and see that Helen bitch over in Greenfield tower, his Lordship wants another one, the sick fucker. When you have her, bring her back here." The younger brother simply nodded, stood up, picked up a long, folded grey coat which he slung over his shoulder, and ambled confidently out of the office.

The three ghosts followed Neal to a huge tower block named Greenfield, the big man pressed the button on the lift, and after a lot of clanking and rattling, the silver doors opened. The smell of stale piss that hit him was overpowering, it was so bad that the big man held the hem of his coat over his nose and mouth, in a bid to try and block the smell out, he travelled noisily up to the thirteenth floor.

Neal walked out of the lift and took some deep breaths of clean fresh air that suddenly gusted all around him, he stood and looked at the view over Newcastle for a few seconds, before he turned and began walking along the walkway that had black steel railings on one side, and different coloured doors on the other.

 He reached the green door that he wanted, and began hammering on it with his huge fist, after only a few seconds he began shouting,"c/mon you bitch, I know you are in there, its time to pay up, now open this fucking door or I will smash it down" he thumped the door a few more times. There was no reply so he stepped back, leaned back against the rails and with an almighty kick with his right foot, he kicked the door open, the big man rushed into the dirty apartment, his eyes searching every recess for his quarry, he tossed furniture aside as if it was nothing, he found a young terrified woman hiding behind a beaten up leather chair.

Neal tossed the chair to one side, grabbed the terrified woman around the throat with his huge hand, and lifted her bodily from the floor dragging her into the middle of the apartment. Holding his face close to hers, he asked with a menacing hiss,"where is she, where's the bairn?" The blond woman was struck dumb with fear, she was terrified and having trouble breathing, her bulging eyes darted from side to side, The big man began screaming at her again, when she did not answer him he threw her down onto the black settee, pointed a thick finger into her face and shouted "I want the fucking bairn and I want her now, so where is she?" The blond woman just shook her head for side to side.

This was when the big man lost it and began tearing at her clothes, he literally tore her white blouse from her thin emaciated body, then her white bra followed her blouse, which revealed her tiny soft breasts, he was literally screaming at her, all the time he did his work. Knowing what he was about to do to her, she knew that it would be best not to resist him, he opened the button on her faded blue jeans, he yanked the zipper down and grabbed the sides of her jeans, he lifted her legs and was about to yank the thin material down her thin legs, when he suddenly went stiff and as if by magic, he seemed to fly backwards across the room and slam backwards into the wall. The big mans eyes were huge, as he looked from side to side, he didn't know what was happening to him, he struggled against an invisible foe as he continued to be dragged backwards, he was pulled backwards out of the apartment door, his back hit the black railing and then he was flying through the air, his eyes bulging as a scream left his throat, he was heading headfirst for a blue car, there was an almighty crashing sound and then there was nothing.

The big mans spirit appeared out of his body, it stood there looking at what used to be himself, then his head turned as he heard the low growling sound of the growlers as they came to collect yet another victim. The three ghosts all stood at the rail and watched the man fly through the air and smash into the roof of the blue car, the, watched as the growlers came and did their work. Kevin thanked the two soldiers for what they had just done, he then turned to enter the apartment of the young blond woman. The terrified woman was still on the settee, only now she was hunched up in the corner, her eyes searching the shattered room for whatever it was that had just saved her from being raped, and then most likely, murdered. Kevin sat down by her side and whispered "please don't be afraid Helen the bad man has gone, we have been sent here to help you, please don't worry about the other brother coming to get you, we are about to go and deal with him also, so do not worry about your debt's either Helen, soon they will all be gone, and you will be free."

Helen turned her head to the left to look at him, but there was nothing there, he whispered "I am about to show myself to you, I will do it slowly, so please don't be afraid, because I need to ask you something very important, Is that ok?" The young woman eyes darted from side to side, Helen was too scared to do or say anything, so she simply nodded her head. He gradually began to materialise by her side, at first the woman recoiled back, he was certain that if she could have, she would have jumped up and run screaming out of the apartment.

Kev then whispered to her "There are two of my friends here with me, we have been sent down from what you know as heaven, we are going to stop this evil man from hurting any more children, we know that he must be sick in the head for what he has been doing to his victims, but he has to be punished, and we are here to do just that. Do you know other mothers that have already lost children to this predator, if so, do you think that you could get them all together, somewhere private, like here at your home? The reason that I ask this question is this, one of the reasons that I agreed to take on this mission, was that I would then be in a position to make certain demands. At my request the powers that be, have decided that these unfortunate mothers can if they do so wish, have the opportunity to see their dead child one last time.

This very rare event was only being allowed simply to reassure those mothers that their deceased child was being cared for by a close relative, and to reassure them that their child's spirit was not just wandering aimlessly in heaven. I know that you yourself have lost a child to this man, do you think that you can do what I ask, Helen? [she nodded her head] I will give you some time to think about what I have just said, and then we will come back, when we have dealt with the other two men. At that time, and only if you agree, we will move forward and make all the necessary arrangements [he moved over and stood by his two friends and said] So this is goodbye for now, so please don't worry" and with that he left the woman to her very confused thoughts.

Kevin and the two soldiers were standing in the office looking down at a seated Arthur Nalmond, standing in front of him were two plain clothed police officers, one a sergeant the other a constable. The senior man had just informed the criminal of his brothers unfortunate death, the sergeant smiled as he explained the manner of which he had died. Arthur never said a word as he was told this news, because sadly in their world of criminality, they accepted that these things happened, what he wanted to know was, who it was that had murdered his brother?

He intended to find out and when he did, by fuck they were going to pay. The two officers smiled and left the big man to his sad thoughts, as soon as they were out of the door he picked up his mobile phone, he pressed a button and held the phone to his ear, after a few seconds he spoke, "Ah, your Lordship, there has been a small problem, but don't worry, I am just about to leave the office to collect your parcel, I will call you when I have it" The big man stood up and placed his mobile phone, cigarettes and lighter in his jacket pocket, he walked across the office, and was just about to lift his big coat from its hanger when a pile of papers that had been standing on his desk, were suddenly tossed high in the air.

Arthur stood and stared at the fluttering papers, when the last sheet of paper landed on the floor, his eyes began to search the office for the source of the activity, as he looked around the untidy room, his personal coffee mug suddenly flew with great force across the room, and smashed into a thousand pieces against the stone wall. The big broad shouldered man looked at the broken pieces, and then around the room again, he slowly turned complete circle, "Is that you Neal, have you come back to tell me who killed you?" There was silence for a full minute and then Kevin made the big man physically start when he whispered in his ear." No, It is not your brother, my name is Kevin West, and I killed your brother, simply because he deserved to die, just as you do, and in just a few minutes time, you will be joining him in hell, along with his lordship, when we finally catch up with him"

A look of sheer terror came into the big mans eyes as he backed against the wall. He pressed himself flat against the wall as his wide eyes searched every corner of his office for the source of the threat. When his eyes moved to the door, he gasped out loud as he saw the key slowly turn in the lock, as if by magic. The big hard man gasped out loud as the key came out of the lock, and he watched wide eyed as the key moved ever so slowly towards him.

The key stopped moving, Arthur held his breath, then gasped again when the key was suddenly tossed into the farthest corner of the room. That was when things really went mad, as boxes and papers all began to fly around the office, the big man stood there, his arms covering his face as different items of office furniture bumped into him, then as soon as the chaos had begun, it ended.

The silence that followed was all too much for the older Nalmond brother, he began to move along the rear wall of the office towards the locked door, at the same time he began muttering, "Im sorry, I was forced to do it, I had no choice but to do as I was told, it was his lordship, he has these papers on me and if I don't do as he instructs, he is going to send them to the police" by this time Arthur had almost reached the door of his office. Then as if by magic, he was grabbed, by both arms, by some invisible source, he was literally lifted into the air, and carried towards his office chair. He was thrust into the chair, he then watched as the roll of brown wrapping tape lifted from the desk and moved around and around him as it secured his arms, one by one to the arms of the chair and then he saw the roll of tape move down to his ankles. He couldn't believe what was happening as he watched as the tape bound his legs. "who are you, what do you want?" Screamed the big man.

Kevin began to materialise in front of the him, a sheer look of terror crossed the terrified man's face, his blue eyes were bulging out of his head as he looked at the growing apparition that now hovered in front of him, the big man stared into the hollow eyes. The so called hard man could say nothing, even though his mouth opened and closed. This was when Joe and Andy began to also materialise either side of him, the only sound that came from the huge criminal was a terrified gasp, as he looked from one to the other of the three dead men, that now hovered near him.

Arthur turned his head back to Kevin, and that was when the ghostly spirit began to speak to him, Kevin snapped,"You are an evil bastard Arthur Nalmond, and you deserve everything that is coming to you, you and your brother have caused nothing but fear and misery amongst the young women on the local estates. You have taken young children from their mothers without a seconds thought, even though you knew exactly what was going to happen to them, you have raped and murdered just to satisfy one mans sick depravity, and you are just as guilty as he is. Up above, from where we have been sent, we have those poor children safe and sound. We are looking after them and as we speak, relatives of each child are being sought, so that they can look after and care for these children. Life is like that up above, calm, peaceful and you want for nothing, but where you are going, there is nothing but darkness, fear and loneliness. We will stand by and watch as the devil himself comes for you, and I can assure you that he will be smiling as he does his evil work.

That is all I have to say to you, so be prepared to meet your new master himself and do your best to smile when he comes for you." Kev nodded at Joe, Joe reached into the bound mans pocket, and took out his cigarette lighter. He picked up some loose papers from the desk and held them up in front of himself, he held the lighter under the papers, turned his head to look at the terrified man and flicked the button, the ghost watched as the flames licked at the dry paper. As the flames began to spread across the pages he held the flame to other loose sheets, which then spread, soon the whole surface of the desk was ablaze.

Joe and Andy picked up burning pages and set fire to anything that would burn in the office. The bound man began to scream at the top of his voice, his eyes bulged as he struggled against his restraints. He watched as the three ghosts slowly faded away, to leave him to die all on his own, a slow painful, well deserved terrifying death.

The three of them stood back and watched the office burn, soon the flames completely consumed everything in sight. They heard the growlers as they approached, long black arms crawled out of the ground and reached into the roaring flames, after only a few seconds, the black fiends withdrew with the spirit of the big man, the look of terror on his face as he was dragged below, a look that if ever seen, would be remembered forever.

CHAPTER 45

The trio of ghosts made their way towards the Watson-Brown estate, the large estate house was fully lit by different coloured, well positioned, ever changing spot lights. Highly polished cars by the dozen, were neatly parked at the front of the house. Two men in bright day glow jackets were in charge of the car parking, both directing traffic from the estate gate house. The three simply entered unseen and made their way to the main ballroom where couples expertly danced the foxtrot, they hovered half way up an unlit ornate staircase and watched the dancing. Andy pointed out a tall, very thin man with longish grey hair that had been brushed under at the sides, he had a pointed nose and wore an ill-matching blue silk shirt and trousers. His Lordship stood chatting to a group of men of a similar age as himself, against the others, he looked very young for his age. "Thats him sir, that's our target."

They watched the condemned man as he enjoyed the company of a young woman, who's false laugh filled the ballroom. His lordship soon became bored of her, and made his way towards a pretty young lady that wore a long black silk dress. His Lordship stood by her side with his right hand casually placed in the middle of her back, as she did not object, he slowly lowered his hand until his soft hand rested on her pert bottom, she let it rest there for a few seconds, and then quickly moved away. It was obvious to the three that the tall man was a sexual predator, and from what that had already seen, always on the prowl.
The three of them were sitting observing the dance floor, patiently waiting for the dancing to end, so that they could then deal with his Lordship. Joe nudged Kevin and pointed across the room to an unused alcove that was opposite them, and in almost darkness, a young female ghost danced along to the music, her arms held in position, as if she was in-fact dancing with a partner.

Kevin said that they ought to make contact with the young woman, as she may come in useful. The trio remained where they were and watched proceedings, it was a short while later that the female ghost opposite acknowledged their presence with a tentative wave, they all automatically waved back, and that was when Kevin decided to go over and talk to the young ghost.

When he had made his way over to her, he smiled confidently "Who are you, and where have you come from?" She returned his smile, "I thought that I was the only one left down here?" Kev moved closer and realised that she was in-fact a very young girl of maybe eleven or twelve years of age. "My name is Kevin, how long have you been here?"

 She looked all around before she answered, "My name's Keira, my mother was a waitress at a ball just like this one, it was four years ago now and it was my eleventh birthday and rather than being left at home all alone, I decided to come here with my mother. I was in the kitchen doing my homework when he found me[she stared hard at his lordship] he took me down into the cellar after he had asked me to help him carry up some wine. Once down there he grabbed me and did some really horrible things to me, he removed all my clothes, tied my hands together and raped me in every way possible, and after he had finished doing what he did, he strangled me and left me down there on my own for two days.

My actual body is buried in the little copse, which is at the very edge of the estate. There have been many other victims, but they have all been so much younger than me, I have tried many different ways to save them, help them, some have been taken by relatives, others still roam the estate grounds, lost and lonely souls. I have vowed to help them and one day I will. As for him down there, I will kill him if I ever get the chance, but at the moment I am not strong enough to do so on my own, I don't know how, but one day I will, and then I shall have my revenge"

Having listened to the young girls sad story, Kevin gently placed his arm around her shoulder in a bid to comfort her, she almost moved away from him, because she wasn't sure at first, but one look at his smiling face, and she rested her head on his shoulder. Kevin spoke quietly to the young girl, saying, "Don't worry Keira, we have come to take care of his Lordship, and when we have done so, we will take you and the others that we can find back with us. Once you are up above your, deceased relatives will be located, and then they will look after you, they will be happy to take good care of you" Keira looked into his dead eyes, she smiled the first time for a very long time, then lowered her head back onto his shoulder.

The dancing finally ended at midnight, and by the time all the guests and the band had departed, and the staff had cleared everything away, it was almost four in the morning. That was when his lordship made his way up the ornate staircase to his bedroom. The four of them watched and waited until all the staff had finally gone home, and the big house fell silent. Now on their own, they made their way down to the now silent dance floor, where they would formulate a plan. Kevin introduced Kiera to the other two, and asked her to tell them every thing that she knew about the man that had murdered her, and anything she knew about his sick habits. Kiera looked from dead face to dead face, before she began talking, she said,"His Lordship, well, he was a creature of habit, he eats the same breakfast every morning, he then takes a long bath before taking one of his many horses out for a ride, at lunchtime he has a meeting with his estate team where they discuss any problems.

At around mid afternoon he spends some time in his office making phone calls, and completing any computer work. Around four thirty, that is when his work day ends, he will most probably leave the estate then. Where he goes and what he does when he is off the estate I do not know, because I can't follow him. When those two brothers arrive his Lordship becomes very excited, he has a summer house down in the wood near the lake, that is where he takes the young girls that the brothers provide for him. I have seen many girls being abused by him, he likes them very young as you know, it's the way that he just murders them for no reason, that part of what he does just makes me cry. I really did try to save them Kevin, honest I did, I just didn't know how, but now that you three are here, maybe you can teach me?"

Kevin looked into the sad eyes of the young girl,"Please don't worry about his Lordship, I promise that we will deal with him, and we will make sure that you are there when we do. Now, can you take us to this summer house, I think that is the most likely place to catch him on his own" Joe coughed politely, "excuse me sir, but how will his Lordship access his victims now that we have taken the brothers out of the picture?" Kevin was deep in thought when Kiera answered," but the brothers only brought the really young ones. The other ones are brought here by Miss Brooks, she was my old school teacher, she used to teach me at primary school. She usually brings them in the early evening where she drugs them, and if they are still alive, she fetches them back later on when he had finished with them,"

Kevin suggested,"in that case I think that we need to set up camp in the summer house, and wait for him to turn up, but we will need a plan as to what we intend to do with him, and this Miss Brooks, maybe they should be together when the time comes?"

# CHAPTER 46

The four of them spent a lot of time together, waiting in the summer house which had all the latest mod cons, there was a large flat screen tv on the wall, refrigerator, the leather chairs and settees were all covered in bright cushions, most had animals printed on them. In one corner, stacked in a box, were a lot of children's toys, from soft cuddly ones to the latest hand held computer games. They spent a lot of time talking to each other about their former lives, and life up above, Kev taught the young ghost the basics of how to communicate with the living, or with any other young person of her own age that she would eventually meet, she would need this skill, once she was living with them up above.

She, as he expected picked every thing up with ease and was soon talking to the other ghosts as if she had been doing it for years. Next he would teach her to move small objects and once she had mastered that skill, she would be able to have some fun with the living.

As for his Lordship, he seemed to be lost, and somewhat nervous now that the brothers had both been mysteriously killed. He had been forced to put his sexual activities on hold for the time being, but Kevin knew that it was only a matter of time, before his desires got the better of him. Kevin roamed the estate and now had a plan in mind, but they would need some help from a living person, they required someone that they could trust to make the plan work, but where to find such a person, and then how to approach them, was a problem.

After a great deal of thought he asked Keira if there was anyone living on the estate that she knew of that they could approach to help them. She thought for a few seconds and then suggested,"the only person that I can think of is Billy, he is one of the young game keepers, he lives on his own in a cottage in the wood, I go and sit with him some times, he talks to himself most of the time. I have accidentally been able to do little things to let him know that I am there, but it scared him more than anything else, I can show you where the cottage is, if you like?"

Keira led Kev and the others down the lanes to the thick wood, and then into Billy's old thatched cottage, when they entered the secluded dwelling a man of around eighteen years of age was sitting eating a meal at the table. He was thin and had a lot of raw looking spots on his chin, his brown hair was long and unkempt. As soon as they entered the cottage, the young man began to look round the room as if he sensed that they were there, Kev sat in the chair opposite him, staring at him, trying to use his mind to make contact, when this did not work he reached out and moved the salt cellar slightly to the right.

Billy almost had a heart attack as he jumped up, his bulging eyes stared at the salt cellar, "Who's there, what do you want with me?" He asked in a trembling voice, Kev picked up the salt cellar and carried it around the table, to finally hover in front of Billy, the young man was rooted to the spot as he stared at the hovering object, "Leave me alone, please. Don't hurt me, what do you want?"
Thinking that the young man would react better to a young girls voice Kevin nodded to Kiera to answer him, she whispered,"don't be afraid Billy, my name is Kiera, and I have been here for a while now. I don't mean you any harm, and I don't want to frighten you, I just want to talk to you, is that ok?" Billy"s eyes would not leave the set cellar, so Kev placed the set cellar back onto the table, and the young girl ghost suggested "Why don't you sit down Billy, so that we can have a little chat?"

The young man sat down at the table, his eyes slowly moved around the room searching for whatever it was that was in the room with him,"Where are you?" He asked nervously," I'm sat in the chair opposite you Billy, please don't be afraid of me, I am only a young girl who was raped and murdered by his Lordship. He has hidden my body in the small copse, myself and a few friends intend to get revenge for what he has done to me. Well, not only myself, he has raped and murdered a lot of young girls, he is a very sick man Billy, and he does not deserve to go on living, but we will need your help, will you help us please?" The young man's brow was furrowed as he thought about what had just been said, he then mumbled,"Exactly how many of you are here then, how many are here right now?" She answered him truthfully, There are four of us here altogether, but only two of us want to talk with you, the other spirits name is Kevin, you can talk to him if you want to, he is very friendly" Billy's eyes again began to search the small room as he asked,"Where is he, is he sat at the table as well?"

She gave a tiny giggle "He is stood right by your side Billy, if he wanted to do you harm, then he could do it now without you even knowing about it, but he does not to want to hurt you in any way, we just want your help" Billy looked from side to side before asking,"You are telling me that there is a ghost standing right by my side, right here, right now?" She answered him,"Yes Billy, he is standing by your left side, would you like him to do something to prove it to you, he could pick up the salt cellar again, if you want, but he really just wants to talk to you without you being afraid. Kevin will even show himself to you, but, if he does it without letting you know, he is afraid that you will run off, and we don't want that Billy.

You tell us what you would like to happen?" Billy sat there shaking his head from side to side,"I am going fucking insane, I am talking to a fucking ghost, what's fucking happening to me?"

Kevin spoke for the first time, all that said was,"Hello Billy" the young man jumped up and backed away from the table, he moved ever so slowly, his bulging eyes searching for this new unseen threat. He reached the wall and stood there terrified, he was literally trembling with fear as he whispered,"Stay away from me, don't hurt me, go away, please leave me alone. I've got to get out of here" that was when his eyes moved to the door, the door that would lead to his freedom.

Billy was just about to make a run for it, but what stopped him was when he saw the large steel key turn in the lock, there was a loud click as the lock turned. He watched the key as if by magic as it came out of the lock and float across the room, only to be placed onto his cheap pine dresser. Kevin spoke quietly, "Why don't you sit down again Billy and I will sit down opposite you, and then I will tell you what we want from you?" Stiff legged Billy moved back to the table and sat down heavily in the old wooden chair. Kevin spoke again,"now don't be afraid Billy, because I am going show myself to you" The young man gasped out loud as Kevin slowly begun to materialise in front of him. His eyes seemed to grow even bigger as the ghost of a small thin man came from nowhere. Billy sat and stared into the dead eyes and asked what he wanted? Kevin sat and told Billy what his employer had been doing, and who he had been doing it to. The dead man then sat and explained to Billy exactly what was required of him. Having listened to the dead mans story, Billy agreed to do whatever they wanted.

Kevin had a plan in his mind as to what would happen to his Lordship and Miss brooks, it would not be a very nice end for either of them, but it was only what they deserved. They had located a large metal box in the wood that was used for storing the feed for the pheasants. It had taken a lot of working out as to how they would get the box to where Kevin wanted it, but with a lot of effort and help from Billy, they had finally managed it, The box was now sitting on a fishing platform, by the deep side of the lake, the water in front of the platform was very deep and a more than suitable resting place for the evil pair.

Their chance came a week later, the four ghosts were sat by the lake in the summer sunshine waiting patiently for their opportunity to catch his Lordship in the act,[so to speak] when a battered blue ford pulled up by the sun house, two young women climbed out of the car, went into the building with two hand held blue tool boxes, filled with cleaning materials, and began to clean the mainly glass building, from top to bottom.

When they had finished their work, they carried two more boxes from the back of their car into the sun house, which contained fresh stocks for the fridge, when they were finally done they climbed back into the car and drove away. Kevin smiled,"It looks like this was what we have been waiting for, he turned to Joe and asked the dead soldier,"can you go and find Billy and tell him that it is time to act, and that we need him to be close by" The deceased soldier simply nodded, and faded away to go and find the young man.

# CHAPTER 47

It was early evening when they watched Lord Cecil walk down the path towards the sun-house, when the thin man reached the building, he stood in front of the glass house and looked all around, it was as if he was searching for any unwanted watchers. When he was happy that there was no-one observing him, he turned and pointed a small remote control towards a black box that was fixed to a thick pole, he pressed a button and small lights came on either side of the long gravel path, lighting the way from the top of the hill, to the bottom.

He turned and aimed the remote back at the box and pressed another button, all the lights in the sun house came on, he pointed at the box again and pressed another button, lights on the roof of the funhouse came on making the whole building look like a palace.

His Lordship entered the sun-house and sat down on the settee, he picked up another remote and pointed it at the large flat screen tv, the tv came on but the screen was blue, he pressed another button, and a drawer of the unit that was positioned beneath the tv, opened. Different games consoles lay in the drawer, he pressed another button and a dance game came on the screen, he froze the game and looked at his watch, he sat there tapping his fingers on his knee, as he waited patiently for his next young victim to arrive. Miss Brooks walked down the lighted pathway, in her left hand she held the hand of a pretty young girl of seven years of age, she was dressed in a pink dressing gown, underneath she wore a pink nighty that had a smiling blue bear on the front. Clutched in her left arm was a much loved teddy bear and on her feet she wore a pair of pink slippers, her long blond hair fluttered in the evening breeze, as they walked down the hill towards the sun-house.

Miss Brooks stopped when they reached the lit up building, she turned and bent down so that she could speak to the little girl. She turned her bodily to face her and warned,"Now Sarah, remember what I told you and you are to be a good girl, remember that your mummy wants you to do whatever his Lordship wants, is that ok?" The little girl looked as though she was about to burst into tears, and said in a tiny scared voice, that she wanted to go home. Miss Brooks told her that she would be ok and not to be so silly, she almost dragged the tiny child into the sun-house. His lordship stood up and smiled,"ah, at last, and who do have we here then Miss Brooks, the school teacher smiled back,"this pretty little girl was Sarah and she loves dancing" The thin man bent down and looked deep into the young girls blue eyes, he touched her on the chin, "Hello Sarah, you are a pretty little thing, do you like lemonade?" The nervous girl nodded her head and gave a half smile, so his Lordship stood up and nodded to the teacher,"Miss Brooks will get you some lemonade.

"Now Sarah, help yourself to chocolate, choose any bar that you want, there is a whole basket full there. Would you like me to put on a dancing game for you?" Sarah smiled and reached into the basket and chose a chocolate bar, she opened the wrapper and began eating, unseen to her Miss brooks poured some lemonade into a plastic cup, she then added a good splash of neat vodka, she then broke a red and white capsule in half and mixed the contents into the cup,  using her fore finger she mixed the drink. This done she passed the drink to the little girl, Sarah took a tiny sip and shook her head at the bitterness of it, the teacher added more lemonade to the cup and this time when Sarah tried it, she drank some without pulling a face, "drink it all up Sarah love" said the teacher, they watched as the young girl finished the drink, and began to play on the dancing game.

Lord Cecil passed the teacher a large wad of cash and said that he would call her when he was ready, The teacher looked back at the dancing girl and reminded her,"remember what I told you Sarah, and I will come back for you later" the little girl did not even acknowledge her teacher as she danced along to the music, and didn't even notice when the older woman left the sun house.

A few minutes later the old man noticed that his intended victim had begun missing steps in the dance routine, he went to her and eased the teddy bear from the child, "Are you not hot in that dressing gown Sarah?" Sarah did not object as he removed her over garment, she continued to dance as he began to remove some of his own clothing. Sarah had begun to stagger as she tried to follow the dance music, he went to her and lifted her night dress up and over her thin shoulders, and dropped it onto the floor. The old man was sexually excited, and stood looking at the young girl with renewed interest, he looked at her almost none existent breasts and then down at her pink pants and licked his lips in anticipation of the delights to come.

Sarah's eyes were almost closed as she continued to sway along to the music, the old man picked the girl up and carried her towards the settee, he was just about to sit down with her on his lap, when Billy burst through the door, he looked at his employer and shouted,"put her down you sick fucker" the shocked old man dropped the girl onto the floor, and fell backwards onto the settee.

Miss Brooks never even looked back as she walked away from the sun-house, she stopped at one point and counted the money that she had been paid, kissed the bundle of notes and smiling to herself, she stashed them in her pocket. She began to walk up the pathway with a spring in her step, after only a few steps she stopped dead as if she had walked into an invisible wall of some kind, she recoiled back at first and then tried again, and again she was stopped dead in her tracks, she looked all around her to see if there was anything that she could see that was causing the obstruction, but she saw nothing.

She reached out in front of her and felt nothing, so she took another step only to once again hit the invisible object. She held both hands out in front of her and moved forward, and as if by magic she felt herself thrown to the rough ground. Unseen hands moved thin blue nylon rope through the air as her hands and feet were bound tight, she went to scream, but a rag appeared, and was tied around her mouth. The school teacher was totally confused, she lay on the ground tied in such a way that she was unable to move, she could not call out to summon help, nor could she see who had done this to her. Sudden panic hit her, at what had happened to her, she became wild eyed as she began to scream from behind the gag.

Joe, Andy and Kiera looked down at the school teacher, none of them had any sympathy for the woman whatsoever, the school teacher tried to scream again, only this time a big invisible army boot silenced her as it hit her hard in the stomach, Miss Brooks grunted, and folded almost in half as the breath was completely knocked out of her, she just lay still and began shaking uncontrollably.

Back in the sun-house his Lordship stood up and said angrily, "Who the bloody hell are you, and what do you think you are you doing, walking in here un-announced?" Billy looked at the old man and said angrily,"My name is Billy Smith you sick bastard, I am your game keeper, and I intend putting a stop to your perverted little games" Lord Cecil made himself as tall as he could, and shouted, "Well Billy Smith, you no longer have a job here on the estate, so get out of here this instant, pack your bags and leave my estate at once" Billy looked down at Sarah who was now fast asleep on the floor, sucking her thumb, he turned around and walked over to the tv and kicked it as hard as he could, sending the now silent flatscreen onto the floor, to the sound of breaking glass.

Billy walked over to Sarah and picked up her sleeping form, he then shouldered the old man out of the way, and lay the almost awake child down on the settee, he picked up her dressing gown and covered her up, she immediately pulled the garment around her and drifted into a deeper sleep. Billy did no more, but walk over to his Lordship and punch him hard on the chin, the old man sank to the floor, and lay still.

Billy picked up the sleeping girl and carried her outside, he stood looking down at the school teacher. He looked up and appeared to speak to no-one,"remove her gag for me please Joe" unseen hands reached down and pulled the rag from her mouth, Billy asked,"whats this poor child's address?" He was told the address without any further argument, he then spat out the words,"I am taking this poor thing home, and then I am coming back to deal with you and that sick bastard in there, and I can promise you that it will not be a pretty ending for either of you" he was about to walk away when a voice stopped him,"Wait" another unseen hand reached into the teachers coat pocket and pulled out the wad of cash, the cash was pressed into the sleeping child's hand. Billy delivered the still sleeping girl to her crying mother, he left her with the reassurance that she had nothing more to worry about as far as further dealings with Miss Brooks and his Lordship were concerned. When Billy left the tiny high rise flat Sarah lay in her loving mothers arms, he took one final look around, and then made his way back to the estate.

When Billy arrived back, the spirits had moved Miss Brooks into the sun -house. The trussed up pair lay side by side on the narrow settee, both pairs of eyes watched the angry young man as he stared down at them. His Lordship was trying to speak, but couldn't because of the gag in his mouth, Billy reached forward and pulled the gag down. "What are you going to do with us?" Asked the old man, Billy smiled and looked around the sun-house,"That is up to my dead friends here, oh yes, you haven't met the ghosts have you, let me introduce them to you" And he did, one by one the ghosts materialised as he introduced them, leaving Kiera until last, using her new found skill, she made the old man gasp out loud, as she hovered in front of him. "But, But you are dead, I know I buried your body" Billy began laughing out loud, "At least Kiera's body will be found now, that was more than can be said about you pair of sick fucks" Billy looked at Kevin,"I will go and fetch the truck, and be back in a few minutes."

Billy reversed the truck trailer so that it was by the door of the sun-house, he walked inside, grabbed the woman by the ankles and literally dragged her outside and dumped her into the waiting trailer, he then did exactly the same to his struggling Lordship. The ghosts followed close behind as the truck made its way slowly towards to lake, Billy reversed the trailer towards the metal feed box.

Billy lifted the teacher up first, and placed her into the metal box and then his Lordship was placed by the side of the teacher, the ghosts and Billy stood looking down at the terrified pair, Billy smiled "Enjoy hell"and closed the lid down and pushed the lock into place, they could hear the muffled cries of the perverts as they desperately called out for someone to help them.

 Billy reversed the trailer until the rear of the trailer touched the metal box, he pushed the box back until it slipped silently into the cold deep water, they all watched as the metal box slowly filled with water and sank, thin lines of air bubbles made their way to the surface as the box slipped ever deeper beneath the surface. Kevin took hold of Kiera's hand and pulled her away from the lake, just in time because the sound of the growlers could be heard coming from the depths of hell. Billy moved back with the rest of them, and watched as the long black fingers reached into the deep water and withdrew the spirits of Miss Brooks, and then his Lordship, both of them clasped in the elongated tentacles of the devils workers.

Back at the inner cloud, Kevin introduced Keira to the nurse Rita

Wood, with the promise that the relevant section would immediately begin searching for her closest relative, that way she would have someone that she knew to take care of her. The young girl ghost instantly took a liking to the nurse and the feeling was mutual, so much so that within a week Keira had been offered the position as the nurses assistant.

The two soldiers were always near Kevin as they awaited further instructions. As for Kevin he himself was waiting to be allowed into the inner sanctum, to find out from the higher authority if there was another victim that needed avenging, or would he be given the time to search for his own family. He had thought about this a lot, and had decided that he would very much like to find his mother and father, although they had been dead for quite some time, he was pretty certain that he would find them. Lady Mary would advise him where to look, she has the contacts to find out on which level they would be on, he would need her help, especially after they had been dead for such a long time.

Lady Mary appeared to Kevin and the two dead army men, and congratulated them on a job well done, she went on to say that plans were almost complete for the revelations to the mothers of the dead children, [the ones that had been murdered by his Lordship] to see their offspring one last time. She requested that Kevin to go back down below, and make certain that Helen had convinced the mothers of the dead children, but only if they wanted too, would be allowed to see their child one last time, and for him to make the arrangements.

Then when everything was finally in place, Lady Mary would complete her part with the correct authority, because what was about to happen with revealing the dead children as they now were, had never been done before. On the rare occasion that an adult had made a reappearance for whatever reason, it had always had a very positive outcome. How the mothers of the dead children would react was unknown, everything would now rest on how Kevin handled the whole affair. How he made his appearance in front of the unbelieving mothers, how he explained to them what was about to happen, and exactly what would happen when their child was revealed to them.

When Kevin had first broached the subject of what was about to happen, Lady Mary was not very happy with him, because what he had requested was so rare and so very difficult to achieve, only a certain few, very high ranking spirits that have God like abilities, have the power to actually create the right conditions for the revelation to take place. The reveal would only happen if this king like spirit himself was convinced that all parties involved, knew exactly what was about to take place, and that the mothers of the dead children's had been fully informed that their child would appear to them as a spirit, and that they would only be able to see their dead child as they were now.

These mothers would also be informed that a close deceased adult relative would be located, one that was willing to look after their child, would also be present on the day, and act as any foster parent would. They would also have the ability to speak to the bereaved parent, before the child was reintroduced to their mothers, if need be, this would be done to reassure the mothers that their child was being properly cared for, and well looked after by the chosen foster parent, and would be until such times that they themselves passed over, and become spirits themselves. Then and only then would the child be reunited with their mother, they could then happily spend eternity together.

Kevin, Lady Mary and the inner cloud senior advisers spent many hours together, as they discussed the best way for Kev to handle the unusual situation down below. The biggest concern for the top adviser being, how would Kevin explain to the mothers exactly what was about to take place, how he did this would be vitally important. In order to cause the minimum of stress to the child, the young sprit would not be able to see their mothers, but the child would appear to the mothers, as they were now, a spirit. A set of strict rules must be laid down, and must be religiously obeyed at all times.

These include a set amount of time available to complete the whole process, this would be determined only by the highest ranked adviser present on the day, and this spirit would be there not only to observe the event, but be in ultimate charge. This spirit would also have the power to put a halt to proceedings at a seconds notice.

Once all the mothers had agreed to follow the strict procedure, a further, most important rule would be explained to them.  An imaginary line would be drawn across the room, any mother that crossed that line to try and make contact with their child, would do so with the full knowledge that they *WOULD NOT* be allowed to return, and therefore forfeit their lives.

# CHAPTER 48

Kevin and the two soldiers were waiting in Helens flat for her to return, as soon as she entered her dwelling she sensed that someone was there, she stood dead still as her eyes searched every corner of the big room "is that you Kevin?" She asked. When he answered her, she gasped out loud, and said "where are you?" He slowly materialised and they stared at each other for a few seconds,

"We need to talk Helen, final arrangements have been put in place for the mothers to see their dead children one last time, but it will be done under strict conditions, one of them is that if any of the mothers leave your flat for any reason, once they pass through the doorway, they will remember nothing of what has taken place.

What we need is for you to gather the mothers here in your flat, where I will explain to them exactly what would be on offer to them, and the strict rules of the occasion that will be fully enforced. The first rule would be that any mother that turned up either drunk or full of drugs, would be asked to leave, Andy and Joe my army friends would be happy to take care of that side of things.

The biggest problem for you would be persuading them to come in the first place, the most obvious way for you to get them here, was on the pretext of discussing the demise of the Nalmond brothers and their debts, you can then leave the rest to me.

The powers that be have made it possible, that when I have the ability to materialise in front of them, and I will look almost alive again, I will have a normal face so as not to appear too frightening. Everything on this side has been arranged for two days time. The event will take place at three o'clock in the afternoon. Do you understand all that?"

She answered without really thinking about it and suggested that it would be best if he explained his presence, and the reason for them being there, because they would never believe her in a million years, especially if she told them that they were about to meet a ghost.

At the prearranged time the mothers were gathered in the flat and chatting between themselves, the main conversation being the welcomed demise of the Nalmond brothers, and his Lordship. When one of the women who's name was Laura said that she couldn't understand how it had all happened, because it appeared that no-one had seen anything, Helen took the opportunity to stand up and say, ”I know exactly how it was done, because I saw it with my own eyes. Neal was in this very flat, he had lost it big time, and was just about to rape me, when he just flew backwards, it was as if some invisible force simply grabbed him, his arms were held outstretched as he was dragged backwards. Neal was screaming out loud as he went out through the doorway, he was then literally thrown over the railings to his death”

The rest of the women sat open mouthed as they stared at Helen, it was Laura that said jokingly ”so you are saying that it was a ghost or something like that, are taking the fucking piss, you mad cow?” Helen shook her head "it was a ghost all-right that saved me, I have spoken to him, his name is Kevin, and he is here with us right now, and he wants to speak to you all. He has an offer that you won't believe, but I can guarantee that you and I will all except it. So if you are ready, he will show himself" Nervous laughter filled the room as wide eyes searched every alcove. When no-one spoke for a few seconds, all eyes were back on the thin woman, it was Laura that spoke,"you'r really fucking serious ain't ya?" Helen just nodded, Laura said jokingly but full of false bravado," c/mon then Kevin, show you'r fucking self"

Kevin ever so gradually began to materialise, gasps and silent screams filled the flat, one woman held her hand over her mouth, she jumped up and made for the door, but she stopped dead when she saw the key in the lock turn all by itself, as Joe locked the door. The room full of women fell silent as Kevin completed the transformation, he looked from women to woman before he began speaking, he explained who he was and about the demise of the Nalmond brothers, and his Lordship.

He went on to tell them that all their debts to the brothers were no-more, and that there would be no further come back. He told the stunned ladies that he had a one time offer for them, and that it would involve their dead children. [again the room was filled with audible gasps]

But I have to warn you that there are strict rules and even stricter consequences. [He looked into the shocked faces] First, all phones and any other recording equipment must be turned off. I have two spirit friends here with me, and they will be checking each of you without you even knowing it. I have a one time offer for each of you, and that is the opportunity to see your deceased child as they are now in heaven. This has never happened before, but because of the terrible circumstances of each child's death, and the depth of your own individual loss, it has been decided by the highest power there is, this rare event will take place to reassure you all, that your children are being well looked after, and are as happy as they could be under the circumstances. The system up above was such that when any child passes over to the other side, a search instantly begins for a deceased family relative, that spirit [once found] was then asked to take care the child.

This selected spirit does this until it is time for you yourselves to cross over, and then you will then be reunited with your child, where you both will then hopefully have a fairly normal child/mother existence. At such times that you yourself pass over to the other side, the rules up above will be explained to you in depth, once the authorities are satisfied that you understand those rules fully, and you are prepared to adhere to them, you will then be allowed to care for your own child.

This next rule is the most important one of all, before any of the children are revealed, I must tell you that my two associates will now appear, one either side of the room and between them there is an invisible line that separates you from your offspring. If you cross that imaginary line at any time, even if it is to go to your child, you will forfeit your lives and remain up above with your sibling. I have to be certain that each of you understand that? [each mother nodded their heads] Next, the door will be unlocked and you have the opportunity to leave, if you so desire, but be warned that once you leave, there will be no coming back, and if you do leave, as you pass through the doorway, you will remember none of what has happened here today. Finally, we will give you fifteen minutes to talk between yourselves, and make your decision, for those of you that are remaining, then we will proceed".

The room became very animated, and two of the women with other children, stood up and left the flat, other mothers sat with their heads in their hands, and cried because in their drug and alcohol fuelled lives, they rarely had to make such an important decision, but today they had to choose life or death. With only a minute to go another mother left the flat, leaving only a few of them. Kevin spoke, "It was time ladies" he waved his right hand and just like a black and white film, the children appeared, each of the younger ones had a toy or comforter of some sort, and each of the slightly older children, seemed perfectly happy.

Mothers stood up and stared at their dead children, others sat and cried but Laura did not hesitate, and stepped forward over the invisible line. The now deceased woman bent over to pick up her child. This sparked the others into action, and three other mothers crossed the line where they instantly turned into spirits, they were now in a place where they no longer had to worry where their next hit was coming from, when their next drink would be, and there would be no need for them to be out in all weathers, selling their drug dependant bodies to all and sundry. The remaining mothers fell to their knees in front of the magical line, arms reaching out, they wept at the sight of their dead children, they begged for longer, as the sight of their dead child, ever so slowly faded away.

As they left the flat that day, all memory of what had taken place was almost wiped from their minds, one day they would remember. Lady Mary led the few mothers that had crossed over and their child, and led them towards the specialist hospital, where they would spend time readjusting to a new existence.

# CHAPTER 49

Time up above passed happily for Kevin, because his search for the sisters was finally over, he spent his days watching his daughter Samantha playing with the ghost children. He saw Tina walking towards him, and was delighted to see that she was pregnant again, she sat down besides him, but did not speak at first, she continued to watch the children" "I'm sorry for what happened between us Kev, what with Petra and all. I will be totally honest with you, I did love her in my own way, but when I found out about the drugs that she had stolen from the Albanians, and what she did with them, I knew then that I had made the wrong decision.

As you can see, I am pregnant. Myself and Ed, we are really happy and can't wait until this little one is out here, playing with her sister and the ghosts. Sam has begun to realise that her play mates out here are a lot different from the friends that she has at pre-school, the problems would come when she wants to invite her friends around to play on her birthday, we would have to ask the ghosts to stay away that day. [she turned her head and looked into the hollow eyes of her dead lover, and said] I am so sorry for shooting you Kev love, I take full responsibility, if I had not got involved with Petra, none of this would ever have happened" They sat quietly or a few minutes before she asked, "whats it like, you know, being dead?"

Kevin looked at his ex lover, "Please don't concern yourself with me luv, to be honest I never could see what you saw in me in the first place, I am happy enough up above, as long as I can come down here, watch the girls playing, see you and Ed getting along, that is all I really want. They have found me a few odd jobs to do, some of which have kept me busy, I think they may have found me some more work, because I have been summoned to a meeting later today" When he stopped talking, she felt no need to say anything more, so she simply smiled at him, and then stood up and walked away.

Kevin stood patiently waiting to be invited into the inner cloud, once inside Kenneth Wattage and all of the other high authority ghosts looked down on him. The loud voice of the Lord Chief Justice echoed around the inner sanctum, as he praised Kevin on his success in dealing with the Nalmond brothers and Lord Cecil. The huge ghost seemed to almost smile as he announced, "I promised you a reward on a successful completion your mission, there will be more jobs for you of a similar nature in the future, but for the moment we would like you to take some time, and explore the many interesting facilities the we have to offer up here. 175175To help you do this we have arranged for someone close to you to show you the way. We have located your parents, and they are waiting outside as we speak, as you leave this room, life will change for you, you will no longer be as you are now, you be taken back to when your life was the most happiest, so go and enjoy. But remember this my friend, should we have need of your special talent in the future, we will find you. And with that each one of the VIP's simply faded away, leaving him completely on his own.

Kevin was really pleased to see his parents, they were just as he remembered them, the three spirits hugged each other, when they parted his father spoke to him" come son, it was time for you to rest now, spend some time with us, and let us show you all the wonderful things to be seen up here. It really is quite fascinating. The trio walked away from the inner cloud, and this begins a new episode in our heroes spirit life, one where life as he now knew it would be perfect. Maybe one day he would be reminded of the great work that he had done, but until then, he was a free spirit.

The End.

# ABOUT THE AUTHOR

Brian is a new author, he is a long-term dialysis patient of over 20 years and uses his 4 weekly sessions of treatment to write his many different genres of books, these include fiction novels, a biography [A Badsey Boy] and many beautifully illustrated children's books.

Born in the mid 50s, Brian is a disabled man with a lifelong passion for angling, when his illness forced his retirement, he discovered his creative imagination, which shows in his love of writing.